Praise for Elizabeth Palmer's
SCARLET ANGEL

"In the deliciously deadpan, confidential tone of an avid gossip, Palmer gives us a world in which the evil are very, very bad, and the good are often portrayed by their own timidity."
—*Kirkus Reviews*

"This is the kind of book where good is good and bad is bad and never the twain should have met, but it builds up a momentum of its own, and carries the reader along with it."
—*The* [London] *Sunday Times*

"Clever…Palmer adroitly captures the nuances of British country life with all its snobbery and pretensions."
—*Orlando Sentinel*

"Full of wit, family entanglements, death, and deceit, it is beautifully executed."
—*Today*

"The characters are remarkable, as is Elizabeth Palmer's prose, frequently and deftly employing wry understatement."
—*Roanoke Times & World News*

ELIZABETH PALMER

SCARLET ANGEL

ISBN 1-55166-456-9

SCARLET ANGEL

Copyright © 1993 by Elizabeth Palmer.

First published by St. Martin's Press Incorporated.

Printed in U.S.A.

To David,
James, Alexander and Marina

Her flowing iridescent draperies,
Add to her grace; walking she seems to dance,
As sinuous snakes, when holy jugglers tease,
Coil round their wands in rhythmic elegance.

Like desert sands and skies, all vacancy,
Both unaware of human suffering,
Like waves whose network surges through the sea,
She goes her way untouched by anything.

Her eyes are polished metals, cold and bright,
And, in this strange symbolic soul that links
The stainless angel with the ancient sphinx,

Where all is gold and diamond steel and light,
Shines, like a burnt-out star eternally,
This sterile woman's frozen majesty.

—Baudelaire

1

His friends sometimes speculated on why, aged forty, George Marchant had never married. Good-looking and rich enough to be considered a catch, he plainly liked the girls and they apparently liked him back. The truth of the matter was simply that he had never wanted to. In the past his girlfriends had been upper-crust English girls, mainly country blondes of the horsy variety, who had eventually got tired of waiting for him to make a permanent commitment and had drifted off to other partners. George hardly noticed. It was true that he liked to have a woman in his life, preferably on a long-term basis, since this meant less effort all round, but he had never felt the remotest desire to legalize any of his liaisons. Then, in Rome, on secondment from his firm, he met Camilla Vane. Her blend of Italianate chic and striking looks coupled with a mind which many admired for its brightness and just as many dismissed as superficial, dazzled George and, in his forty-first year, he married her.

Like him, Camilla was English, and the daughter of diplomatic parents, both of whom were dead. She fitted seamlessly into the Italian scene and, George was to discover, had a spectrum of acquaintances which ranged from the respectable to the raffish. At thirty-four Camilla had been around. George, who was beginning to feel as though he had been asleep for years, rather enjoyed all this, and certain things which he probably would not have condoned in London seemed in the rather louche atmosphere of Roman society, and in particular of Camilla's set (or those of them he was allowed to meet anyway), to be acceptable. Of course, George had been around too but not, it could be said, with Camilla's avid curiosity and lack of scruple. George was really very conventional. For her part, having once decided that, if she could, she would marry him, she was careful not to expose George to more than she thought he could stand. It was not until they had been seeing each other for some time that she invited him into her bed, after which exotic happening George was lost. Her sensuality and appetite were counterpointed by a feline reserve both mental and, at times, physical, and an unpredictable intermittent coolness which, at the height of what had become, certainly for George anyway, a very hot affair, was at once fascinating and unsettling. When she finally told him of the existence of her son, Anthony, and her first marriage, the upshot was a very unpleasant quarrel. George, for years such a lethargic suitor, found himself tortured by possessive jealousy such as he had never encountered before. Of course he knew that there had been lovers prior to him, but a husband and child were something else again. In his calmer moments he tried to understand why he was so upset. Perhaps it was because she had only just thought fit to tell him. Whatever the answer to this was, it put him in touch with himself and his real feelings. He discovered that he could not bear to be away from her. At the end of a separation which lasted a week and nearly killed him, he asked Camilla to marry him, and she accepted. When they finally had a rational talk about it, it transpired that her son was at an English prep school, and the former husband was dead. She was a widow. This made the whole thing easier for George. It had a finality and respectability about it which put an end to further discussion. Obsessed as he was with making her his wife, his mind veered away from how much he did not know about Camilla, and, if he had only been prepared to think about it in those terms, how much of her past did seem to be (literally) buried. As only those can who have fallen violently in love late, he put all of this to the back of his mind and concentrated on the entrancing present.

For her own part, Camilla was well satisfied. At thirty-four it was definitely better to marry for money than to be unmarried with no money. Of this she was sure. As usual, though, there were two sides to it, the upside being that he was rich enough (just), presentable and besotted with her, the downside that not infrequently he bored her and, furthermore, she recognized a probity about George and his dealings which could seriously cramp her style. *Still, nothing is for nothing,* thought Camilla. *I'll just have to put up with that. For a while.* And, just as she had had to gauge the right moment to tell him about Anthony's existence, she would have to pick the right time to tell him about her debts. After that, maybe, certain old friends kept for the moment right out of George's orbit in the interests of a stainless image might begin to filter back.

It was while all this was happening that the news of his father's death arrived. Because of this George suggested to Camilla that they should marry quietly and at once, which they did. He did not, however, go into the other implications of his father's demise, the principal one of which was that he would inform the firm that it was no longer possible for him to continue working in Rome and they would go home to England. When he did tell her she was thunderstruck. It had never occurred to her that they would leave Italy. Equally it had never occurred to George that they would not eventually return. The matter had not been discussed during the course of their affair. It was the one thing concerning which the usually malleable George was absolutely immovable. Camilla felt trapped and infuriated. Essentially an urban animal, the prospect of English country life filled her with panic and gloom. Most of this she concealed by means of a great effort of will, and with her customary calculation settled back to play a long game, at the end of which she hoped to get her own way. Even so, she had not come to terms with the new turn of events enough to feel like accompanying him to his father's funeral. It was a small revenge but she decided to take it all the same. Accordingly she went to bed with what she described as an August fever.

Sweetly she said, 'I'm so sorry, darling, but do give my love to all your family, and tell them how much I look forward to seeing them in September.'

So George went alone, with a feeling that although she was not reconciled to her new life at present, she soon would be. After all, she was his wife and where he went she would have to go too.

George's mother was at home when he finally arrived at the house. Sarah looked tired and strained but was not distraught. Osbert had been ill for some months and his death had not been unexpected. She had had time to prepare herself for the inevitable.

She kissed her son. 'How very sad that Camilla couldn't come with you,' she said. 'The family are dying to meet her. We're so happy for you, George.'

George could imagine. He knew perfectly well that they had all given up hope that he would ever marry, and that speculation concerning Camilla and what sort of a person she was must be intense. He looked forward to the day when they would all meet her for the first time. Meanwhile, Sarah was saying, 'Tell me all about her. Where did you meet? What are her family like?' Typical Mother, that last question. She had always been a great believer in the importance of family. Answering the first was easy, the second less so and after the words 'dead' and 'diplomatic service', he rather ground to a halt. Both of them were suddenly struck by how little he seemed to know about her, although neither put it into words. Sarah experienced a faint flutter of apprehension.

'Does Camilla work?' she asked, getting off the unsatisfactory subject of family. This was, in fact, another poser for George since Camilla apparently lived off thin air. Well, no, not quite. Camilla earned herself some money advising well-heeled Romans on the decoration of their houses and palazzos. What her qualifications were for doing this sort of thing he had no idea, and it could never have been called anything remotely like a full-time occupation and certainly couldn't have funded Camilla's life-style, never mind Anthony's education. George, child of the upper class, supposed she must have some kind of private income, and said as much in those terms to his mother. Sarah was amazed that her eldest son, normally so punctilious about that sort of thing, should know so little about his own wife. She decided to drop the matter. After all, in a few weeks' time she would meet Camilla for herself and could make her own assessment. The talk turned to arrangements for the funeral, after which George was flying straight back to Rome to settle his affairs.

Her husband having finally left for Fiumicino, Camilla lay in bed in the flat in Trastevere. The faint hum of traffic came through the open window across which the heavy curtains were partly drawn. In the half-light the pretty things she had collected from the Porta Portese and various antique shops while searching out more exclusive treasures for her clients stood upon the polished dark wood floor and decorated the old rose of the walls. Her favourite possession, a carved and gilded angel the size of a small child, stood on an apple wood chest in one corner beside a large jug filled with scarlet flowers. With its pageboy hair and sightless eyes, the angel faced Camilla across the room, wings furled. A pencil of light from the window traced the golden outline of its full, sensuous mouth and the folds of its robe and formed a nimbus around its head. Looking at it, Camilla had an idea. On impulse she picked up the telephone receiver and rang an old friend.

'Julius? Camilla. Yes, I know it's been a while. Look, George has gone to London and I'm here by myself and very bored. Why don't you come over and amuse me?'

He must have said that he would for she got up,

checked that there was a bottle of champagne in the fridge, put on the lightest touch of make-up and scent and then rearranged herself on the bed, heaping up her soft pillows against the rococo mirror which formed its head, before lying back luxuriously framed by the dark cloud of her hair. Half an hour later Julius let himself in, still having a key from the days when he was one of Camilla's regular lovers. Since her marriage he had seen virtually nothing of her in the interests of discretion and landing George. Being a penniless descendant of old Roman aristocracy, he had perfectly understood this. Without preamble he walked across the room and sat down upon her bed. Without hesitation he kissed her hand, kissed her lips, kissed each shoulder and then, very slowly, slid down the thin silk straps of her robe and kissed her white breasts. With a sigh Camilla gave herself up to the intense pleasure of making love to a man who was not her husband.

How desirable she is, thought Julius, looking at her as they lay in bed afterwards, sharing a joint and talking. But not to be trusted. A ruthless, worldly woman who knew what she wanted. In spite of her beauty one could not on reflection say that Marchant was a lucky man. Devoid of hypocrisy concerning matters like this, the reasons for Camilla's marriage were obvious and perfectly acceptable to Julius. Eventually he himself would have to do something similar and marry for money. But not yet. He won-

dered how long it would be before she reverted totally to type and, try as he might, he could not imagine her in an English country setting, though it was
easy to see how her life with Marchant could have
been conducted here.

Eventually he prepared to take his leave. When he
was ready to go he once more bent his sleek head
over her slim hand adorned with George's large generous emerald. His key lay at the feet of the angel
and he stretched out his hand towards it. As he did
so, Camilla got there before him, picked it up and
dropped it into her small crocodile handbag, whose
little golden jaws she shut with a snap. Nothing was
said. He looked at her with a mixture of chagrin and
admiration. So that, for the time being at any rate,
was that.

'*Ciao,* Julius,' said Camilla, and saw him out.

When he had gone she went back upstairs. Standing before the angel she drew her red fingernail down
the classical nose stopping at the curved lips where
she let it rest a minute. Then she dressed and went
out.

Two days after this interlude had taken place,
George arrived back. By this time another bottle of
champagne lay coolly in the fridge, replacing the one
drunk previously by Julius and Camilla, and the
smell of Julius's interesting cigarette had quite disappeared. George kissed his wife, opened the cham-

pagne and raised his glass. 'To going home,' he said, and began to talk about his journey. As he spoke she stood looking at him, her mind in furious turmoil her face inscrutable. There was, she knew, no point in saying anything. They had been over it all before. Camilla had been too subtle to let George see the true extent of her loathing for the whole idea, but had done her best both in bed and out of it to dissuade him. All to no avail, it seemed. To a cosmopolitan nomad such as Camilla, George's ingrained Englishness and strongly entrenched family ties were quite incomprehensible.

'The family' (he made them sound like the Mafia) 'were very disappointed that you couldn't come,' George was saying. 'I've told them to expect us back in roughly three weeks' time. The idea is that Mother will move into the Dower House, though probably not until after Christmas since a lot of work has to be done on it first.'

It was all she needed, thought Camilla crossly, the prospect of sharing a house with her mother-in-law. She stared moodily into her drink. By this time George had woken up to the fact that she had not uttered for the last twenty minutes. Wisely, he decided to drop the subject. They were going and that was that. He would have given Camilla anything within reason, but on this front he was absolutely inflexible. There could be no question of not going home to take up his inheritance. Besides which the house needed a face-lift and Camilla would enjoy doing that. She would also do it very well. A little time was all that would be needed, he felt.

He looked at her. She stood by the fireplace sipping her drink, one elbow on the marble mantelpiece. Apart from her silence and the faintest of shadows between her eyebrows there was no outward sign of the anger within. She was wearing black, which suited her. Around the stalklike neck, just below the chin, a satin ribbon was tied in a bow and secured with a pearl pin. Above the bow the face reflected in the old grey glass of the overmantel mirror was not merely that of a pretty woman, but that of a beauty with all the aloofness and finely drawn severity that this implies. The dark hair swept shining back from a pronounced widow's peak and fell to the shoulders, framing a face that was notable more for its strength than its softness. Camilla's eyes were grey, her nose straight and her cheekbones high. The mouth then came as a surprise being full and curved and painted very red. There was a hint of cruelty and appetite about it reminiscent of certain classical statuary. A pagan mouth. A man who had taken the trouble to understand women in a way George never had, a man like Julius, for instance, would instantly have seen Camilla for what she was—a formidable woman, and, if thwarted, quite possibly dangerous with it. All this passed George by. He adored her.

Putting down his glass he walked across the room

and took her in his arms. With inward rebellion and outward compliance Camilla let him. 'Darling,' was all she said. George picked her up, carried her into the bedroom and laid her down among the embroidered cushions on the bed. Here he slid her sheer black stockings down to her painted toenails, and kissed her narrow feet, then very slowly he undressed her until she wore nothing but the black satin ribbon and the pearl pin, and began to make love to her. In spite of her bad temper, it seemed wise to respond and Camilla did so.

Lying in his arms when it was all over, it was clear to her that now was the time to tell him about her debts. He might, after all, never be this much in thrall again. She got up, put on her robe and went to fetch the remains of the champagne. Then she sat on the bed beside him and said in a faltering, contrite voice, 'George, I have something to tell you.' He listened indulgently, his mind half on something else, until she got to the actual amount, at which point he was quite shocked.

'Good God!' said George. Five seconds at least passed, during the course of which he did not, as she had hoped he would, immediately take her into his arms again. He looked grim. By the time another five had elapsed she could see that drastic action was needed before stupefaction and disapproval became active condemnation. Camilla took a deep breath, put her face in her hands and began to sob. George had never seen her cry before, and was not seeing her cry now though he did not know this. He gathered her to him. What a brute he was. It was not as though he did not have the money to bail her out. He said as much. Her sobs began to subside and finally ceased altogether to his great relief. She turned her face up to his. Kissing her, he noticed with some surprise that, despite her distress, there were no tears.

Eventually she got up and went into the bathroom, where he heard her turn on the shower. Lying on the bed, the flicker of unease signalled its presence again. Why had she not told him all this at the beginning? It occurred to him to wonder what else he didn't know about his wife. He stared at the angel and the angel looked ironically back. Suddenly unwilling to confront this particularly uncomfortable line of enquiry George got up and hastily began to get dressed. He looked at his watch. Time for dinner. Drawing back the curtains he found it was already dusk outside. Leaning through the open window he breathed in the spiced warmth of the indigo Roman evening. Like her, he thought, he would be sorry to leave. Eventually turning back into the bedroom, he was disconcerted to find Camilla silently watching him. She had lit the tall church candles on either side of the angel. The pale light burnished the rosy interior of the bedroom, gilding the flowers and delicately highlighting the gold thread of the cushions. Camilla was wearing something high necked and black, and above it her face appeared to float in the dark, a third oval flame. A light air from the window caused the candles to flicker and almost go out and as the shadows were tossed around the room, it seemed to George for one startling moment that the angel laughed.

2

And so here they both were. Going Home, as George so irritatingly phrased it. Travelling towards Marchants in his large comfortable Jaguar, he felt his heart lift. Sitting by his side, Camilla felt exactly the opposite. So far she had seen only one blurred photograph of his family which George carried about in his wallet. They had seen no pictures of her at all. Camilla assumed herself to be about to live among country bumpkins and felt something like desperation at the prospect.

The cold weather had come freakishly early this year and outside a light frost had already iced the English countryside. In the west the red and wintry sun was beginning to sink, preparing to give way to a silver slip of moon. Cocooned within the warm car, Camilla nevertheless shivered. What am I doing here? she wondered. Joylessly she put a hand on her husband's knee. There was, after all, no point in having a fight about it at the moment. George's latest present to his wife, a black kitten named (ridiculously in his view) Frescobaldi, looked at him jealously from his comfortable seat on Camilla's lap.

The Marchants had always had dogs, never cats, which were regarded as inferior animals and relegated to the outhouses as ratters. However, having insisted on the move to England he felt it would have been curmudgeonly to have refused such a simple request, though he wished he had put his foot down where the name was concerned. Like many of his wife's simple requests, it had turned out to be not so simple after all. Perhaps, he thought hopefully, Frescobaldi would run away.

By this time they were approaching the local village. Past the Norman church and through the market square with its pump in the middle, known locally as The Pant from time immemorial, they swept, down the cobbled main street where the houses were all built of the local grey stone, and out into the countryside. George drove very fast and very well. Although there seemed to be nobody much about, behind the lace curtains much curiosity was generated as the racing green car disappeared in the direction of the big house. Three miles further on he swung expertly through a fine cast-iron gateway, roared up the long drive and finally crunched to a halt in a shower of gravel.

Camilla stared at Marchants with a feeling of pleased surprise. In the half-light the white stuccoed façade, over which climbed a majestic *Magnolia grandiflora,* shone faintly. Tall English trees grouped darkly and protectively around the house, gracefully framing its Georgian elegance and symmetry. In front, beyond the drive, which was apparently lined with rhododendrons, a park stretched as far as the eye could see.

Leaving his wife sitting in the car, an unusual lapse of manners on his part, George ran up the front steps two at a time and, as he reached it, the door was opened by the housekeeper, Mrs Melbury, who had been on the lookout for them. The Melburys had been employed as a 'couple' years before, Henry Melbury having been the butler until he had collapsed suddenly of a heart attack, anticipating by only a few months Osbert's own death. Sarah had not replaced him, rather assuming that George would want to make his own arrangements when he returned.

'Welcome home, sir,' said Mrs Melbury. At this point the family came out onto the steps. As they did so, Camilla, svelte in grey, swung her long legs sideways and, with the poise of a model, got out of the car still holding Frescobaldi in the crook of her arm. As she walked towards it, she ran a critical eye over the small family group waiting to welcome her, which consisted of Sarah, Tom and Marcus who were twins, and Marcus's wife, Diana. A slightly awkward silence had fallen. Tom whistled under his breath. Well, well! To think that dull old George had married someone like this. Not Tom's own type, of course, but even so! They all began to speak together. Amid laughter, George introduced his family to his wife. Sarah and Camilla kissed. Marcus watched. Camilla's immediate reaction to her mother-in-law was one of grudging admiration. Clearly in her day Sarah Marchant had been a beauty rather in Camilla's own mould. No fluffy blonde she, but a tall, striking woman in her sixties with the stern profile of a warrior queen. Sarah's figure had thickened slightly with the years, and the long hair which Osbert had always refused to allow her to cut had gone grey and was gathered into a soft knot at the nape of the neck, emphasizing the imperious nose and jutting cheekbones. Partly owing to her height, Sarah had always had presence and now, with advancing age, she was an imposing and even a daunting figure. Camilla felt that it would not be as easy as she had hoped to manipulate her mother-in-law.

Sarah, whose snap character judgements were famously accurate, made one now. She thought, *Camilla's hard and bright, like a diamond. She will be too many for him. George just doesn't know enough about women to be able to cope.* She was conscious of a feeling of foreboding and deep disappointment. It had taken him so long to marry, and from a family point of view whom he married really was important. Having airily handed Frescobaldi to a disapproving Mrs Melbury to be borne off to the kitchen, Camilla was talking animatedly to Sarah's other daughter-in-law, Diana. From the way in which he looked at his new wife, Sarah could see that George, dependable, unromantic George, was quite infatuated.

Sarah said briskly as they all walked into the hall, 'George, I've put you and Camilla into the main bedroom.' (She forbore to say 'my bedroom', although, of course, it had been.) 'Perhaps you would like to show her where it is.' Turning to the new daughter-in-law, she said, 'I expect you would like a bath and a rest after the journey, Camilla. Dinner will be at nine tonight instead of eight-thirty as usual. We normally make a habit of all meeting in the drawing room beforehand for drinks.'

She smiled and Camilla smiled back. Sarah headed off in the direction of the kitchen and Mrs Melbury, having suddenly remembered the unwelcome presence of Frescobaldi. She wondered as she hurried along whether he was housetrained or not, and was informed by a purse-lipped housekeeper on her arrival that he was not. Sarah cast her eyes to heaven.

Camilla and George ascended the wide staircase. So far the inside of the house was more or less what she had expected. Everything looked comfortable, faded, and rather tired. Some of the paintings she had seen so far were good but probably not, she thought, exceptional. There were, however, one or two interesting pieces of furniture none of which was much enhanced by its surroundings. She would soon change all that, Camilla decided, as they arrived at what George still thought of as Mother's door. The bedroom was much less shabby than the rest of the house, probably because only Sarah and, until lately, Osbert used it. The ceiling was lofty and moulded and unusually painted with a delicate flower design, putting Camilla in mind of certain Italian houses. On either side of the fireplace where the fire had been lit were two pretty windows which, Camilla guessed, must look over the garden at the back of the house. On one wall hung a painting of Venus with cherubs. Camilla looked at it with appreciation. Venus herself, eyes downcast and flesh rosy, held an apple in one hand. With the other she fondled one of the golden-winged cherubs. The effect was, paradoxically, both chaste and sexual. She said so to George, who mistook the signal and began to unbutton her silk shirt.

'Not now, George.' She slid away from him and went into the bathroom. As she had expected it was pure 1920s. She would keep the taps, she thought, but get rid of the tiles. Camilla began to run a bath and, while it was filling up, went back into the bedroom, kicked off her shoes and lay down on Osbert and Sarah's large bed trying to decide what to wear.

When Sarah had set off for the kitchen in pursuit of Mrs Melbury and Frescobaldi, the others had wandered into the library.

'What a turn-up for the book,' said Tom.

'I know,' said Diana. 'She's so different from the others too.'

Rather to her relief Tom said, 'She certainly isn't my type.'

His eyes rested on Diana with approval. *She* was. A blonde of the petitely pretty variety with good legs, which was how he liked them. Diana, who had grown up with the Marchant twins, had been in love with Tom for years. When Tom, after seducing her at the age of fifteen, had made it plain that he had no intention of settling down, then or ever if he could help it, Diana had done the next best thing and married Marcus instead. She had, however, in no way allowed this fact to interfere with her affair with Tom, and so with or without Marcus's knowledge (no one was quite sure) the two brothers had effectively shared her for years. Diana's conscience did not bother her for she had the perfect amorality of someone who knew exactly who she was in love with, and therefore where her loyalty lay, namely with Tom not her husband. Making love to Marcus in her capacity as his wife, which happened less and less frequently anyway these days, was not a betrayal either since Tom knew this happened and said he did not mind. Although alike to look at, Tom and Marcus were in fact unidentical twins, Tom being the elder by nineteen and a half minutes. They had divided everything since childhood and sharing the same woman seemed to Tom a perfectly logical extension of this. Temperamentally, though, the two were quite different, the turbulence of the one being totally contrasted by the steadiness of the other. Through Tom's uneven, and in the end disastrous, school career his brother had always defended and stood up for him, sometimes taking the blame for Tom's misdemeanours, and even, on occasion, doing his work for him.

'What do you think, Marcus?' enquired Diana.

Here she received an answer she could have done without for her husband said, 'Rather decorative. Wonder what on earth she sees in George.'

'Money, probably,' said Tom briefly and rather enviously.

There was a silence. Tom got up and began to walk restlessly about the room. Diana watched him. He was wearing an old burgundy velvet smoking jacket which looked as though it had come out of the dressing-up box and probably had. This was teamed with narrow black cords, a pink shirt and a red paisley neckerchief which gave him a gypsyish look. A lock of brown hair fell over one eye and was constantly and impatiently brushed back. Whereas Marcus looked more like George, and all three brothers were unmistakably Marchants, Tom had a distinctly wolverine look about him, accentuated by his leanness and height. He prowled. It was true to say that keeping Tom out of trouble had been something of a family preoccupation almost ever since he was born. Currently suspended from the City firm for which he worked pending an investigation into insider dealing, it looked as though the new broom

which was sweeping the City clean might brush Tom
away too. Sarah had been mortified by this. Knowing
her son as she did, she had been careful to steer clear
of anything in which Tom was involved, but to
someone as upright as she was this was small consolation. Diana hoped he would get off with a warning. Her feelings about this were mixed since the
suspension of Tom meant that he was around all the
time, while Marcus, of course, still went up to London as usual, he being a barrister of impeccable integrity.

Diana and Marcus lived in a cottage in the
grounds. Tom, as a bachelor, had retained his bedroom in the main house. Tonight they were all staying with Sarah, or, rather, now he was back, with
George. Where Camilla was concerned, Tom's less
than ecstatic reaction was not surprising. As time
went by and it looked less and less likely that George
would marry, he had allowed himself to grow used
to the fact that the lion's share of the inheritance plus
the house would, since he was the elder twin, eventually come his way. Large overdrafts can be built
on such assumptions and, fuelled by expensive tastes,
Tom's was one of these.

Diana's heart had also fallen like a stone when she
heard about the marriage. With the advent of a new
mistress at Marchants, it was obvious to her that the
old regime was now over and, with it, her protracted
childhood. Like all who are themselves unfaithful she

took a pessimistic view of fidelity generally, and the sight of her new sister-in-law's beauty and self-assurance filled her with insecurity.

She stood up. 'Come on, Marcus. Time we got changed for dinner.'

Left alone, Tom helped himself to a whisky and soda and sat down in one of the comfortable old armchairs. As he did so, Sarah entered holding a chastened Frescobaldi who was full of stolen steak.

'You'll have to get rid of that cat, Mother. It's a ludicrous animal with a ludicrous name.'

'You forget, Tom, that I'm no longer mistress of this house. Camilla is. If she wants him to stay, he'll stay. For what that's worth, my guess is that she'll lose interest in him.'

'I can't imagine what George was thinking of to allow it,' grumbled Tom.

'Well, he did,' said Sarah shortly.

Tom gave her a long look. 'You don't approve of her do you?'

'It's not that exactly,' said Sarah carefully. It was hard to defend a first unfavourable impression on such short acquaintance. On the other hand Sarah was a perspicacious and usually accurate judge. She tried to pin down what it was that had alerted her. The high gloss perhaps? Something about the eyes maybe? Trying to be fair, Sarah said, 'She's very good-looking in such a cosmopolitan sort of way that

I just think she may be too much for George and too much for the country.'

On second thoughts it hadn't been the eyes but the mouth. Well, they would all meet Camilla properly over dinner. Meanwhile she must follow Marcus and Diana's example and get ready.

Tom kicked the logs into a blaze with a handmade shoe. Good-looking? He supposed she was. And she certainly had style. Not for the first time in his life he felt covetous; at the end of the day George seemed to have everything.

Upstairs Camilla was putting the finishing touches to her ensemble. George, who had been mildly miffed by the earlier rebuff, had now got over this and was putting on his tie. He looked forward to making love to Camilla after dinner. She was wearing a short black dress of exquisite, clinging cut which showed off her breasts and small waist around which was tied a crimson sash. Her only jewellery, apart from the emerald, was a single strand of pearls, and the scarlet mouth echoed the sash. Sheer black stockings (George found suspenders sexy) and Gucci bag and shoes completed the whole. A handsome couple, they went to the drawing room together where Marcus was dispensing drinks.

'Campari and soda, please, Marcus,' said Camilla when he asked her what she would like. She smiled at him, an ingenuous, wide smile. A lawyer to his

finger-tips, Marcus considered her for a second or so
before smiling back. Having carefully observed her
earlier, he was not deceived by her apparent openness, and in that short space of time, just as though
he were assessing a witness in the box, instinctively
judged her to be probably devious and certainly hard.
Camilla, who was very acute when it came to re-
cording this sort of negative vibration, however mo-
mentary, noticed, and was instantly alerted to the fact
that he had not endorsed her. Still, his new sister-in-
law was extraordinarily fetching, no doubt about that,
and Marcus, who liked pretty women, had no reservations on that score. Maybe, after all, she was just
the sort to get old George going.

Old George at that moment was talking to Diana
though his eyes were on his wife. He was listening
with a serious face to her toned down version of
Tom's problems in the city. To George the whole
thing had a very familiar ring. While regaling him
with all the details in so far as she could without
being disloyal to her lover, Diana was also eyeing
Camilla. She felt suddenly dowdy and dispirited. The
dress she was wearing which she had always thought
suited her so well looked provincial and even frumpy
beside that of the dashing new arrival. Somebody,
she couldn't for the life of her think who now, had
once advised her never to buy evening clothes in the
country. Whoever they were they had been right. Di-

ana felt her self-confidence, always precarious, begin
to ebb away.

At this point Tom, like an actor, made his entrance. Watching him walk across the room to organize himself a drink, Camilla conceded that he was
attractive. He reminded her of a large, muscular cat
with a grace and languor of movement which she had
encountered often in Europeans and seldom in Eng-
lishmen. Things were looking up, she thought. Turning her gaze elsewhere she caught Diana anxiously
staring at Tom. Camilla, for whom intrigue and nu-
ance were second nature, immediately intuited that
an affair either had taken place or was taking place
between these two. *Fascinating.* Sipping her drink
and answering Marcus's polite questions concerning
Rome, at the same time she summed up Diana. Un-
remarkably pretty was her contemptuous opinion.
And that dreadful dress. Where could she have
bought it? Camilla was not, in fact, a clothes snob
as such, but she was a style snob. She knew that an
inexpensive dress could still look ravishing provided
it was tasteful to begin with and *worn* rather than
just put on. During her penniless twenties in Europe
Camilla had become a mistress of the art of looking
millions of lire on a shoestring. Now, of course, the
indulgent George's ample bank balance kept cheap
frocks at bay. All the same, money could not buy
taste and Camilla knew hers to be exquisite.

They all went in to dinner. The table being D-ended and by ordinary standards very large, the six of them sat at one end of it. To begin with, the talk was general, mainly Sarah bringing George up to date concerning the house and estate. Tom, who had heard it all before, took the opportunity to engage his sister-in-law in a separate conversation. Camilla had already decided to amuse herself with Tom and Diana. To produce a situation where one was enslaved and one palely loitering would do to begin with. She began to charm Tom, regaling him with a highly selective account of life before George, listening, amusing, flattering, not quite flirting. Powerless to intervene, Diana watched all this from her seat on the other side of George, unable to hear most of what was being said but painfully conscious of the fact that her lover had not once looked in her direction, so deeply engrossed was he by Camilla and whatever it was she was saying. Finally, with one last seductive, slanting grey glance she turned away from Tom and towards Sarah with a question about a painting which had caught her eye.

The ritual of dinner continued. The pudding followed the cheese, and finally they all stood up and went back into the drawing room for coffee. George, who had been oblivious to any provocative behaviour on her part, felt proud of Camilla. He knew that she had not wanted to come to England to live, yet so far she appeared to be trying hard, even succeeding in apparently captivating Tom who could be very prickly. He did not notice Diana's depression.

Marcus who had seen her humiliation but had been unable to stop it even if he had wanted to, now did. 'Are you all right, Diana?'

'Not really. I've got a perfectly bloody headache. If you'll all excuse me, I think I'll go to bed.'

Without enthusiasm Marcus said, 'I'll come with you, darling.'

It was the last thing she wanted and in the grip of her self-obsession was unaware that it was the last thing he wanted too. 'No. No, honestly, I'd rather be left alone. Sorry to be so feeble.' She kissed him. 'I'll see you all in the morning.'

She walked to the door. Once outside it, she leant for a few seconds against the wall with her forehead pressed to its coolness before going slowly upstairs to the bedroom she would share with her husband. She felt as if the last eight years of loving Tom and being married to Marcus, both of which situations had seemed so easy and so right in the enclosed existence of Marchants, had, in fact, all the time been taking an immense toll. She shut and locked the door. Tears of despair began to trickle down her face. Roughly she unzipped the green dress, tearing it in the process, took it off and dropped it in the bottom of the wardrobe. She would never wear it again, never. Diana began to sob now in earnest, with the loud, unbridled woe of a five-year-old. Slowly she took off everything else and when completely naked stood evaluating herself in the cheval glass. The young woman who looked back at her was a little on the plump side with full, high breasts, a trim waist and shapely legs. It was, in a word, a rather Edwardian body topped by a charming blonde head whose hair was looped up like that of a Degas *danseuse*. Around her dilated eyes the mascara had run. Noticing this fact made Diana pull herself together and she went to wash her face. By now thoroughly exhausted, she unlocked the door, climbed into the freezing cold country house double bed and fell into a disturbed and unrefreshing sleep.

3

Camilla got up early or, rather, early for her. It had been agreed the night before that Sarah would continue to organize the house until she moved out. Camilla would learn the ropes by watching Sarah. This arrangement was due to begin on Monday morning, which Sarah usually commenced by going through the week's menus with Mrs Melbury. Today being Sunday, George proposed to show his wife the house and grounds. Accordingly, Camilla poured herself into a pair of jeans and a tailored jacket. When she appeared outside, George looked askance at her narrow patent pumps.

'Darling, you can't tramp through fields in those shoes. Haven't you got a pair of wellingtons?'

Wellingtons? Camilla had never owned such a thing since she was six and said so. Tom watched this little scene from his bedroom window with some amusement. George and Camilla disappeared into the house and reemerged some ten minutes later with Camilla wearing someone's highly polished riding boots, having considered gumboots inappropriate with the Armani jacket. Husband and wife went off arm in arm towards the back of the house.

As Camilla had suspected, here was a formal garden the central feature of which was a large old stone sundial surrounded by flowerbeds. Beyond this, and leading out of this particular part of the garden, there stretched a long avenue bordered by high hedges of yew, at the end of which stood a lifesize classical statue. Mossy arms upraised, she seemed like some high priestess invoking the gods of the garden. They both regarded her without speaking for a short while. She really should have been garlanded with myrtle, thought Camilla. The face of the statue was reminiscent of that of her own angel with its straight nose and voluptuous mouth. It was reassuring to find this pagan echo here in an English country garden.

Eventually they turned away and retraced their steps along the yew walk. The day was overcast, and, despite the fact that the weather was much milder than it had been, Camilla, who was underdressed for an English autumn, felt cold and shivered. Gallantly George took off his jacket and put it around her shoulders. Together, walking quickly, they skirted the end of the house and continued until they were once again at the front. Really studying the park for the first time in the daylight, Camilla was struck by its tranquillity and beauty. She imagined the rhododendrons in May, massed blooms of red, cyclamen, cream and purple. She would fill the house with their

resplendent colours. Naturally Marchants would have
to be substantially redecorated, though she supposed
tact dictated that this would have to wait until Sarah
moved out. She spoke her next thought aloud.

'How are they getting on with it?'

'Who getting on with what?'

'The builders. With your mother's house?'

'Oh, the Dower House. Faster than we thought. It
will be ready for her by the end of the month, hopefully.'

Camilla thought, *I'll believe it when I see it.* Builders being what they were that meant after Christmas.
Well, that was all right. After all, a substantial
amount of planning and thought would have to be
put into the refurbishment of Marchants before anything actually happened, and Camilla was too old a
hand to rush things. All the same, she could start on
the bedroom. She decided to broach the subject with
George that evening.

'Why don't we tackle the park next?' he suggested.

'I think I'll have to change these boots first,' said
Camilla who had remembered that riding in riding
boots was much more comfortable than walking substantial distances in them. 'Let's go back into the
house anyway. I'd like to look at the drawing room
again.'

Pleased that she was taking this amount of interest,
George complied. Once there Camilla began to vi-

sualize how it all could look. Of course those awful
moth-eaten old curtains would have to go and the
sofas must be reupholstered. The fireplace was a particularly fine one, though, and the ceiling mouldings
and cornices were magnificent. Interiors were one of
Camilla's passions. She estimated that this one would
take at least a year and thousands of pounds to do
properly and she intended to enjoy herself, but was
well aware that, however grand her surroundings, at
the end of the day she would still be living in the
country. With George.

Frescobaldi suddenly sashayed light as a leaf into
the room. Camilla, who had forgotten all about him,
in common with everyone else except the unfortunate
Mrs Melbury whose responsibility he had become,
picked him up and put him on her shoulder where
he stood like a small black figurehead, his amber-
eyed profile silhouetted against her ivory cheek.
George, who did not like cats, had a sudden sense
of…what? Isolation? Not exactly. In so far as one
could feel close to Camilla, he did. And, in any case,
her very coolness had been one of the things which
had attracted him to her. Others had been known to
substitute the word 'calculating' for 'cool'. Frescobaldi, whose dignified stance had not lasted long, had
begun to play with Camilla's earring and was smartly
put down. Immediately he began to run madly
around the drawing room almost as though her proximity had given him an electrical charge, and without

warning, to Camilla's amusement and George's annoyance, he streaked up the velvet curtains and then, all claws unsheathed, slid straight down them again deeply scoring the thick material as he came.

Camilla laughed.

'Camilla! Don't let him do that,' shouted her husband aiming a copy of the *Field* at the cat. Frescobaldi, by now expert at dodging an irate Mrs Melbury, effortlessly avoided George's missile and shimmied off in the direction of the kitchen.

'Don't be so *cross,* darling. You know it's all going to be replaced in any case. You must admit that this room is awfully run down, and look at the rest of the house. Shabby. It needs redoing from top to bottom. And I have to tell you that, much as I admire your mother, I really can't endorse her taste.'

George, who had grown up in Marchants and for whom it was like an old, profoundly comfortable and much-loved shoe, could not frankly see much the matter with his surroundings. However, redecorating being a small price for keeping his wife happy, he let it go. Sarah, who had been about to enter the room and who consequently had heard Camilla's words, did not in fact do so but turned on her heel and walked off again. Neither of them was aware of her presence.

Sarah felt inordinately upset. *Bitch!* She was, of course, (she knew it!) being unrealistic. After all she had always recognized that the next mistress of Marchants would want to change it. The real reason was that she instinctively saw Camilla not as a potentially admirable daughter-in-law but as an interloper and adversary who probably despised not just the house as she found it, but all of them too, and that probably included George. And he, she now saw, would let her get away with it. Still feeling furious, she made her way to the library where she sat down in front of the fire. Looking around, she supposed it *was* shabby. Over the years she had rather ceased to notice her house after her own decorating blitz when first married, and had more or less let it look after itself. And bringing up three boisterous sons within it hadn't improved its looks either. Not usually the despondent type, Sarah had a sudden feeling of bereftness, a sense of the end of one cycle and the beginning of heaven knew what. She saw, as had Diana, that life at Marchants was to be entirely different. Nothing would ever be the same again. She acknowledged to herself that, albeit on short acquaintance, she did not like and, she felt, never would like, her new daughter-in-law. This was a pity, for Sarah had made Marchants and the village her life. She had earnestly hoped that the next chatelaine of this house would do the same and that she could retire to the Dower House knowing that the old ways would go on more or less as they always had. Given the sort of man George was and the sort of girls he had liked in the past, this had not seemed an unreasonable expectation in the way it did now.

Placing a couple of logs on the fire and trying to analyse her feelings, she decided that change itself was not really the problem, but more the manner of its coming. She divined Camilla to be a frigid personality with, as her grandmother would have quaintly said, no bottom. It was plain that the normally sensible George was putty in her hands and, suppose it were to be needed, she felt there was unlikely to be any correction from him. And then there had been that little scene over dinner. Sarah had never enquired too closely into the relationship between Tom, Diana and Marcus, mainly because she preferred not to know. Generally regarded in the village with affectionate respect as a hard worker for the common good and a believer in the old values of the rather staid community in which she had lived for so many years, Sarah was at the same time not a prude. Sensitive and intelligent as she was, she recognized the complexity of the twins' relationship and had, almost without realizing it, assumed Diana to be a common romantic factor. Like Diana herself, Sarah had no idea whether or not Marcus knew it. In a very English way sleeping dogs had been allowed to lie for a long time and, but for the arrival of Camilla, this would have continued to happen. Now that she had seen Camilla bent on mischief, it was obvious to Sarah that there was nothing she could do to contain matters. If only George were more perceptive or more masterful, or both, and therefore more of a match for his wife. It was not as though she could alert him to the instability of the situation, since he had apparently not even noticed his wife flirting with his brother, and anyway would have been outraged to learn that Tom and Marcus had effectively been sharing Diana, of whom he was very fond, for years.

It was a depressing prospect and so very different from her own marriage. In her youth Sarah had been one of the beauties of the county set, though not a wealthy member since her father had managed to gamble away most of the family money on the stock market. As was the way for many girls of her class, she had been given very little formal education, and although a love of books and her own innate wit had largely overcome this, she had always keenly regretted it. Good at tennis and riding, she was a popular guest with the result that a great many invitations came her way. It was at a houseparty, the culmination of which was to be a dance, that she had met Osbert. And had fallen in love. It had been just as simple as that. In her mind's eye Sarah saw it all as if it had been yesterday. She remembered dancing with him, and not just once either but three times in a row, followed by wallflowering envious eyes, for he was, after all, the most eligible bachelor in the room.

'Isn't it very bad form for you to dance only with me?' she had teased.

'I haven't danced only with you. I have danced once with our hostess.'

'That probably isn't good enough. In fact, looking at her face, I'm sure it isn't. What about the girls with whom nobody has danced?'

'And what about all the men who are being deprived of you?'

She laughed joyously. 'I think they should all dance with each other.' His arm encircling what was in those days a small waist for her height, tightened around her, and she was conscious of being, though only temporarily, alas, under his protection and of wishing that the evening would not end because at the end of it she would probably never see him again.

'It's far too hot in here.' He took her hand. 'Let's go out onto the terrace.'

In fact he walked straight across the terrace, pulling her after him, and down the stone steps into the garden.

'Where are we going?'

'Does it matter?'

Entering into the spirit of it, she said, 'Of course not. Doesn't the garden smell heavenly? It must have been raining.'

'Only a light summer shower.'

By now the hem of her ivory silk trailing on the lawn was damp and the new ivory satin shoes were becoming muddy and covered in grass stains. Registering the expensive fact that they would be ruined, Sarah decided to disregard it. Under a huge gnarled old apple tree, which put her in mind of one of her childhood Arthur Rackham story books, they stopped and, turning her round to face him, he had silently looked at her for a minute. Then, taking her face in both his hands, he had quoted:

> 'I did but see her walking by,
> And yet I love her till I die.'

after which he had kissed her.

'I've been wanting to do that all evening.'

'Do it once more!' Suddenly frightened by the intensity of her own feelings, she had looked up at him blushing and very desirable. 'After all, I may not see you again.'

Amused he said, 'You will see me again. Once more, but then I must take you back to the dance, otherwise I might not be responsible for my own actions.'

This time she had kissed him back passionately, and then, dazed with happiness, had allowed him to escort her through the sweet-smelling September garden to the house and the censorious looks of their hostess. Four months later he had married her.

Recalling how handsome he had looked that evening, tall, dark and very much at ease with himself, extremely like Tom in fact, Sarah suddenly felt her heart contract with the pain of her loss. Following the short courtship, their wedding had taken place in the little family church at Marchants, which was still used in those days and had been filled with expensive winter flowers. Afterwards they had gone on honeymoon to Venice which, out of season, had been faintly melancholy and very, very romantic.

How innocent I was, she thought, *and how gentle Osbert was. The physical passion which he awakened in me lasted throughout my married life. Though we did, of course, have disagreements, especially in the beginning when I was very headstrong, and knew so little. Usually, though, if he couldn't persuade me out of some course of action he just let me find out the hard way. And quite often we laughed about it afterwards.*

His death, with which she thought she had finally come to terms, suddenly seemed impossible to bear all over again, and her eyes filled with involuntary tears.

Sympathetically it had begun to pour with rain outside. Water sluiced down the library windows and, through the torrent, Diana, who was running across the garden towards the stables, became a streaming Niobe-like figure. Resolutely putting her memories aside, Sarah walked across the room and stood, uneasy and restless, at the window. What exactly was it about her new daughter-in-law that made

her so wary? The sky was a bruised violet fading
into yellow. After a while the downpour stopped as
precipitately as it had begun and lustrous sunshine
suddenly irradiated the garden with the intense brilliance of a Vlaminck. Lost in her own thoughts, she
was startled to hear a low voice behind her say,
'Sarah?'

Despite the clarity of the light outside, or maybe
because of the contrast, the interior of the library was
still storm dark. Camilla was standing in the shadows
by the door.

'Do you mind if I join you?'

'Of course not.'

The room was slowly beginning to lighten along
with the sky outside, but even so Sarah put on one
of the lamps.

'Why don't you sit down.'

She supposed Camilla must have something particular to say, and wondered what it was.

4

Tom lay on the bed watching Diana undress. It was a Tuesday and Marcus had departed for the City whence he would not return until eight o'clock that evening. Tom's room was a relic of his school days. Brownish school team and house photographs lined the walls and there was an old cricket bat, long since discarded, leaning against the wardrobe. For Tom the room was so familiar that he had never noticed that effectively he lived in a time warp. Only the clothes in the cupboards had moved on since Eton and quite a few of those, in addition to the ones he had just taken off, were strewn all over the floor waiting for Mrs Melbury to pick them up. His old school tie was knotted around the neck of his ancient balding teddy bear, which leant rather drunkenly against the Georgian dressing-table mirror and was called Icarus. Diana had long ago given up trying to stem the flood of Tom's untidiness, and the only concession to femininity and order in the whole room, apart from her own presence there, was a flown blue jug of anemones, whose deep pinks and reds and purples glowed against the rich patina of the mahogany chest and pointed up the extreme grubbiness of Icarus's left foot in front of which they stood, like a votive offering to Tom's childhood. Ironically the very vividness of these flowers provided by Diana reminded him of Camilla. Tom had thought quite a lot about his new sister-in-law. Rather more, in fact, than he cared to admit to himself.

Diana lifted her white broderie anglaise petticoat, which smelt faintly of one of Mrs Melbury's lavender bags, over her head and came to the bed where her lover lay. Tom usually liked to take the rest of her clothes off himself, but this time as he did so he mentally undressed Camilla. Not much of a thinker, more a man of instinct, Tom nevertheless understood women in a way George never had. He recalled how she had leant towards him at dinner, and the iridescent gleam of her eyelids as she turned away from him to talk briefly to Sarah and then had drawn his attention back to herself again with a sidelong, frankly flirtatious invitation from narrowed grey eyes. And he also remembered how she had tilted her head back and pushed up the dark mass of her hair, revealing high cheekbones and the classical severity of her profile. In that instant he recognized her to be an emotional freebooter, a sexual mercenary who would probably go along with almost anyone provided there was enough in it for her. In short, she was very like himself. Tom felt a rush of lust. He wanted to kiss Camilla's peony-painted mouth.

Without knowing why, Diana benefitted. They made love with the ease and skill of long practice, and all her misgivings receded as the tide of her pleasure came in.

How she loved him! And he loved her, she felt sure he did. Not for the first time she thought about Marcus and wondered if he knew. She had always assumed that he did. After all, he and Tom had always shared everything, why not her? On the other hand, this being the case, why had she never been open with Marcus about it? Why had *they* not been open with each other about it? It was certainly true to say that the clandestine quality of her assignations with Tom heightened her enjoyment, and making love in the afternoon reminded her of playing truant from school, sitting in the local cinema, head well down, guilt sharpening appreciation. But, if she was perfectly honest with herself it had to be admitted that unlike certain other things the twins had divided between themselves, this was not true sharing because Diana loved Marcus like the brother he should have been, but was in love with Tom, so the division of her particular spoils was not and never could be equal. She, Tom and Marcus had been inseparable as children, Diana having come to live with the Marchants as Osbert's ward after both her parents had been killed in a motorway car accident. So they had run wild together, climbed trees together and ridden together and, life being what it is, Diana had fallen in love with Tom and Marcus with Diana. Marcus, who was no fool, had in fact recognized her infatuation with his twin but typically had kept his own enigmatic counsel, probably hoping that she would get over it in time. Tom, deeply in love with himself then as now, suffered from no such emotional inconvenience, though this did not inhibit his seduction of Diana, and when he eventually made it plain that marriage was not on offer, it had seemed perfectly logical to her that she should accept Marcus instead, thereby preserving her proximity to Tom and ensuring that life went on much as it had before.

She lifted her head to smile up at him only to find that he was already looking at her, but not with adoration. The expression was a disconcertingly detached one and when he turned his face away without returning her smile, she realized in that second that she had lost him. The contentment which had filled her was replaced by panic. She felt that she could not live without him. Being well aware that Tom disliked women who made scenes, even when his own behaviour had caused them, or perhaps especially then, Diana was silent, her heart palpitating like that of a sparrow in the jaws of a cat.

Tom got out of bed abruptly, letting her head which had been resting on his arm fall back upon the pillows. He put on his silk dressing-gown, tapped a Gauloise out of the packet which habitually sat on the bedside table and lit it. There was hostility in the way in which he did not so much as glance at her again, but walked to the window where he stood with his back to her, smoking and looking out. Taking this as a sign of dismissal, Diana also got up. She began to draw on her tights. Spirits drooping, she moved slowly like one in a bad dream. When she was fully dressed again and had looped up the loose strands of her hair, she went over to him and put a light, beseeching hand on his arm. When this mute appeal was not in any way acknowledged, she let herself quietly out. He did not even turn round.

In the privacy of their bedroom Camilla was saying to George, 'I've told your mother about Anthony, by the way.'

Ah! He wished she hadn't. George had meant to tell his mother himself about the existence of Camilla's son and had rather been waiting for an auspicious moment which, up till now, had never presented itself.

'What did she say?'

'She expressed surprise without really saying anything very much. You know the sort of thing, a raised eyebrow here, a long look there. I received the distinct impression that she felt you should have told her yourself. I must say I'm not quite sure why you didn't.'

George shifted in his chair. He wasn't sure either but had to admit to a feeling of ambivalence concerning this ready-made child whom he had not yet met. He could see the scene in his mind's eye. Mother could be very starchy. He would have to apologize to her after dinner for this sin of omission.

Meanwhile Camilla was saying, 'Anyway I told her that they'll all be meeting him soon. He has a long exeat from school coming up so we'll have to go and pick him up and bring him back here for the week.'

This last piece of information may have been news to Sarah, but it was also news to George. He received it with mixed emotions. The thought of sharing Camilla with anyone, specially a previously unencountered ten-year-old at this early stage of their marriage rather dismayed him. And the thought of the forthcoming interview with his mother during the course of which she was bound to enquire why on earth he hadn't thought to mention all this before, made him feel positively fugitive.

These days George was under fewer illusions concerning his wife. He cast his mind back to the photograph of Anthony which she had shown him but which was not, as it might have been, displayed in their bedroom. A solemn little face had stared back at him, frowning under the traditional prep school fringe and singularly lacking in the carefree quality one normally associates with the age of ten. George hoped Anthony was not going to be one of those wet miserable children who moped about the house and never did anything. Well, he was about to find out. It suddenly struck him, as it had already struck Sarah, how odd it was that the first thing Camilla had not done on arrival in England was to contact either Anthony or his school. Nor had he ever seen her write to the little boy, which wasn't, of course, to say that she hadn't done so. Other boys' bracing upper-class mothers had been legion during his own prep and public school days, but this was something else again. Sarah herself had largely expected the Marchant boys to get on with things and not complain, but the weekly letters from home had always come, the Fourth of June and the like religiously attended, and when a crisis arose such as the time when Tom had been caught cheating in his exams and nearly expelled, it was mainly due to Sarah and Osbert's positive relationship with the school that a combination of his housemaster and the Provost had reluctantly agreed to give him a second chance. It had been, he reminisced, a different matter later though when Tom and Michael Hardwick-Smith had been found smoking cannabis in Tom's study. Nothing had been able to save him then, and Tom had been shipped off to a crammer to confront the problem of his A levels in a much less congenial atmosphere than that of Eton.

Camilla's lack of overt maternalism disturbed George. 'Darling,' he said, 'don't you think we should ring Anthony's housemaster and let the school know we are back in England?'

Sensitive to the unspoken reproof in this question and thoroughly irritated anyway at the prospect of entertaining a ten-year-old for a week, Camilla snapped, 'And what leads you to think I haven't already done it? How do you think I know about his exeat?'

George, who had rather assumed that she knew about it as a result of opening some post which had been sent to Rome and then forwarded back to England by the long-suffering tenant in the Trastevere flat, did not want to have a quarrel about it and therefore did not pursue this. He felt the point had been made. All the same, he was displeased with her and frankly disappointed by her *laissez-faire* attitude, and made a mental note that when they had children of their own a more committed approach would be expected. Much more committed. For the moment this would do as a warning shot. Presumably if, as he assumed, she had in fact done nothing so far about contacting the school she would now make it her business to do so, although without telling him.

Sitting on the end of the bed feeling mutinous and that George was interfering where he had no business to do so, Camilla nevertheless perceived that as a mother she had been found wanting. The time would come, she thought, when she would be so secure as mistress of Marchants that she would be able to do exactly as she pleased but that time was not yet. It would come when Camilla had another child, as she fully intended to do—George's child, and with a bit of luck that child would be a son. She did not relish the idea of another pregnancy, having neither wanted nor enjoyed the first one, but, with the practicality and calculation which characterized most of her actions, could see that, in the context of her situation, there was nothing else for it.

Accordingly, she stood up and put her arms around the silently disapproving George. Rather reluctantly he turned within them to face her and to give her a searching look, and found her downcast and, apparently, contrite.

'I'm sorry, George,' (in spite of the necessity to correct the bad impression she had made, she couldn't on this occasion bring herself to call him darling) 'you mustn't think that I don't love and miss Anthony, but a great deal has changed and there has been so much to understand and to adjust to, and, instinctively, I feel it will be much easier for me to build a closer relationship with him when I am truly at home here.'

It didn't occur to him to wonder what she meant by the last few words. In fact what she meant was *when I have finally got rid of your mother and I am at last running this house the way I want to.*

Disarmed in spite of himself, and after all, though he often didn't understand her at all, deeply in love with her, George kissed the full, inviting lips. He wanted her and, as usual, her remoteness gave this need an edge of insecurity and, therefore, a feeling of urgency. Slipping his hands inside her cashmere sweater he made the interesting discovery that she was not wearing anything underneath it, and desire conclusively overtook disapproval.

'Let's go to bed,' said George.

After she left Tom, Diana, shying away from being alone, went in search of Sarah. She discovered her where Camilla had also found her a few days earlier, in the library. Beset by her own problems, Sarah was nevertheless struck by the look of misery on her daughter-in-law's face and thought she could probably guess the cause of it. Intrusion, however, was not her style, and so she said nothing and when it became obvious, so great was Diana's distress, that she could not, rather than would not, speak, Sarah simply took her hand. The inevitable tears began to fall. Ignoring these Sarah said, 'She has been married before. She has a son.' There was no need to ask who she was. Sheer astonishment made Diana stop crying. Camilla had a son! Try as she might she could not imagine Camilla pregnant, could not imagine such a glossy bird of passage having any truck with children at all, in fact.

'What surprises me is that George never saw fit to mention it.'

'Well, he's told you now,' said Diana, feeling suddenly better, and sensing that in her mother-in-law she had found more of an ally than she could ever have hoped for.

'He didn't tell me,' came the terse reply. 'She did.'

'Oh, I see.'

'It makes me wonder what else he hasn't told us.' Diana noticed the word *us*. So that was how it was to be. Her and us. She experienced a sudden surge of optimism, and the dreadful leaden feeling of isolation began to lighten. She said rather daringly to Sarah, 'You don't like her!' This assumed a lot but Sarah did not contradict her.

'It's instinct. I thought at first that I was being unfair and I did examine my own motives. After all, I've lived in this house all my married life and beyond it. But I've always known that one day George might marry and that when Osbert died the house would pass to him and his wife, whoever she might be. I've really had plenty of time to get used to the idea, so I honestly don't feel it's that. It's just that, well, I've watched her. I think she's avaricious, and not just for things either.'

It was the nearest Sarah felt she could get to mentioning the first moves in the seduction of Tom as she had witnessed them over dinner. And the spitefulness of doing this right under Diana's nose had not escaped her either. Certain it was that Camilla had the social sophistication to have picked up the sexual vibration between Diana and Tom and, having done so, had set out to enjoy herself. She really had not wasted any time where mixing it was concerned. Sarah foresaw a lot of trouble unless George was able to control his wife.

'If only George were firmer. More aware,' she said aloud.

'Why on earth do you think she married him?' asked Diana. Neither of them actually mentioned Camilla by name. 'It's my observation that very few people marry for love,' commented Sarah obliquely, and could have added *as I don't have to tell you* but forbore to do so since Diana's liaison with Tom was still officially a secret from her. *Though Osbert and I did marry for love,* she thought, *and maybe it's because of that that I can see through other people's motives with such clarity.*

'They marry for all sorts of reasons,' she continued. 'I think you'll find Camilla spends a great deal of money. She's a very expensive lady.' She shrugged. 'Enough said.'

'Not much opportunity for that here,' remarked Diana, 'and no audience to speak of for her sort of display either.'

No indeed, that could certainly be conceded. Suddenly Sarah saw what had happened. Of course. They had met in Italy. Camilla had never expected to live in England. She had expected to spend George's money in Rome. It must have come as quite a shock when he insisted on the move home to Marchants.

While Sarah was picturing this piquant little scene, Diana stood up, and announced that she intended to hack out on one of the horses. She looked altogether calmer and Sarah thought this a good idea. Riding for her had always been a panacea. It would take her mind off her troubles, imagined and otherwise.

'I'll come to the stables with you when you're ready and help you tack up if you like.'

'Fine. Thanks. I won't be long.'

In fact, Diana, who kept her riding clothes at Marchants, took rather longer than either of them anticipated and returned looking irritated. Her boots had not been in the usual place, and when finally located, thrown down carelessly in a corner without their trees, were found to be covered in mud. They could only have been borrowed by one person since the rest of the family had their own of both the riding and wellington variety. Diana, who had been brought up not to sit on a horse unless she looked immaculate, fumed. However, having kept Sarah waiting this long, there was now no time to do anything much about them. She decided to ride Othello, a seventeen-hand black gelding originally purchased for Tom. Sarah buckled on the horse's head collar while Diana got the tack, and led him out of his box to an iron ring in the stable wall to which she tied his leading rope via a loop of baler twine. She hoofpicked him

and then began to groom him prior to putting on his
brushing boots while Diana sorted out the bridle.
Gracefully Othello bent his massive handsome head
to receive the bit. Standing beside him Diana looked
diminutive. From an upstairs window where the old
servants quarters were situated opposite the stables
Camilla, who had been exploring this part of the
house, watched. There was no doubt that Diana did
look good in riding kit, very good in fact. The hack-
ing jacket, an old herringbone tweed of Sarah's, was
sharply cut with its tiny waist and vented flared back.
Immaculate buff jodhpurs set it off perfectly. *Pity
about the boots, though,* thought Camilla, and
laughed to herself. She, who had not sat on a horse
since she was a child, made up her mind to ride
again. The temptation to upstage her new sister-in-
law, if not at the sport itself then certainly in the
clothes, was not to be resisted.

Unaware that she was under observation, Diana
tucked her hair into a net, put on her hat, pulled on
her gloves and then, using the old brick stable mount-
ing-block, swung herself lightly into the saddle. She
leant down and said something to Sarah, who handed
her a whip, and then walked Othello who was beginning to fidget out of the stable yard. Camilla lost
sight of them as they turned the corner, Diana checking the girth as they did so. The show was over.
Turning away from the window she was disconcerted, though only momentarily, to find Tom, a

squirming Frescobaldi under one arm, leaning against the wall of the passage watching her.

As was her habit, Diana walked Othello for the first ten minutes or so, before stepping him up to a steady rising trot along the road. There was a chill in the air, a forerunner of the white frost to come, and the hedgerows, which were thickly berried this year, blazed with their own inner fire, reminding her that Christmas was only a couple of months away. From her point of view, Diana had always found this a rather depressing festival probably because, with its emphasis on family, it indelibly underlined for her the fact that she was in love with one man but married to his brother. As well as inviting one or two house guests, Sarah had usually organized a drinks party for friends and neighbours and now, presumably, George and Camilla would take on this task. Or perhaps the celebrations would be toned down this year because of Osbert's death. Underneath her she felt Othello's eagerness to get going. He pranced a few steps forward.

'All right, old boy,' she murmured, checking him. They turned right past the little church, the family church used by generations of Marchants who had worshipped and been buried there until two parishes merged and the spiritual centre of the village had shifted to the larger St Cecilia's. Once out of the lane, they took the bridle path up the hill and through a small wood, after which the moors opened up before them. From a sitting trot, the gelding struck off smoothly into a faster canter. Feeling the initial surge of power and then settling into the rhythm of his movement, Diana was reminded of her lover. She began to cry again. She seemed to cry all the time these days. Impatiently she brushed the tears away. She must stop this. Nothing bored a man more than a miserable woman, especially a man as self-centred as Tom. In defiance of her own anguish and determined to blot it out, she urged Othello on to a gallop, knowing that as long as this lasted, her mind would be empty of everything except the need to concentrate absolutely on the physical activity in hand. But then, at the end of it, as the sweating horse slowed down and eventually stopped, blowing hard, she shouted at the top of her voice to the deserted, darkening countryside, 'How can I live without him?' Answer came there none and, putting her head down onto the rough black mane, Diana wept as though her heart would break.

Sometime later, when she had finally calmed down, rider and horse, iron shoes sparking on the cold winter stones, turned for home through the glittering purple evening.

After Diana's departure, Tom lay on his bed for at least half an hour, smoking and thinking. He had not taken the trouble even to open the door for her when she left. The absence of a parting kiss had been seen by both of them without anything being said as a valediction, a seal set on an old love now grown, on his side anyway though maybe not hers, cold. It had all gone on too long, he recognized. He had desired her and enjoyed her for years, and now he could see that he had slowly been falling out of love with her for at least half that time. In the end Camilla's dark sun had eclipsed Diana's moon and finished it once and for all. Dishonestly Tom told himself that, whatever she thought about the situation as it stood, Diana would come to acknowledge that things had, in fact, turned out for the best. After all, she was married to his brother. Amoral, and therefore unaccustomed to feeling uncomfortable with himself, Tom nevertheless felt mildly uncomfortable now. It was not a sensation he enjoyed.

There had, of course, been other girls over the years, stylish, shallow London girls mainly, whom Diana had not known about, but she had been The One, and Tom, rather like George until George had met Camilla, preferred his pleasures to be on hand when he wanted them. He very much hoped Diana would be civilized about this and not make scenes. Quite apart from himself, there was Marcus to consider. Typically, with a hot pursuit of his second sister-in-law in view, it never occurred to Tom to extend his new-found consideration for his twin to his elder brother. Confident of success, and not without reason, for he knew himself to be very attractive to women, he looked forward to the chase, and having no intention of taking George's wife away from him but only of amusing her while George was worthily working in the City, was quite untroubled by any scruples concerning loyalty.

Feeling suddenly dynamic, he decided to start *now,* and got off the bed, removing his robe as he did so, and selecting a shirt from the heap on the floor. Putting it on, he looked with approval at the lithe frame reflected back at him by the wardrobe mirror. Not bad at all for thirty-seven was his verdict on himself, and with the considerable charm which Tom could deploy when meeting a desirable woman, or someone he felt was important enough to impress, for the first time, he smiled at himself in the mirror. Wandering about the bedroom selecting his clothes from the polished floorboards or the Turkish carpet, depending on where he had dropped them, he began to formulate a plan of campaign.

When he finally found Camilla, having first located a sleeping Frescobaldi, she was staring out of a window at someone or something he could not see. So intent was she on whatever it was that she did not hear his approach and he was able to stand at the end of the passage for some time watching her, unaware that she was, in her turn, watching his former mistress. When she finally turned round, he was amused to see her jump slightly. It was the first time he had seen her ruffled but, on the other hand, it couldn't be said that Tom had much of an advantage. Holding a comatose cat was one thing but by now Frescobaldi had woken up and could not have been less interested in meeting Camilla who never fed him anyway. It was difficult—no, impossible—Tom discovered, to look like a debonaire man of the world while battling with an intransigent animal such as this was. To cap it all he thought he detected amusement in Camilla's eyes. Neither of them spoke as they moved towards each other. At her approach Frescobaldi had become quiescent and was regarding her with watchful topaz eyes. Perhaps unnerved by the total silence in which this all took place, Tom, who had had every intention of simply handing her cat to his sister-in-law and then, perhaps, suggesting a walk in the grounds before they all changed for dinner, suddenly lost his head. By now Camilla was so close to him that he could smell the scent she wore, and, tall as she was, to look at him she had to lift her chin. As she did so, he could have sworn he saw a look of invitation. Unable to resist the impulse and at the same time aware that he might be making an error (for hadn't he decided to play a long game?), he caught Camilla around the waist with one arm, the other being out of action since it was still wrapped around the cat, and began to kiss her red mouth greedily and hard.

The slap was very hard and very well aimed. It landed on the left side of his face encompassing his ear as well and making his head ring. Caught off balance Tom staggered sideways, dropping her cat which raked him with its claws on its way down. Frescobaldi made his escape. He was followed by Camilla, who did not run but walked very fast indeed, and the purposeful tapping of whose high-heeled shoes on the lino which was still down in this part of the house could be heard receding. Face on fire and both eyes filling with water, Tom prepared to follow her at a rather slower pace. He had no desire to encounter Camilla again until she had cooled down. That is, if she was in fact angry. Thinking about it, he wouldn't have put it past her to give him a come-on and then hit him for the hell of it, or the practice perhaps. It suddenly occurred to him that not a single word had been exchanged during the whole incident. He could not fathom her. It was at that moment that lust turned into obsession. Come what may, he would have her.

In London Marcus, having rung home to inform Diana that he was obliged, unexpectedly, to have dinner with another member of the Bar, was, in fact, dining with Jane Prior. Scrutinizing the wine list he said, 'We may have a cuckoo in the nest.'

'A cuckoo in the nest?'

'Yes. At Marchants. My brother George's bride,

though bride is a very virginal word and, as such, hardly applies to Camilla, I would have thought. What about a claret?'

'Fine.' Like all mistresses, she was inordinately curious about his family. Occasionally he talked about them, but never about his wife. Jane had not even seen a photograph of Diana. 'What makes you say that?'

He narrowed his eyes. 'Because she has the face of an angel, a very materialistic angel, though, and, unless I'm much mistaken, the morals of an alley cat. George, naturally, hasn't noticed.'

Shocked, Jane said, 'Don't you think that you are perhaps being rather unfair. After all, she is your sister-in-law and you hardly know her yet.'

'Ah, but I do know her. Every so often her type crops up in court. Beautiful, assured, so slender that you feel you could snap her in two, and made of sprung steel. What makes her so threatening is that, on top of all that, she is intelligent. And grasping. It's really a question of whether George can handle her. On the whole I think not. I think she'll handle George.'

'Do you have to be so waspish?'

Their first courses arrived. Watching him eat, Jane whose first, unsatisfactory marriage had failed after five years, reflected, *I wonder if Marcus will ever leave his wife. I am so tired of being a mistress and I would like to be married again.* She found his dispassionate summing up of this newcomer to his family unnerving. *It makes me wonder what he really thinks of me.* This didn't bear contemplating.

Noticing that she had hardly eaten anything, Marcus said, 'Isn't that any good? Let me order you something else.'

'No, no, it's delicious. You know I adore quails' eggs.' She peeled one. 'I was thinking, that was all.'

'What about? You aren't allowed to have thoughts and not tell me,' he teased. 'They might be subversive.'

Impossible to tell him.

'I was remembering the time we first met,' fibbed Jane. 'At Jack Carey's exhibition at The Gallery.' He had been standing talking to James Harting who owned it, and, looking at his elegant suited figure, she had judged him very handsome and had wanted to know who he was. Now she did.

'Do you have to go back home tonight?' The archetypal mistress question. She could have kicked herself.

'No. I've told Diana that I'm staying in town.' He took her hand. 'With you, I hope.'

She thought, *I know I'm in love with him, but I have no idea whether he is in love with me. He's so hard to read, I may never ever know.*

Picking up her wine glass, without much hope in her heart, she raised it.

'To us.'

'To us.'

5

When the weekend of Anthony's exeat arrived, George and Camilla drove to Kent to fetch him. He was waiting in the main hall of the large old house which constituted the school building.

'Hello, darling,' cried Camilla with uncharacteristic effusiveness, more for George's benefit than Anthony's.

'Hello, Mummy,' replied the little boy without moving towards her. Quite determined to appear the perfect mother, Camilla caught her son up in a restrained hug, for there was, after all, her hair to consider. George could not help noticing that the hug was not returned. Anthony simply stood there with his arms by his sides and let himself be clasped. It seemed odd to George when one considered that the child had not seen his mother for months. George extended his hand to Anthony who shook it gravely and then stepped back a pace, rather as though he had just laid a wreath on the Cenotaph. He stood solemnly regarding George. As had been previously arranged, Camilla went to keep a long overdue ap-

pointment with her son's housemaster, leaving the
two of them together.

'Come on, Anthony, old boy,' said George, 'let's
put your kit in the car, and then you can show me
the school while we wait for Mummy.'

It had to be said that the word 'mummy' sounded
odd in connection with Camilla. George wondered if
Anthony thought so too. He picked up the tuck box
leaving Anthony to bring up the rear with his holdall
and, one after the other, they made for the car. At
the sight of the Jaguar, the boy showed the first sign
of animation.

'Wow! Is this yours?' He hesitated not knowing
whether to call his new stepfather Mr Marchant, or
maybe even sir. Daddy, Anthony had decided, lying
on his narrow bed in the dorm thinking over the unexpected news of his mother's marriage the day the
letter had arrived from Rome, was not on. On balance he decided not to call George anything for the
moment.

Fitting the tuck box, which felt empty, into the
boot, at the same time reflecting that such things
hadn't changed at all since his day, George said
kindly, 'I'll show you how it all works when we get
home if you like.'

'Brill and ace! Thanks! Does it have electric windows?'

George laughed, unexpectedly finding himself enjoying Anthony.

'Yes. Yes, it does.'

They went back into the main building where the parquet floor smelt of wax and the silver sports trophies gleamed in the darkness of a large bow-fronted mahogany display cabinet. Not for the first time George wondered why on earth schools were always painted cream and dark brown. The entrance hall was filling up with parents and boys. Running past, one small boy caught at Anthony's blazer collar.

'Hi, Ant,' he shouted and like a comet rushed on.

'Who was that?' enquired George.

'Oh, that's Pemberton minor. Ned. His family used to have me for the holidays when Mummy couldn't.'

'Was that very often?'

'Quite often,' said Anthony vaguely, without volunteering any more information.

Anxious to make contact with the Pemberton parents, George looked around the seething hall. There was, however, according to his stepson, no sign of them or their sons for the moment. Anthony led the way up the wide, polished uncarpeted staircase, towards the dormitory wing. As soon as he stood in the long bare room, George realized that not only tuck boxes had remained the same. Except for the new-fangled idea of duvets, it could have been the dormitory in his old prep school thirty or so years ago. Eight beds stood in two rows of four facing each other. At one end, the window stood open, rendering the temperature subzero. In spite of this the pungent

smell of socks permeated the air, and so did another
one that he couldn't at first identify. Surely it
couldn't be carbolic? Hadn't that gone out with Dickens? The general dinge and decrepitude filled George
suddenly with a feeling of nostalgia mixed with melancholy. He had never been sure at the time whether
he enjoyed his school days or not, having no point
of reference. Anthony, who had been searching
through a collapsing cupboard while George looked
around, pulled out a dog-eared football magazine
with a whoop of triumph and began to show it to his
new stepfather. Watching him as he turned the pages,
George pictured the endless school weekends, especially the dead Sundays, and the holidays when,
hopefully, the Pembertons would rally round yet
again. What had happened when they did not? He
wondered how often the little boy had gone to Rome
to visit his mother, but shied away from asking him
in case the answer reflected badly upon his wife. The
unwelcome knowledge that Camilla had been an offhand, not to say absentee, mother filled George with
dismay. Everything looked so different in England,
and there was, he was beginning to realize, a much
wider chasm between an affair and a marriage than
he would ever have supposed.

With difficulty he refocused on Anthony, who was
saying, 'I support Spurs. Ned says they were rubbish
last season, but I don't care. Who do you support?'

George resolutely pulled himself together in an ef-

fort to put his demons behind him. 'Arsenal,' he said
automatically. 'Let's go and find your mother.'

They found her in the main hall talking to a rather
untidy woman whom Anthony identified as Joan
Pemberton. Among the other mothers, many of
whom were decidedly tweedy, Camilla looked as if
she had stepped off a Paris catwalk, the ankle-length
silver fox coat (a present from generous George) giving a vulpine quality to her beauty and causing second glances from both the women and the men. Conscious of the small stir she was making, and rather
enjoying it, especially the flattering contrast provided
by Joan's sensible pleated skirt and Barbour, Camilla
waved to George and Anthony to join them. George
noticed that Anthony had fallen silent at the sight of
his mother. This was so marked it was almost as
though a light had failed. All animation had gone and
had been replaced by a facial expression George
could only describe as apprehensive. Politely the boy
extended his hand to Mrs Pemberton.

'Hello, Mrs Pemberton,' he said formally. He
wondered if his mother was about to palm him off
on the Pembertons again.

'Come on, Anthony,' said Joan robustly, 'you can
do better than that.' She extended her arms and Anthony gave her a hug, the real warmth of which could
not be doubted.

'Now Mummy is back, we'll be seeing less of you,
I expect.'

George looked sidelong at his wife. Camilla, who hated being called mummy, was staring into the middle distance.

Here George stepped in. 'On the contrary, I hope Ned will come and stay with us at Marchants. It's a large house, and after all the hospitality you have shown Anthony, we'd like to offer some back. Wouldn't we, darling?' By neither look nor word did Camilla associate herself with this invitation. He began to search for his diary.

Sizing him up as he did so, Joan Pemberton decided that she liked George. Apart from his undeniable good looks, there was an openness and normality about him which had always seemed to her to be conspicuously lacking in his wife. Without ever having let this fact influence her treatment of Anthony, who she rather pitied as well as liked, Joan disapproved of Camilla. Lavish presents from Italy to the Pembertons' farm, thanks for her son's keep, had in no way mitigated this view. She hoped that the advent of George heralded some happiness and stability for the child.

Once they were in the Jaguar and on the way home, silence fell. Driving with his usual speed and efficiency, George reflected that Camilla had a lot of fences to mend with her son. It troubled him that there should be such a gulf between the two of them, and it was symptomatic of his changing view of his wife that he could now confront his own frankly critical attitude about this without pushing it out of his mind as he once would have done. He decided to speak to her about it when he thought the moment was propitious.

Anthony stared out of the window. For the first time for two years he was going to spend a week with members of what he supposed he must now call his own family. And then there would be Christmas. Loneliness had made him in some ways a very elderly small boy, and the fact that his mother viewed him and his interests with unconcealed boredom and impatience was to affect him for the rest of his life. Camilla could have a very sarcastic tongue and, because of this, he feared her attention almost as much as he lamented her indifference. Christmas with the Pembertons had always been jolly, but in the same way as Diana had her reservations about this particular season of the year, so did Anthony, and for very much the same reasons, although he was not yet old enough to analyse and understand them fully. On the other hand he had perceived his parent's attitude to be more motherlike with his new stepfather in the offing. Rather as though her marriage had made her less unkind. Or perhaps, he thought, George had indicated that good behaviour was expected, rather as Mr Cazalet, his housemaster, did in speeches to the house before Founder's Day and the like. Mulling it over, he hoped that he had remembered to pack his puffer. Anthony knew from experience that his asthma was usually at its peak just before and during his mother's infrequent visits. For the last year he had been virtually free of it. All the same, one could never be sure, and Anthony was very frightened of the attacks when they did come.

As the car finally drew up outside Marchants he was found to be asleep. George lifted him out, carried him into the house and set him on his feet in the hall. To Sarah, waiting to welcome him, he looked curiously careworn for a ten-year-old, and really, in spite of the dark hair, not very like his mother at all. Anthony rubbed his eyes, pulled up a sock which had slid down to his ankle and then, remembering his manners said, 'How do you do,' and extended his hand towards Sarah. Looking at his intense, withdrawn little face, she felt a sudden compassion for him. This was a child who had learnt to tread softly early. Bending down she put one hand on his shoulder and took the proffered brown paw with the other. 'Welcome,' was all she said, meaning it. Children had always liked Sarah and this included her own sons as though, rather like animals, their emotional antennae told them who to trust. To this vibration Anthony was no exception and the touch of her lips on his face irradiated a smile of such brilliance that Sarah was momentarily taken aback.

At this moment Camilla swept through the door unencumbered by anything as mundane as a bag, calling to George who was unloading the car, 'Bring my gloves with you when you come in, would you, darling?' Anthony's smile dimmed and went out. He disengaged his hand from Sarah's and stood looking mutely at his mother. *He's afraid of her,* Sarah suddenly thought. To Camilla she said, 'It seemed to me that the old night nursery would make a perfect bedroom for Anthony. What's your view? If you think it's a good idea, we could ask Mrs Melbury to make up the bed.' It was extraordinarily difficult, she thought to herself, this business of the old regime coexisting with the new. Even though Camilla was now thoroughly briefed and perfectly capable of running the house, Mrs Melbury, whom Sarah suspected of not liking her new mistress, still came to her old employer for her instructions. It would be a relief to move into the Dower House. She decided to have a word with the builder tomorrow to make sure they were still on course for completion straight after Christmas.

Interfering old bat, thought Camilla. Aloud she said, 'I think that's a good idea. Shall I take Anthony along to see it or shall you?'

'I'll take him,' Sarah immediately offered. She picked up the empty tuck box, making a mental note, as had George, to fill it up, Anthony slung his holdall over his shoulder and together they set off in the direction of the back stairs.

He began to talk again. It was as though the further away he got from his mother the more relaxed he became. Looking around him he began to ask her questions about the house.

'It's very big, isn't it? I don't think I've ever been in such a large house before. Have you always lived here, Mrs Marchant?'

'Not "Mrs Marchant", Anthony,' Sarah said kindly, 'it makes me feel very ancient. Which I am, of course, but I prefer not to be reminded of it. Besides, you are now a member of the family and I should like you to call me Sarah, the way everybody else does.' She smiled at him. 'The answer is since my wedding day. When I married Osbert I married Marchants as well. Now I am handing it over to George and your mama, and they will run it.'

Concerned, he said, 'But it's your home. Why should you have to move out?'

'Firstly, I'm not moving very far, only to the Dower House in the park, and secondly, this is a quite usual arrangement where houses the size of this one are concerned. Now you tell me a bit about school. What do you like doing best?'

'Rugby.' With pride he added, 'I'm in The Squad, you know.' It was the first time he had told anybody outside school except for Joan Pemberton. There had never been any point in passing this information on to his own mother who simply wouldn't have known what he was talking about, and probably wouldn't have wanted to know either.

Sarah, whose sons had all played rugby at their

prep schools, keyed in immediately. 'The Squad!
That means you're one of the best. Well done you!'

Gratified, Anthony responded, 'Well, really I prefer football, but they don't play it there.'

'That's a pity. Maybe they will at your next
school.'

They had reached what he supposed must be his
bedroom door. Putting his hand on the brass knob,
he said anxiously, 'I wish you weren't moving out.'

Touched, she set down the tuck box and put an
arm around his shoulders. 'Don't worry about it. The
Dower House is really very close and I don't give
up my friends that easily, you know. Especially not
new friends like you.'

'Me neither,' said Anthony stoutly. They went in.

The night nursery would have looked spartan to
many eyes, but not to Anthony who was used to the
rigours and lack of privacy of his prep school dormitory. This room was comfortable but dilapidated,
having been well used over the years by Sarah's own
sons. One of the single beds had been made up by
Mrs Melbury who had simply gone ahead and done
this without debate because it was obviously the sensible thing to happen. In the middle of the clean
counterpane lay Frescobaldi, blissfully asleep with
all four feet in the air. Anthony's face shone with
pleasure. He picked up the little cat which was so
relaxed that it appeared to be boneless, and cradled
it.

'Oh, he's great. Is he yours?' he tentatively asked Sarah. 'You don't mind if I hold him, do you?'

'Actually he's not mine,' Sarah replied. 'He's Mummy's cat.'

'Mummy's cat!' Anthony looked amazed.

Sarah said, 'Shall we unpack your things?'

'Yes, all right,' he said, and began to unload not the holdall but the pockets of his tweed school jacket. These yielded a miniature mountain of screwed up sweet papers, half a shoe lace, a Greek coin ('it's my lucky one') and what looked like the remains of a small but probably lethal little catapult. Tackling his bag, Sarah encountered an object which she didn't recognize.

'What's this?' she asked Anthony.

'Oh, that, that's my puffer,' he replied without much interest. Then noticing that she was none the wiser, he elucidated, 'I get rather bad asthma. It makes it better.' And then, after some thought, 'Sometimes it does, anyway.'

Asthma. Sarah was not surprised.

It crossed her mind that Mrs Seed might be able to help here, but she would have to talk to Camilla about that. Putting this to one side for the moment she continued to concentrate on the job in hand. All his washable clothes had the threadbare look of fabric which had been relentlessly boiled in Matron's twin tub.

'Put these in the top drawer over there could you,

please, Anthony?' requested Sarah, handing him three limp shirts. 'No, not that one, the top one I said. You need some more clothes. Good heavens, look at this!' She extracted a matted object which according to its label had, in its day, been a rather expensive pure wool sweater. Matron, it seemed, treated everything she put into her machine to the same pulverizing programme. 'I think we'll throw this out, don't you? So you play rugby in the Michaelmas Term. What about the Summer Term? Cricket, I suppose.'

'Well, actually I'd rather do tennis next year.'

'Really! It's a marvellous game. I used to absolutely love it. Osbert and I played quite regularly years ago. We have a court on the other side of the vegetable garden. Perhaps we could have a knock-up some time. When the weather improves.'

'Oh, yes please.' His face lit up.

Still delving about in the holdall which was apparently bottomless, Sarah said, 'And what about work? All that boring reading, writing and arithmetic that you've been sent there to learn. How are you getting on with all that?'

'Quite well.' Like all small boys he wasn't very interested in education. And then, anticipating the question every grown-up always asked, 'I'm about halfway up my form. I really like English and History. Not much good at Maths, though.'

'It was ever thus,' said Sarah, unconsciously echoing Osbert and mindful of Tom's dismal performance which had culminated in extensive tutoring to propel him through his O levels. 'You wouldn't be the first small boy to say that by a long chalk. What about Latin? And French?'

'French is all right.' He thought for a moment and then resumed moodily, 'There seem to have been an awful lot of Gallic wars, though.' Catching his gloomy expression, Sarah suppressed a desire to laugh. Getting up to her feet, she announced, 'Right, that's that. If you stand on a chair, can you reach high enough to put your bag on top of that cupboard?'

'No probs.'

'Let's go and have some tea. Tell me, Anthony, do you know how to ride? I only ask because we have an old pony in the stables whose name is Blue, and I thought you might find it fun to sit on him.'

'Oh, wicked,' was Anthony's response, treating her to another dazzling smile. 'But I don't know how to do it, though. Does that matter?' He seemed to worry a great deal about being a nuisance.

'No probs,' said Sarah, easily slipping into his vernacular. 'We might organize you some lessons at the local riding school.' Or maybe Diana would teach him. On second thoughts perhaps not. Diana had been conspicuous by her absence lately, and Tom had also kept, for him, a low profile. Once or twice Sarah had noticed him staring at Camilla with an intense gaze though what he was thinking she couldn't begin to guess. There was an unnatural stillness about the house of the sort that sometimes occurs before an electrical storm.

Watching Camilla pour out the tea which had just been brought in by Mrs Melbury, Sarah tackled her on the subject of Mrs Seed's Spiritual Healing Sanctuary and Anthony's asthma, and was intrigued to learn that Camilla herself had consulted a healer some years ago, though with negative results. Sarah wondered what the problem had been. Camilla did not enlighten her.

'So you would have no objection if I took Anthony along with me the next time I go?'

'None whatsoever,' replied his mother absently. 'Though why it should do anything for him when it did nothing for me, I can't imagine.'

'Perhaps you were unlucky. All I can tell you is that it did a great deal for me when I had a desperately painful back and I tried absolutely everything else before finally finishing up with Honoria Seed, including a very expensive osteopath who actually succeeded in making the whole thing even worse. I practically crawled out of his clinic.'

'Healers are everybody's last resort,' remarked Camilla, studying her fingernails, and noticing that one was chipped.

'That's what she said,' said Sarah remembering

Mrs Seed's exact words: *I'm everyone's last resort, dear. Until they experience the power, that is.* Well, she had experienced the power, and, whatever it was, it had worked for her, and in the course of doing so had caused her to re-evaluate her Christian faith, mainly because of her discovery that her own church disapproved totally of Mrs Seed and all her works, even going as far as to say that these were satanic. Ridiculous, was Sarah's verdict. How could somebody who did so much good be satanic?

'Who told you about her?' Camilla's voice broke into her train of thought.

'Mrs Melbury. She had some rheumatoid relation who claimed to have been cured.'

'So what actually happened when *you* finally got to her?'

'It was really quite extraordinary. She asked me to lie on the bed and when she ran her hands over my back, although without actually touching at first, I could feel the heat coming from them. The whole session took up about fifteen minutes, I think, and the pain began to recede almost at once. Afterwards I felt wonderful, rejuvenated.'

'And your back was better?' Camilla sounded sceptical. 'Of course, psychosomatic ills, in which I include slipped discs and probably Anthony's asthma, about which he has always made a massive fuss, may well simply be cured by the power of suggestion, don't you think?'

Nettled by the inference that she had imagined the whole thing, and that there was nothing really wrong with Anthony either, Sarah said coolly, 'My back was not cured by the first visit, as a matter of fact, but by the end of the third it was definitely much improved. And now it doesn't cause me any pain at all unless I really overdo things. May I ask why you went to see a healer?'

'Secrets of the confessional, I'm afraid,' said her maddening daughter-in-law with a languid shrug. 'May *I* ask how you square all this with your Christian conscience as a regular churchgoer and pillar of the community?'

Keeping her temper with difficulty, more for Anthony's sake than anything else, Sarah said, 'As I don't have to tell you, everybody knows everything about everybody in a village the size of ours, and it's certainly true to say that the vicar and I did have the odd debate about it. Spirited rather than spiritual discussion, I'm afraid. Never a very sensitive man, in the end even the Reverend William Gilbey realized I was quite inflexible on the matter and, more in sorrow than in anger I suspect, stopped raising the subject.'

'That must have been a relief.' She now sounded bored.

'It was,' answered Sarah shortly, feeling like pouring Camilla's China tea over her head. Never mind. She had got the parental approval more easily than she expected, and decided to change the subject adroitly before Camilla, who could be very perverse, altered her mind. Turning to George who had just entered the drawing room, she asked, 'Do you intend to organize anything special for Christmas this year?'

'Yes, I'd like to, so long as you don't feel that it is too soon after Father's death to jollify.'

'Of course not. Osbert loved entertaining. Sackcloth and ashes were never his style.'

The whole idea struck Sarah as good thinking on the part of her eldest son since maybe Camilla would take the opportunity to spread her net elsewhere and might even throw Tom back, thereby releasing some of the pressure Diana was under.

Pursuing it, she enquired, 'What did you have in mind?'

'I should have thought a drinks party, probably, to introduce Camilla to the local families. You know Canfords, Kirkpatricks, Fordyces et al. What do you think, darling?'

Whatever she might have been going to say in response to this was interrupted by the arrival of Tom. He kissed Sarah, made an ironical half-bow in the direction of Camilla, who said nothing but only gave him an inscrutable lynx-eyed look in return, and then was introduced to Anthony by George. Anthony seemed to be tongue-tied in the presence of his mother, and after a couple of attempts to initiate a conversation Tom rather gave it up. It surprised him that someone with as much *savoir-faire* as Camilla should have produced such a gauche son.

Forgetting about the party for the moment, George said, 'What's happened to Diana lately? I feel as though I haven't seen her or Marcus for ages.'

Tom said easily, 'Oh, I think she's staying with friends in town while Marcus is away seeing a client.'

Putting down her cup, Sarah added, 'That's right. She and Marcus are turning up for lunch on Sunday to meet Anthony. That's correct, isn't it, Camilla?'

Camilla nodded, her mind clearly elsewhere.

Satisfied with this information, George enquired, 'Who's exercising the horses while she's away?'

'A girl from the village who grooms and mucks out. It's a marvellous opportunity for her to get some riding in.'

Apropos of nothing in particular, George said, 'Time those two started a family. Diana can't have much to do with Marcus away in London all week.'

Tom laughed into his tea and was quelled by a look from Sarah. Into the thoughtful pause which followed, Camilla said conversationally, '*I'm* pregnant.'

As one they all turned and looked at her. There was an astounded lull.

Suddenly nervous, although not sure why, Anthony said to Sarah, 'Can we go and see Blue now?'

6

The news of Camilla's pregnancy took everyone by surprise, George included, but the person on whom it indubitably had the most effect was Tom, for it was then that he realized he must be in love with his sister-in-law. In terms of shocks this was practically as major as the news of the forthcoming baby since Tom was well aware, principally from the deleterious effect he had seen it have on others, that only pain and humiliation trailed in the wake of hopeless passion. Diana, who appeared to be having some sort of nervous breakdown, was a good example of this sorry state.

Covertly watching Camilla who was sitting demurely, and rather suitably as things had turned out, on the old Victorian nursing chair serenely sipping her Lapsang Souchong, it occurred to Tom to ask himself if she was actually telling the truth. Here he was nearer the bone than he knew for she had not yet had a test, it being too early for such a thing. Still, she was sure she was right. She had known instantly the first time she was pregnant, and she knew this time too. On reflection he decided she probably was, for what would be the point in lying about it? Curiously, her pregnancy made her more desirable rather than less because she now seemed to be, for the time being at least, quite unobtainable. Or was she? For as George disappeared to fetch a bottle of champagne and Sarah procured appropriate glasses, Camilla deliberately sought, and caught, Tom's eye and shot him a look which, combining as it did detachment from the current proceedings with amusement, bound them together for its short duration in a cynical complicity which effectively excluded the others and the event they were all about to celebrate. *Nothing has really changed,* the look said. Extremely interested but wary, remembering the last invitation he had taken seriously from her, Tom responded with what he hoped was a non-committal smile. He began to see that staying ahead of the game with Camilla was going to be exacting, but, in spite of this and the fact that she was pregnant with his brother's child, it never occurred to him that he might throw in his hand and pursue his pleasures elsewhere. Bored and restless, just like her, it was still his intention to entertain them both.

George returned. The cork was released. The moment passed. They all raised their glasses. Even Anthony had some champagne, frankly baffled, though, as to why Mummy wanted another child when she really couldn't be bothered with the one she already had.

George kissed his wife. Her announcement, which
had clarified his own emotional situation to Tom, had
unquestionably done the same for George. All misgivings concerning her offhand attitude to Anthony,
and her cavalier disregard of certain responsibilities
which George saw as *de rigueur,* were pushed to the
back of his mind by the knowledge that she was carrying his son. For, naturally, it would be a boy. As
far as Camilla was concerned it had to be a son too.
She was quite determined to consolidate her position
at Marchants with one blow. As soon as possible she
would have the appropriate tests. Should the foetus
prove to be female she had no intention of allowing
the pregnancy to continue.

There was, Sarah noticed, a marked absence of the
sort of euphoria one normally associated with this
sort of event about Camilla. It also struck her as odd
that George, and even more especially Anthony,
should have been included in the common procla-
mation and not privately informed beforehand. She
glanced at Tom. He was staring at an elaborately
framed oil painting of a Victorian Marchant, with a
look of moody preoccupation, dark brows drawn together very much in the way they used to be when
he was a small boy having a battle of wills with his
father. Prosperously, the nineteenth-century ancestor,
another George as it happened, stared back. Not for
the first time Sarah wondered how the same upbring-
ing could have produced unsatisfactory Tom and sat-

isfactory Marcus, almost as though they were, literally, opposite sides of the same coin. A head and a tail. As usual she gave it up. Going back to the general conversation, she heard George saying, 'But, darling, do you really think it's wise for you to take on all the organization of a large party. Wouldn't it be more sensible for you to take things easy for the first few months?'

'Well, I don't agree,' said his wife quite crossly. 'Pregnancy isn't an illness, you know, George, and I really don't think I can be expected to drop everything for the next seven months because of it.'

This speech was delivered with considerable irritation, and it occurred to Sarah that Camilla resented the whole idea of a baby, or, at best, was ambivalent about it. George looked as though he might be about to say something else and then, probably wisely, decided not to.

There was an awkward pause.

Evidently realizing that she had sounded more than a little tart, Camilla said in mollifying tones, 'After all, I shall need something to occupy my time, and I promise to take on lots of help. And a Christmas dance would be such fun. Please don't be grumpy about this, George.'

To be accused of being grumpy when all he had been trying to do was to stop her overexerting herself seemed rich to Sarah. However, pouring oil, she said, 'We'll all pitch in and help, and I'm sure Camilla will know if she is overdoing it. It's not as though it's her first child, after all.'

No, thought Camilla, *but it's going to be my last if I have anything to do with it.*

Changing the subject completely having got her own way, she flashed a smile at her son. Not accustomed to this unpredictable beam swinging in his direction Anthony was immediately on the alert. In fact her question when it came was quite innocuous. She said, 'What do you think of Marchants, Anthony?'

Unused to his mother's full attention, Anthony hesitated. Camilla gave him a withering look. Swiftly speaking up for him, Sarah said, 'He's been asking me all about it. Of course the house and grounds are heaven for children. With your permission I'd like to arrange riding for Anthony. He tells me he likes his sport so he should make a competent horseman.' She smiled at him. Anthony blushed with delight, and gave her a grateful look.

'Oh, good,' said his mother vaguely, immediately losing interest.

Sarah stood up. 'Now I think we could go and give Blue his feed, if that's all right with Mummy.'

'Sure,' said Camilla. 'Run along. George, there's something I want to talk to you about.' She rose and rang the bell for Mrs Melbury to come and clear away the tea, and then she and her husband went from the room together.

Tom was left alone looking morosely into the fire.

He felt sorry for himself. The woman tantalized and tormented him. Quite possibly she even laughed at him behind his back. He had lost the initiative and could see no immediate way of retrieving it. Frescobaldi slipped noiselessly into the room and, recognizing a cat-hater, jumped onto Tom's knee where he made himself comfortable purring loudly. Apart from uttering the words, 'Bloody cat,' Tom felt too dispirited even to push the animal off.

A log fell causing the heart of the blaze to disintegrate with a sunburst of sparks, and reinfusing the room with the fragrant smell of burning cherry wood. Automatically Tom got up, and wearily began to reassemble the parts of the fire. This positive act of movement revived some of his pride and resolution. On the spur of the moment he made up his mind to get out of his sister-in-law's orbit for a few days and go to London. He would put her out of his mind. He would look up some old cronies. Girlfriends too. Why not? He would paint the town very red. Kicking Frescobaldi cemented the decision. He went off to pack his bag.

The weather continued to be raw all that week and one day there was a fine powdering of very dry snow. This was evanescent though; for the rest of the week the fiery orb of the October sun rose in the morning and sank in the evening, and as it came and went with the tranquil days of his first holiday at Marchants, Anthony discovered that he was actually enjoying himself. Apart from anything else he counted a room of his own a great luxury, and Marchants was a big enough house for him successfully to avoid his mother except at mealtimes when she was considerably diluted by the rest of the family. Most importantly, though, he had now established that he should call George 'George'. This was a great weight off Anthony's mind. As a child who had spent a lot of time on sufferance in other people's houses, he was more alive than most to the importance of getting this sort of thing right and Camilla could be very scathing about social gaffes.

On the Friday before he was due to return to school which was also the day on which Sarah had booked him an appointment with Mrs Seed, she went in search of him and finally ran him to earth in Blue's stable. He was standing with his arms around the old pony's neck, face buried in the rough mane. Standing watching him for a brief moment before he became aware of her presence, Sarah thought that Anthony might be crying, but when he raised his head she saw that his face was clear.

'I love him so much. You won't ever sell him, will you?'

'No, I'll never sell him. Quite apart from anything else he's too ancient to be sold. It would break his heart. As a matter of fact I've spoken to George and told him that I want to give Blue to you. And I've decided that I'll teach you too.'

Anthony's face looked doubtful and then, when he saw she meant it, became incandescent with joy. Without a word he went to Sarah and silently hugged her. Hugging him back, she said, 'Now listen, if he is to belong to you, you must learn to look after him. Let's start by giving him some hay. Tonight when we get back we'll give him a proper feed.' Undoing the knot of the empty hay net she handed it to the little boy. 'Go and fill it from the hay store and when you've done that bring it back here and I'll show you how to tie it up. It's important that it's high enough off the ground so that he can't catch his foot in it.'

Later, while Anthony was wrestling with the knot, he said conversationally, 'Do you think Mummy's happy about having another baby? It's just that I never thought she liked them very much.'

'Why do you say that, Anthony?' queried Sarah, her attention arrested.

'She never seemed to have much time for me, that's all.' This last was delivered totally without rancour but as a statement of fact.

'It was rather difficult for her, being in Italy and all,' she excused.

He wasn't having it. 'There are lots of boys at school whose parents live abroad but they visited much more than Mummy did. And some of them lived further away. Although,' he added inconsequentially, 'when she did come she was the prettiest. And she had the nicest clothes. Everyone said so.' This took Sarah back to the Fourth of June, before which event the boys had always anxiously quizzed her about what she planned to wear, particularly her hat.

'You must have been very proud of her.'

Significantly he did not answer this. Then he said, 'Do you think there is a difference between *loving* someone and *liking* them?'

With Tom in mind Sarah said, 'Yes, I do. That's a very adult question, Anthony.'

Pleased, he said, 'Do you think so?'

'Yes. What made you ask it?'

All at once he looked confused. 'It's just that at weekends, when there wasn't anything else to do, I used to think a lot. I mean I used to think about *her* and that I must love her because she's my mother and everyone loves their mother. But I wasn't very clear about the liking part.' He gave Sarah a guilty look. 'Sometimes I used to wonder if there was something wrong with me.'

She pictured him kicking his heels on his dormitory bed during the dead Sundays when friends such as Ned were taken out by grandparents or whomever. Feeling unable to comment reassuringly on Camilla's dismal performance as a parent, Sarah said robustly, 'You can take it from me that there is nothing the matter with you except that you think too much.'

Giving her a searching look, he said, 'Are you sure?'

'Absolutely sure. Have you ever talked to anybody else about this, Anthony, or has it been something you've tried to sort out in your mind all on your own?'

'Well, I couldn't really talk to Ned about it because his mother isn't the same. She's,' here he searched for the words and came up with, 'she's sort of more ordinary, more like everyone else. Do you know what I mean?'

She knew exactly what he meant. Camilla was certainly unlike anybody she had ever met before.

Sarah said, 'If ever anything like that is on your mind and you think it would help to tell me about it I'm here and willing to listen. And it would be our secret. Even at my great age, when I have a problem, it's often useful to talk things through with someone else if I can't immediately see the way forward. And, by the way, George is very stalwart and would always sort you out if you were ever in any kind of trouble. So, you see, you have a marvellous backup system going for you should you need to use it.' She took his hand and squeezed it, and received in return the brilliant benediction of his smile.

'Thanks, Sarah!'

'My pleasure. I really mean that. Now if you wouldn't mind filling up Blue's bucket with water and saying good-bye to him I think it's time we set off for Compton.'

Later on, driving rather fast along the country lanes towards Compton and Mrs Seed's clinic, Sarah wondered about Anthony's father. The little boy himself hadn't mentioned him and neither had Camilla. It was not the sort of thing she felt she could bring up, or, rather, her relationship with Camilla would have had to be very much more cordial than it was for her to have even contemplated doing so. And George wasn't very approachable these days either. All his old openness appeared to have deserted him, and it seemed to her that more and more was being left unsaid at Marchants just lately.

Stealing a look at her as she drove, Anthony wondered if he had upset her in some way. He thought her profile very stern and rather dreaded that he might have disappointed her. Perhaps he hadn't thanked her enough for the wonderful present of Blue. Whenever he thought about the pony, Anthony was suffused with happiness, and the idea that Sarah might think he had been casual in his acceptance of such a generous gift was too awful to contemplate. As he turned his head to elaborate further on his gratitude and delight, Sarah felt his gaze upon her and suddenly became aware that she had not addressed a word to him for at least twenty minutes so preoccupied had she been with her own anxiety

about the way things were going at Marchants. Pre-
empting him she gave him an oblique, companionable grin. Relieved by the knowledge that whatever
was the matter, and plainly something was, it was
not his fault, Anthony relaxed in his seat and began
to talk about his prep school.

'Where do you want to go at thirteen, or haven't
you thought about that yet?' asked Sarah eventually.

'Not sure. Where did George go?'

'Eton. And so did Tom and Marcus. Tom was a
very naughty boy indeed at school. At both schools,
in fact. I was always having to travel down to sort
things out.'

Anthony was entranced. 'Was he? Was he really?
What sort of things did he do?'

'If I tell you you must promise not to copy him.
It may sound amusing now, but at the time he was
a serious pain in the neck. He was always smoking
and cutting lessons. He and his father used to have
monumental rows about the fact that Tom never did
any work and was quite content to bump along the
bottom.' Deciding to omit the fact that Tom had been
sacked, she continued, 'In the end we sent him to a
crammer in order to get him through his exams.'

'And did he? Get through them, I mean?'

'Yes, he did. But by then Osbert was threatening
to cut off his allowance and turn him out of the house
unless he buckled down.'

She braked slightly to avoid a resplendent cock

pheasant which ran across the road and fluttered into the field. 'Oh, look! Wasn't he handsome? Did you see him, Anthony?'

'Yes, and there's another one, a brown one. In the ditch.'

'That's the hen.'

'What about Marcus? What did he do?' He was clearly very interested.

'Marcus was quite different in that he was self-motivated. He always knew what he wanted, and went for it. At the same time he was very loyal to Tom. Marcus,' here she broke off summing him up for a minute, and then resumed, 'was much more intelligent than his twin, though they were both good at games. Like Osbert, he loved poetry, though I don't know if he ever reads it now. I would say of him that he was one of those unnerving children who watched and assessed from a very early age and kept his conclusions to himself. Rather subtle. Tailormade for the Law in fact. It has always struck me as odd that they are so completely different. Tom looks very like Osbert, but in terms of character Marcus is much more like his father.'

By now they were approaching Compton, which was the nearest medium-sized town to the village, providing such amenities as a swimming pool, a small town hall and a large supermarket. The outskirts of the town, through which they were now driving, were mainly new housing estates with small redbrick houses and equally small square gardens, but as they got nearer the centre these turned into Victorian terraces, most of which had been gentrified and presented painted middle-class faces in wisteriaed uniform rows to the weak sun. Mrs Seed's home was on the other side of Compton and was a large detached Edwardian house called Shangri-la, long since divided into flats of which she occupied only the ground floor plus the basement which she used for her healing centre. The garden around the house, currently in autumnal decline, was cultivated by her alone since none of the other occupants of Shangri-la were interested in horticulture, and its fertile blaze of summer flowers every year bore testimony to her green fingers.

Sarah and Anthony made their way carefully down the steep outside staircase leading to the basement door on which was a notice saying *Compton Healing Sanctuary.* Inside, a gas fire surrounded by a semi-circle of chairs hissed quietly, and they settled down to wait. Nobody else was there. Sarah made a practice of arriving early in order to avoid what she called Mrs Seed's scrum. After ten minutes, a door opened and a voice said, 'You can come in now, dear.'

Honoria Seed was of medium height. Her hair was grey and immaculately arranged, and she wore a long white coat of the kind doctors in hospitals have. To Anthony, aged ten, she looked ancient and was, in fact, a very well-preserved seventy.

'Take off your shoes and lie on the bed, Anthony,' she ordered.

The bed was high, and Anthony needed the wooden step she pulled out for him to do as she asked. It was very comfortable. As Sarah had told him to, he lay back and closed his eyes.

'Uncross your feet,' said Mrs Seed. Primed by Sarah to expect a sensation of heat, Anthony was surprised to find that her hands, as she moved them over his body, at first made him cold. He began to feel very peaceful, and behind his closed eyelids flowed waves of shimmering colour. Finally the hands, which he was coming to think of as disembodied, stopped and were placed lightly on his chest. The sensation of cold changed to one of heat. Anthony began to feel sleepy.

'They are saying that this is an emotional problem,' pronounced Mrs Seed. Who were 'they', he wondered drowsily. And then, 'Yes, yes, I can hear you. Yes, I'll tell them.' Sarah was quite used to 'them'. Mrs Seed claimed to perform what she described as clairaudient operational healing guided by a doctor or sometimes doctors in the world of spirit. She turned to Sarah now and said, 'They say that the mother is the problem. It is not an allergy. Anxiety is the activator.' She paused. It was quite a significant pause, and Sarah was beginning to wonder if she should break the silence when Mrs Seed finally began to speak again. To her stupefaction the voice had

changed completely and had acquired a different tim-
bre and resonance, as though someone else entirely
was there. With a not altogether pleasant thrill of
apprehension, Sarah realized that Mrs Seed must
have slipped into trance. The healer's eyes had a curiously sightless yet, at the same time, distant look,
rather as though the room in which they were gathered no longer existed for her and she was peering
down the centuries instead. This must have been how
the Pythoness at Delphi looked, thought Sarah, actually feeling the hair on the back of her neck rising.
The disconcerting new voice deepened and gathered
strength, rather as though a charge had shot through
its medium. Patrician vowel sounds had replaced Mrs
Seed's flatter London variety. With a shock of recognition Sarah realized that the voice she was now
listening to *was that of Osbert.* She glanced at Anthony who seemed to have fallen asleep. Mesmerized, she transferred her gaze back to the healer.

Still staring with the same blindness, apparently
oblivious to her immediate surroundings, Mrs Seed/
Osbert was saying, 'No good is going to come of
this. That woman is malign, a bloody menace, in fact.
And there will be tragedy. You can't stop it. Death
in the family. It can't be avoided, it has to be. His
time has come. It's going to be underground war.
You've got a fight on your hands.'

Sarah stood immobile, unable to speak. She felt
profoundly shocked and moved by this communica-

tion from her husband, if that was what it was. It was either that, or Honoria Seed was mad.

There was a pulsating silence. The healer leant against the bed as though drained of energy. When she spoke again the voice was once more her own though she herself looked white and depleted.

'Was any of that any use to you, dear? I have no idea what I'm saying in trance, you know.'

This at any rate was a great relief.

'Very helpful, thank you, Mrs Seed,' replied Sarah faintly. She shook Anthony who sat up looking rosy and refreshed.

'I think you'll find that will improve matters,' said Mrs Seed. 'Come and see me again if you have any more problems.'

So ordinary was this exchange that Sarah began to wonder if she hadn't imagined the whole episode and its unnerving prophesies.

'Now, what about a booster for you?'

Sarah politely but firmly declined. The thought of possibly exposing herself to another bout of Mrs Seed's clairvoyance was quite sufficient to put her off. She put the usual note in the donation saucer and they made their farewells and departed.

Judicious questioning of Anthony on the way home in the car elicited the fact that he had dozed off and had not heard any of it. And even if he had, Sarah was pretty sure he wouldn't have understood it. The whole thing gave her much food for thought as she drove. As a Christian, Sarah believed in the afterlife of the spirit, and the notion that someone who had been as close to her as her husband had should continue to care for her and watch over her made sense. She pictured the puce face of the vicar should she tell him that Osbert, one of the most correct and reliable of his flock, had made a reappearance on earth through the mediumship of Mrs Seed, and for the first time for months spontaneously laughed out loud.

This sort of lightness of spirit was something she had always associated with her husband and experienced all too rarely these days. It took her back to the early years of her marriage. *I was so happy,* thought Sarah, *and I really didn't appreciate it enough at the time. It seemed to me that those blissful days would simply go on for ever. It could have been, as so many are, simply an ambitious marriage on my part, and I expect a lot of the girls who set their caps at Osbert thought it was, but I loved him. To have so much is to provide a hostage to fortune. Yet even during the war years I felt impregnable.*

Reflecting on all this reminded her of a particular wedding anniversary. It must have been their fifteenth. He had taken her out to dinner, to what was in those days the best local restaurant, on the other side of Compton. Afterwards they had driven back to Marchants, and walked in the winter garden the way they had walked in another summer garden the night they first met all those years ago. Strolling up the yew walk towards the stone goddess, his arm around her waist, he said, 'She has always reminded me of you. Wonderful breasts and long legs. I shall never tire of your body.'

'I want you. Let's go back to the house.'

'I should really have liked to have made love to you here.'

'Osbert, it's January! Perhaps we should have an unanniversary, the way the children have unbirthday celebrations if they happen to be away on the day.'

'Maybe, but never mind about that now. I'll race you!'

Arriving, laughing hysterically, in the bedroom just after him, with her hair beginning to come down, she felt as though she was twenty again.

'We're *far* too old for this sort of thing!'

'We're *never* too old for this sort of thing. Come here.'

Slowly he had taken off all her clothes, with the exception of the sapphire necklace he had just bought her, and then he had removed, one by one, the grips in her hair, which was very long in those days, so that Rapunzel-like it uncoiled and rippled down almost to her waist.

Running his hands over her body, the body which had born three children by then and was no longer as firm as it once had been, he said, 'Do you think it is ridiculous that I am still in love with you after all this time together?' and, suddenly lost for words of her own, she had said, *'My true love hath my heart and I have his.'* Of course she knew this would please him and was enchanted when he capped it, cleverly misquoting,

> *'By just exchange one for another given;*
> *I hold hers dear, and mine she cannot miss,*
> *There never was a better bargain driven.*
> *My true love hath my heart, and I have hers.'*

Strange that I should remember that now when I haven't thought about it for years. Even the poetry, which he loved. 'Oh, Osbert, how I miss you!' She had inadvertently spoken the last few words aloud. Woken up by the movement of the car swinging through the gates, Anthony looked at her in wonderment.

She drove round to the back of the house, put the car away in the garage and got out. The light was fading and the electric-blue cold of the evening exhilarated her. She felt full of the sort of energy which had seemed to desert her lately. Ever since Osbert's death, in fact. Delineated by frost, the house glittered palely. Perhaps she would take Anthony out for a sedate hack on his pony tomorrow. Remembering that he had not had anything to eat, she turned to him.

'Go and let Mummy know you're back and then

ask Mrs Melbury if she will please organize you some tea. When you've had something to eat we'll go and feed Blue.'

Still thinking about the extraordinary thing she had witnessed at Honoria Seed's Healing Sanctuary, she let them both into the house.

7

Having marshalled her thoughts and made several telephone calls to make sure that what she wanted could be achieved at such short notice, Camilla ambushed George with her Christmas plans. Faced with the prospect of a full-blown ball for the county when what he had had in mind was a rather staid drinks party with canapés, George was temporarily rendered speechless. On the other hand, Camilla's renewed enthusiasm and interest disarmed him for lately he had found her lackadaisical and more than a little fractious. This he had put down in a vague and rather Victorian way to Her Condition, but that being said it didn't make her any easier to live with. And so he agreed.

'We'll stipulate that everyone must dress the part,' she said, 'and masks will be worn. Oh, and I'll organize appropriate music, early music. Perhaps we could recruit some students from the Royal College of Music to play it for us. What do you think?'

George didn't know what to think at first, but then felt disposed to draw the line here. Left to himself he would have said he was a Puccini man, and the

thought of an evening of the sort of esoteric music
his wife was proposing filled him with cultural panic.
In the end they compromised. Renaissance music
would welcome the guests and would be played
through drinks and dinner, and in another room there
would be modern music for Philistines such as himself and younger members of the party. Warming to
her theme, Camilla began to elaborate on the food.
By now he wouldn't have put it past her to organize
roast swans borne aloft on silver platters, and decided
to impose a budget, albeit a generous one. What she
did within it would be her affair. With such a short
time to go before Christmas she would have to get a
move on, he thought.

She did. Sarah, whose advice was not sought, had
to concede that her daughter-in-law was efficient, and
Tom arrived back at Marchants after a week of dis-
sipation in London to find the whole place fairly
humming with activity at the centre of which was
Camilla, very secretive. Seeing her again, he was
forced to concede to himself that a week away from
her had not cured him. Tom was beginning to regard
love more and more as an illness, and the sight of
Diana's depression only served to underline this dismal fact. He avoided her and her reproachful look as
much as he could.

The days wore on towards Christmas. At George's
insistence a secretary was employed to cope with the
huge amount of paperwork generated by Camilla's

ambitious project. She took none of the family into her confidence, which infuriated Sarah, but spent whole days closeted in George's study giving mysterious briefings to the various firms she intended to employ. Sarah and Diana travelled to London, escorted by Tom, to meet Marcus and George for lunch and to hire their costumes. Nobody had any idea what Camilla was doing about hers. Not even George seemed to know. Diana did her own research and decided to appear as Gaspara Stampa, a Renaissance lady from Padua who had been as unhappy in love as she felt herself to be.

In the event, Camilla had her dress made for her. If George could have seen the bill he would probably have passed out, but it was her firm intention that he should never see it. The gown was copied from a portrait of Lucrezia Borgia, and became her mightily. Having got that out of the way, she felt free to concentrate totally on the rest of the organization.

His mother having declared herself too busy to go, it was Sarah who went to collect Anthony from school for the Christmas holidays. On her arrival after a slow journey due to the wintry weather, he ran up to her and hugged her.

'I've been so looking forward to seeing you.' He brimmed with pleasure. 'How's Blue?'

'Missing you, what do you think! Is this your bag?

Okay, you take the tuck box, which I assume is
empty. Let's get going.'

In the car and heading for home she said, 'Great
excitement at Marchants. Mummy is giving a costume ball.'

'Wow!' Then with trepidation: 'Will I have to
dress up?'

'We all will!'

They arrived home in time for dinner and the first
real snow fall of the year came with them from Kent.
Overnight, large flakes continued to drift slowly and
lightly down. Even though this meant that Anthony
could not ride, it excited him beyond measure and
he whirled like a dervish around the garden, kicking
up powdery flurries and falling into the soft white
folds of the drifts. He wished Ned Pemberton was
there to share it with him.

As usual, apart from hiring him a page's costume
which was important because it had to complement
her own, Camilla took scant notice of her son, and
it was left to the combination of Sarah and Diana to
entertain the little boy. It seemed to Sarah that a
change had come over Anthony. The tentativeness
and introspection had been replaced by a more normal robustness. Without becoming in any way a brat,
he had lost the desperate desire to please, perhaps
because he felt himself to be not only accepted but
lovingly accepted. She also noticed that he had be-

come quite expert at avoiding his mother, so that they only ever met at mealtimes, a fact that Camilla appeared not to have registered.

On the morning of Christmas Eve everyone rose early to watch the transformation of Marchants. Great branches of fir and thickly berried holly were brought in from the park and, when the snow had been shaken from them, used to decorate the hall so that the whole house smelt of the fragrance of trees. A swag of evergreen leaves was artfully wound and plaited around the bannister of the main staircase and bound with ribbon rather in the way the Florentine ladies of the Renaissance period used to bind their hair. And tall brass candlesticks, which Sarah had never seen before but assumed must have come from the attic, stood everywhere with their creamy waxen candles waiting to be lit. Sheer scale and artistry rendered the whole effect both natural and sumptuous at the same time. For the first year since the idea was imported from Germany there was no Christmas tree in the hall at Marchants, Camilla having decreed it unRenaissance and banished it to what she contemptuously referred to as the disco room. A correct, if unpopular, decision, Sarah felt, in the light of what she saw. Caterers took over the large old kitchen, supervised by the competent Mrs Melbury. The food, it turned out, was to be served banquet style on long tables in the dining room. When the fires and the candles were lit the effect would be darkly splendid.

By the end of the day, even Anthony who, being ten, hankered after paper chains and a thoroughly gaudy tree more than most, could see that Mummy had got it right. But then, he thought to himself, Mummy always did get that sort of thing right. It was being a mother where she didn't measure up. Lost in thought, he suddenly realized that Sarah was speaking to him.

They went upstairs together, since it was her intention to help Anthony into his costume before tackling the complications of her own. This outfit, chosen for him by Camilla, which consisted of a cream shirt with long padded sleeves over which was worn a red thigh-length tunic loosely gathered in at the waist by a brass-buckled belt, suited him. From his shoulders swung a short cloak and the whole ensemble was finished off by a small red hat and tights of which one leg was black and the other red. For a second, as she watched him strut in front of the mirror, she saw his mother in him. He wore clothes well, just as she did. Thinking how charming he looked, she adjusted the hat above his thick fringe and stood back to admire the effect. Anthony also viewed himself in the glass, and in the parlance of his prep school thought he looked a wombat. He was extremely glad that none of his friends could see him.

One by one the Marchants filtered down to the hall where they formed a handsome group containing a Medici, a Ricasoli (Marcus), a Gonzaga (George), a Borgia (Tom, unconsciously echoing Camilla, had chosen to appear as Cesare) and a subdued Stampa. The log fire had been lit and so had all the candles and the hall glowed and pulsated with the flighty movement of the flames. Above them the high ceiling, which was beyond the range of their light, was lost in shadows. As Camilla had foreseen it would, the glossy sheen of the aromatic evergreens formed a perfect foil for the richness of the costumes.

Tom found himself looking forward to the evening ahead, and, in spite of everything, so did Diana who was clutching a stiff drink and had avoided taking tranquillizers all day in an effort to rise above her lethargy and depression, and actually enjoy herself again. To her surprise she found that this did appear to work and Marcus, who had been extremely worried about his wife lately, was relieved to see how much more cheerful she appeared to be.

The musicians arrived and began to set up their music stands and instruments. Ideally they should have played from a minstrels' gallery, but since Marchants did not possess such a thing, Camilla had placed them to the right of the fireplace. The music began and, as the stately opening notes of a stanza originally composed for Lorenzo de Medici wound gracefully through the pine-scented air, Camilla

made her entrance stepping down the wide polished
oak with Anthony, her page, in her wake. Shyly he
followed his magnificent mother. Willow slim, there
was no sign of her pregnancy as yet except, thought
a dazzled George, that her breasts looked fuller. Her
hair was drawn back and formed into a high, bulbous
shape artfully bound with gold ribbon. It seemed to
defy all the laws of gravity. Beneath its stark shape
the imperious face and high forehead with its pronounced widow's peak were accorded the sort of ex-
posure that only a beauty can withstand. Camilla's
dress was of wine-red velvet, long sleeved, with a
skirt which fell in soft gathers from a small, spectacularly low-cut bodice embroidered with gold flowers,
above which her white breasts were displayed to
great advantage. Tom, who had hoped he was re-
gaining some sort of equilibrium, was lost. George
walked forward, took his wife's hand and, bowing,
kissed it. Anthony, who had never wanted to be part
of his mother's court in the first place, slipped away
and positioned himself by Sarah, imposing and stat-
uesque in black as Catherine de Medici. The first
guests began to arrive and shortly a few became a
throng. Welcoming and introducing, George stood by
his wife. Outside, the snow which had been falling
steadily all through the day before but had since
stopped, formed glistening frozen swathes. In the
flowerbeds and the yew walk, it royally iced the
shrubs and hedges and encrusted the garden seats,

and, at the end of the yew walk, the stone goddess, mantled in white, lifted slender, icicled arms and hands full of snow to the new moon.

Inside Marchants the revels were now under way in earnest. A striking couple, George and Camilla moved through the crowd followed by admiring looks. Everyone there knew George, of course, but hardly anyone had met his wife and there was a great deal of curiosity about her. Camilla played the role as one born to it, well aware that the success of this night's extravaganza would be her passport to some sort of social life while she waited for her child to be born.

Standing together, the Bulstrodes, the Kirkpatricks and the Harringtons, all old friends of the Marchants, watched her progress. Ogling his hostess and wearing what his wife disapprovingly thought of as his goaty look, Colonel Bulstrode said, 'She's a real stunner. Good for George! Where did he meet her?'

'Rome apparently.' The speaker was Desmond Kirkpatrick.

'Oh, *abroad*,' said the Colonel, looking dubious. 'She is British though, isn't she?'

Concealing a grin, for the Colonel's prejudices were well known, Desmond responded, 'Yes, she is. And you're quite right, she is spectacularly good-looking. She'll make a very stylish hostess for Marchants.'

'She's got breeding,' pronounced the Colonel, ris-

ing above his distrust of all things Continental. 'As
a racing man I can spot it a mile off. She's a high
stepper. Could be quite a handful I should judge.
Think George can cope?'

Marcus, who had just joined the group and over-
heard him, riposted drily, 'I think George is enough
of a horseman to prevent Camilla breaking into a
gallop. But perhaps we should open a book on it,
Colonel.'

'Certainly not,' said Violet Bulstrode, oblivious to
any ironical intent, and giving her husband a censorious look. Bunny Harrington, an ex-fashion model
who did not perceive herself to be threatened by the
newcomer, unlike Violet Bulstrode and Vanessa
Kirkpatrick, neither of whom had any claim to good
looks, observed, 'Camilla has great presence. She
performs within a force field all of her own.'

Marcus, who had always known that Bunny was
a clever girl, was struck by this description. She had,
he thought, holed in one. His eyes dwelt on his sister-
in-law for a brief appreciative moment. Could
George cope? The jury was still out on that one. As
she wove a path through her guests, the perfect hostess, though currently without her husband, Tom also
watched and hovered hawkishly, wondering how on
earth he could get her to himself. In the grip of this
obsession, he took no notice whatever of his last love
who was thereby thrown back on the company of her
own husband. It occurred to Diana that it was a very

long time since she had really tried with Marcus. Looking at him with rekindled interest and a large gin in her hand, she wondered what her marriage would be like if she really gave it her best. It was, after all, all she presently had.

In the mêlée Tom had lost sight of his other sister-in-law. Masks abounded but with her dramatic hair she should not have been difficult to spot. After a spin around the hall and the drawing room it became apparent she was not there, and she was not in the dining room either, where food was just beginning to be served. Noting that George had been cornered, and was being held conversational captive by Colonel and Mrs Bulstrode, Tom strode off towards the main staircase, and taking the steps two at a time, mounted it in search of Camilla.

Meanwhile Sarah, in common with her eldest son, was also doing the social round, but with Anthony in tow. Many of their friends and acquaintances either had children or, in the case of her own generation, grandchildren, and she was anxious to put him in touch with other boys of his own age who lived locally. The musicians took a break at this point in the proceedings and moved off in a group to the kitchen where Mrs Melbury had organized a meal for them. George finally managed to effect an escape from the Bulstrodes, only to be immediately button-holed by Hugh Fordyce, the self-satisfied and, in his view, monumentally boring local Member of Parliament. Sighing inwardly and wondering where on earth Camilla was, he allowed himself to be led off in the direction of Miles Canford whom Fordyce wanted to interest, along with George himself, in some business scheme of his.

Without knocking, Tom quietly opened the door of Camilla's bedroom where he guessed she might have gone to repair her make-up. In this surmise he was proved right for as he did so, she materialized on the other side of it. Swiftly he stepped forward, causing her to move back a pace, and shut and locked the door behind him. Camilla tipped her head back and looked up at him. He thought her smile was mocking and this flicked him on the raw.

'Who are you?' she suddenly asked.

Momentarily at a loss and then remembering he was in fancy dress, Tom answered, 'Cesare Borgia. What about you?'

'Lucrezia!' she said and burst out laughing.

Tom was not amused. They were wasting time. He felt this was do or die. The room in which they were standing was one of those being used for the ladies' cloaks, but he was willing to lay odds that while dinner was being served no one would disturb them. For the second time he caught her to him. This time she did nothing but went on looking at him, sphinx-like, and still smiling. Full of pent-up lust and at the same time angry, Tom kissed her savagely. As he did so, the fantastic hair began to come adrift and very slowly, like a ship going down, descended to her shoulders with the gold ribbon still winding through it. Camilla swore. Tom took no notice. Adept as he was at this sort of exercise, he located immediately a row of tiny velvet-covered buttons at the back of her dress and undid them one by one. The wine velvet fell in soft billowing folds around her feet and, following it down, the gold and bead embroidered bodice hit the floor with a faint rattle, rather as though a snake had shed its skin. As they fell together onto the bed, Tom, who had no idea that in sixteenth-century Italy knickers were considered indecent and worn only by courtesans, was fascinated to behold that she had been wearing absolutely nothing underneath it. There was no time to speculate on that now though. He took her (or did she take him?) on Violet Bulstrode's mink coat.

Having successfully got rid of both Fordyce and Canford at last, George followed in his brother's footsteps and also went in search of Camilla. Concerned about her since she had been nowhere to be seen for at least the last forty-five minutes, he located her in the end coming along the corridor from their bedroom. The first thing he noticed was her hair, which now fell in waves to her shoulders. The gold ribbon had been removed and artfully redeployed to form a band. Camilla, mindful of where he had just found her and conscious that this had been a close call, prayed that Tom would not issue out after her. Slipping her arm through that of her husband, she gave him a kiss and then steered him back along the corridor in the direction from which he had just come.

Her colour was high tonight, he noticed. This was unusual for Camilla, who normally had to resort to the artificial variety because of her natural pallor. George thought he had never seen her look more desirable. On impulse he suddenly said, 'Let's make love.' He surprised not only himself, but Camilla too, who did not feel up to the whole thing again quite yet.

Thinking quickly, she said, 'I feel a little unwell.' It was one of the oldest tricks in the book, practically ranking alongside the convenient headache, but she couldn't think of anything else in time. Watching his apprehensive look, she followed this up hastily with, 'I think I'm probably hungry.' Camilla cursed herself. Now he would start banging on that she was doing too much and would endlessly exhort her to rest more. It was all too tiresome. Not for the first time she wondered if this was all worth the candle. With George fussing and Camilla leaning on him, they turned the corner at the end of the corridor. Hearing their footsteps receding either loudly or softly, depending on whether they were treading on

one of the Turkish runners or the wide oak floorboards, Tom, who had been effectively treed by the
arrival of his brother, cautiously let himself out of
the bedroom and, having ascertained that the coast
was indeed clear, sauntered off in the opposite direction. By now the dancing was well established. Even
Camilla who had initially opposed the Renaissance
impurity of a disco had to admit that George had
been right. The musicians were due to depart anyway
at 11.30 and, on current form, the assembly looked
as though it might go on until at least two or three
in the morning. Everyone was showing signs of wear
and tear. Costumes were coming adrift and tights
were snagged. Anthony had put his hat down and
couldn't think where. He hoped no one had sat on it.
Tom's saturnine face reappeared among the throng
and Diana who was currently dancing with Miles
Canford wondered where he had been all this time.
He had a look about him which she recognized, and
which could only be described as replete. The fact
that Camilla's hair had come down did not escape
her either. Surely, even Tom wouldn't have…? Oh,
no, surely not!

She was still speculating about it when twelve
o'clock struck. Anthony was beside himself with elation that it was now Christmas Day. As George had
instructed, he opened the front door so that they
could all hear the village church bells peeling
through the crystalline night. George kissed Camilla,

Marcus kissed Diana, and, for lack of anyone else to kiss, Tom kissed his mother. When it became his turn to kiss his sister-in-law, he said *sotto voce,* 'When next?'

Before kissing him back, Camilla gave him a level look. 'I do hope you aren't going to become a bore, Tom,' she said sweetly without even troubling to lower her voice.

A bore? He couldn't believe his ears! Hadn't she enjoyed herself? He certainly had. Mortified he moved on to Diana, who saw him coming and made for George instead. The rest of the guests began to drift back to the dance floor, while some of the more elderly revellers, now that midnight had struck, felt they could legitimately depart. Among them were the Bulstrodes, she wearing the new mink the knowledge of whose recent baptism would have shocked her beyond measure.

Camilla felt well satisfied. Her ball had been, and indeed still was, a triumph. She had no doubt that it was years since the county had seen one organized with so much lavishness and style. Well, it would give them all something to aim for. Noting Tom's hungry eyes upon her she took George's hand.

'Won't you come and dance sedately with your pregnant wife?'

They moved off together. Marcus who, along with Diana but without revealing the fact, had also noted Tom's return to the ball together with the wreck of

Camilla's hair, sardonically watched them go, and then asked his own wife to dance. Everyone but himself seemed to be having a good time, thought Tom sourly. Left to his own devices, he was unable by now to decide whether from his point of view the evening had been a success or not.

8

Sarah moved into the Dower House at the end of January, with a feeling of relief. Even though the builders had not quite finished she was in no doubt that she would rather be there than at Marchants. Anthony had gone back to his prep school and really there was nothing now to detain her. Also she sensed that Camilla was waiting, probably at George's insistence, for her departure before commencing the interior facelift. Sarah was ready to concede that the house was certainly due for a new incarnation, and having seen how her daughter-in-law had tackled the ball, she was confident that Camilla would probably make a superb job of it. So something good might come out of what was otherwise, in her view, a misalliance.

Camilla existed rather than lived through the colourless days of February. Collected by Sarah, Anthony came home for half term, which was only a brief three-day exeat, most of which he spent at the Dower House. By now Camilla knew that the baby was a boy, so there was nothing left to do but get on with it. All the same, she resented the self-imposed pregnancy. And then there was the little matter of her unpaid dress bill for there had been no question of the money for the wine velvet coming out of the budget that George had set for the ball. That had been supposed to cover everything and for most other people would have done so. Although George currently doted in a way which set her teeth on edge with irritation, nevertheless she didn't think a request for another substantial amount of money on top of his initial generous outlay would be well received. Maybe if they agreed another budget for the revamp of the house, she could siphon some money out of that. Since the demands for total or even partial settlement from the dressmaker were now becoming quite pressing, she would have to think of something, and this might be one way out. Accordingly, she sat down at the little kneehole desk which had once been Sarah's, and began to work out some figures.

The other question occupying her mind was what to do with Tom. Tom currently either palely pined or ferociously sulked. She had managed to avoid being alone with him so far, but with Marcus and Diana and Sarah around less and less this had become virtually impossible. Allowing him to make love to her had been an amusing diversion, although she had not meant to allow things to go so far so soon. Tom in his melancholy frame of mind she felt she could handle, but Tom after a drink or two, glowering and smouldering, had all the unpredictability of an unexploded time bomb. Since his moods seemed to swing alarmingly from one extreme to another to the extent that even George had noticed and had asked her what she thought might be the matter, it was difficult to know how to defuse him. On reflection, the only way to do it seemed to be to let an affair continue on an intermittent basis which, as her pregnancy progressed, *force majeure,* would become less and less frequent and finally cease altogether. Or maybe not. It would depend what she felt like. Consequently several otherwise empty afternoons were wiled away in just such a fashion, though not in Tom's den. Camilla, whose surroundings were of importance to her, drew the line at that and insisted on her own bedroom where they made love presided over by Venus and her cherubs. This was a dangerous practice, but risk taking had always appealed to both of them, and with George safely stowed away in the City of London all day, why not?

As her pregnancy advanced, langour had taken possession of Camilla. Perfectly relaxed, she was content to let her lover kiss and touch and stroke her until her body hummed with anticipation so that, when he finally entered her, this slow accumulation of sensual pleasure took on its own impetus and exploded almost immediately into climax. It was an education for Tom who had always put his own pleasure first before. He had never encountered a woman like her, he thought, and probably never would again.

Perhaps because they mirrored her own, he was oblivious to her essential greed and selfishness, and saw only a beautiful face and body and the expertise, when she could be bothered, of a houri in bed. But, strangest of all, with a perversity he couldn't explain to himself, he found himself enjoying her because she was pregnant rather than in spite of it. Camilla, who had never loved a man in the true sense of the word and did not even like most of them very much, simply used others for her own gratification and gain, and Tom was no exception to this. In this respect he and George were absolutely equal. When she was not with him, Tom thought of her constantly. When Tom, or George for that matter, was not with her, neither entered her mind as she sat drawing up lists and comparing fabric samples. Hers was a totally self-centred existence. Except in financial terms, Camilla did not need a man to complete her. Her circle was perfect already.

One blustery day in the middle of March, travelling up to the office on the 6.45 a.m. train accompanied as usual by *The Times* crossword, George felt unwell. It was nothing he could put his finger on exactly, just a slight tightness about the chest and a general sensation of being below par. This was out of the ordinary for him since, in common with the rest of the Marchant family, he normally enjoyed robust good health. He shifted in his seat, moving his left arm as he did so which felt as though it might be about to go to sleep. Perhaps he was getting the flu. There was quite a bit of it about in the office just now. Resolutely he went back to the convoluted clue for three down, and by the time the train drew into the London terminus had practically finished the puzzle. Feeling marginally better, he caught a taxi and settled down in the back of it to read the day's *Financial Times*.

At Marchants, Camilla decided to make this a Tom day. She would work in the morning, tie up the loose ends of the rehabilitation of the drawing room ready to present to George that evening, and would then, as a reward, give herself a thoroughly self-indulgent afternoon in bed. This decided she sorted out her files and got going.

Sitting at the mahogany partners' desk in his office, George felt decidedly odd again. His chest was still constricted, rather as though it had a tightening iron band around it, and he thought he might be going to pass out. He stopped midway through the letter he was dictating, and when his secretary looked up enquiringly from her pad, she was horrified by his colour. On her advice, and feeling something of a wimp, he curtailed the dictating session and instructed her not to put any calls through for the next hour. Then he shut and locked his office door and lay down on the large, leather-covered Chesterfield. Immediately his breathing became easier, although the pain persisted, and eventually he fell asleep to wake an hour later feeling much the same. It was at this point that George resolved to give up the unequal struggle and take the rest of the day off work. Tomorrow he would go and see Desmond Kirkpatrick, the Marchants' GP. Not up to the train, he reappeared in the outer office and, having asked his secretary to organize a company car to take him home, went back to his own room to clear his desk and pack into his briefcase the papers he intended to work on that evening.

One hour later, sitting in the back of one of the firm's cars, making various telephone calls, one of which was to Camilla who was apparently out, he decided that the whole thing had been a fuss about nothing. All the same, he thought, he would go and see Desmond, just for an overhaul. At approximately four o'clock, the car drew up outside Marchants.

Entering the hall, George was struck by the extreme quietness of the house. Putting his briefcase down, he looked around the door into the library where his wife was often to be found working at her desk. Here was evidence of industry and recent occupation, but no Camilla. It occurred to him that maybe she had gone upstairs to lie down, and holding the afternoon's post which he had picked up from the demi-lune table in the hall, he began slowly to climb the broad staircase. Reaching the top, he walked along the passage towards his bedroom, footsteps muffled by the Turkish runner.

The pain had returned and had become sharp and insistent. Suddenly feeling breathless again, he placed his hand on the door handle, and as he did so Camilla, whose hearing was acute, caught the familiar vibration of George's heavy signet ring striking brass. Instantly on the alert, she turned to face the source of the noise and, amid an appalled silence, she and Tom, who was clad only in his socks, watched the knob turn and the door open.

Downstairs in the pantry, Mrs Melbury was peacefully doing some ironing. On a chair beside her lay Frescobaldi. While it was not exactly true to say that the two of them were friends, a standoff had now been achieved after the initial hostilities. A number of hefty thumps on the back with wet tea towels at various times had given Frescobaldi a good idea of what was and was not acceptable behaviour in the kitchen. Since Camilla appeared to have forgotten all about him, Mrs Melbury had rechristened him Frisky, deeming his original name daft, and this part of the house, plus the stables, had become his beat.

Singing to herself, she put the iron down and switched it off. Then she picked up the ancient portable radio which she listened to while performing mindless activities such as the one she had just completed, and switched that off too. Just as she did so she was startled to hear a loud scream and then the sound of running feet upstairs. Taking off her apron as she made at the trot for the door, she almost collided with Tom.

'There's been an accident. Mr. George. Ring for an ambulance.'

Mr. George? She hadn't even realized he had come home. Conscious of the fact that she had never before seen Mr Tom in such a state, Mrs Melbury stepped her stout frame up to a sedate run. Once she had made the call she followed Tom's retreating form upstairs. George lay just inside the bedroom door where he had fallen after opening it, the letters he had been holding scattered all around him. At his side lay something that Mrs Melbury couldn't at first identify, and then she saw that it was Madam's carved wooden angel which she had brought with her from Italy. The head, which was lying some distance away, must have broken off it when Mr George knocked it over as he fell. Camilla was lying on the bed sobbing hysterically. She was wearing a grey silk wrap, and must have been having her afternoon rest when whatever did happen, happened.

Arthritically Mrs Melbury got to her knees beside the lifeless form of her employer, and felt for his pulse. Nothing. She decided not to voice her opinion that it was too late for an ambulance. It was coming now, so let it come. It suddenly occurred to Tom, who was standing irresolutely by the door, that he should phone both Desmond Kirkpatrick and Sarah, and that Camilla could do with a brandy. Mrs Melbury went off in the direction of the library, where the drinks cabinet was, to get one. While Tom was telephoning, Camilla got off the bed and went to sit on the little gilded chair in front of her dressing-table mirror. The shock had been cataclysmic. All the colour had drained away from her cheeks leaving her face stark white, and the black pupils of her eyes were enormous. With shaking hands she pushed back her dishevelled hair. The wildness of her stare and the red pointed fingernails made her look like a witch. Still trembling violently, she stood up. Tom came back. They faced each other. They had seen the slight shake of Mrs Melbury's head as she had taken George's wrist, and both knew that he was dead.

Camilla said, 'Nobody must ever know you were here.'

'Nobody ever will,' said Tom.

Both realized that the enormity of what had just taken place would link them together for the rest of their lives. Even if they never saw each other again they would always have this dreadful thing in common. Tom wished he could erase the memory of George's disbelieving look as he had stood on the threshold. Alas, there could have been no misinterpretation of the scene which had confronted his brother. He saw again (would he ever forget it?) the tumbled bed, Camilla wearing nothing but the silk wrap which was undone so that her full breasts and the swell of her belly, pregnant with George's child, were visible, while he, Tom, had been in the act of picking up his shirt from the floor. On the bedside table was half a bottle of Chablis which he had had the presence of mind to remove to his own room before summoning help. Tom groaned aloud. He wished that he and not George were dead. For virtually the first time in his life, he felt shame and remorse. Camilla on the other hand seemed to have got a grip on herself. Having drunk at a swallow the very genteel tot of brandy brought by Mrs Melbury, she had gone into her bathroom to dress. As she went, the doorbell sounded, heralding the arrival of Dr Kirkpatrick and the ambulance crew, who had coincided on the doorstep. Mrs Melbury led them upstairs to where George lay and Tom and Camilla, wordless and ashen, waited. They both had a shocked, stranded look, like fish beached by a freak wave. As had the housekeeper before him, Desmond knelt down and after a quick examination rose to his feet again.

'I'm afraid it's too late. I'm so very sorry, Camilla. Tom, could you help me lift him onto the bed? It looks like a heart attack, but because there has been no hint of this sort of problem before, there will have to be a post mortem.'

What an extraordinary thing, he thought. George who had always had the constitution of an ox, and who had been a friend as well as a patient, was the last man he would have expected to go like this.

The doorbell rang again.

'That will be Mother,' said Tom, looking distinctly fugitive.

Desmond said, 'Do you want me to break the news to her?'

'No, I'd better do it.' He went reluctantly towards the stairs.

As he left, Camilla was standing immobile by the bed. She looked as though she might be about to collapse.

Tom led Sarah into the library and told her without preamble. He felt that if he had tried to wrap it up he would never have got the words out. She listened to what he had to say without comment, staring out of the window. Osbert had died here at Marchants too. Not in their bedroom, though. By the end he had been so ill that Sarah had had the bed moved downstairs. Exhorted by his doctors to send him to hospital, she had refused to do this and with the aid of some professional live-in help had supervised his nursing herself. During the long months of his illness she had read to him. Poetry, lots of it, and Trollope.

I loved him so much, yet the day Osbert died I couldn't grieve. I felt, in a curious way, at one remove from myself. Maybe that was just as well since otherwise I might have behaved the way they do in the East, and shrieked aloud and torn my clothes. And now it's the same again. George is dead and once again this very English paralysis of all feeling has set in. George. She saw him, aged ten, the same age as Anthony was now, jumping his pony. As he had grown up he had, of course, had three or four. This was the very showy one called Johnny Belinda which won most of the gymkhana prizes one year, and she, as the owner of the house in whose grounds the event had been staged, had handed out the rosettes and prizes. Those had been carefree days.

She became aware that Tom was speaking to her, and when she eventually turned back to him he saw that she, who had looked the way she was now ever since he could remember, suddenly appeared much older. She was remembering Mrs Seed's prophecy.

'I'd like to see him,' was the only response she made.

Her composure threw him. He would have given a lot for a stiff drink.

They went up the stairs together.

The post mortem and the evidence of George's secretary confirmed Desmond's diagnosis that George had suffered a heart attack. Hitherto apparently in good health, and notoriously indifferent both to doctors and to the need, at his age, for reasonably regular check-ups, he had now paid the price. His widow re-engaged the same woman who had assisted her with the organization of the Renaissance ball to help her answer the letters of condolence which poured in. It was lucky after all, reflected Camilla, who had got over the loss of nerve which had afflicted her when George collapsed, that she was pregnant, for, even if her husband had not updated his will after his marriage, her position as his wife and the mother of his unborn child must now be absolutely secure. Of course the family would not like it. Well, they would have to lump it. So it was with a high degree of confidence that she looked forward to the reading of the will, which was to take place the day after the burial. Camilla could have gone to see Miles Canford, who was one of the family solicitors, before then but felt that this would be a lapse of taste. Anyway, so certain was she of the outcome that she felt she could afford to wait with equanimity. It would not do to appear too eager.

The morning of the funeral was fair and almost warm, a portent of the hot summer which was to come. Galaxies of daffodils starred the park, and Sarah and Diana who had arranged the flowers together, had filled the family church with them, reserving forsythia for the large displays on either side of the altar. The air was fresh with the smell of spring, a time of year which George had particularly appreciated. By the time the family arrived, the church was already more than half full, and as Camilla entered, escorted by Marcus and becomingly attired in black with a bunch of snowdrops in her hand, a sympathetic silence fell. She took her seat in the front pew beside her mother-in-law.

Sitting watching a shaft of sunlight within which oscillated a million shining particles of dust, Camilla reflected that had her husband not died as conveniently as he had, her marriage would have been irretrievably over and so would any hopes she might have had of getting her hands on the Marchant money. Avoiding the eye of Tom who was sitting on the other side of Diana and Marcus, she twisted round in her seat, her eyes scanning the faces of the mourners at the back of the church where people were now having to stand due to lack of space. Sarah following her gaze, wondered who on earth Camilla could be seeking. Evidently she had not located whoever it was, for, with a small impatient grimace, she went back to studying her fingernails, which were long and pointed and very red as usual. Noting her tearless profile and calm demeanour from his seat by her side, Marcus wondered about George's death. He had observed Tom's mounting desperation over the past few weeks and had assumed his twin to be infatuated with their sister-in-law. In the light of all this, the fact that Tom had been in the house the day George died was not insignificant. The question was, thought Marcus, exactly *where* he had been at the time.

The vicar entered and the organ, which had been

quietly playing in the background, now struck up in earnest and the haunting strains of Crimond hung in the golden, scented air. From somewhere in the congregation muffled sobbing could be heard. Inwardly suffering but determined not to weep in public, Sarah held her head high and stared straight ahead, her eyes moist. Noticeably dry eyed, Camilla did the same, while Diana whose nerves were in shreds after this latest blow, sat with her face in her hands and Marcus's strong arm around her shaking shoulders. She felt that her world as she thought she had known it all these years had had, after all, no substance, and had only existed within the fragile glass bubble of her own imagining. The renewed enthusiasm for her husband had proved fleeting, but therein had lain security of a sort, and although she had no overpowering desire to share his bed, she had no particular wish to leave it either, for after all, where would she go?

She forced her mind to concentrate on the service. Marcus delivered the eulogy, Tom for reasons best known to himself having declined to do so, and now the vicar was preparing to read from Corinthians. He commenced. The words were wonderful, thought Camilla, but completely spoiled by the dirgelike delivery. She had hired the organist from London and would have liked to hire another vicar while she was at it. She fixed him with a basilisk stare. Oblivious, he chanted on, *'For now we see through a glass,* darkly; but then face to face: now I know in part; but then shall I know even as also I am known.'

Camilla specially liked this passage which appealed both to her sense of mysticism and the dramatic. Listening to it, Tom stirred uneasily. For him it conjured up an uncomfortable image of George standing before his Maker, being debriefed. He still wondered how he could go on living with himself, though less and less frequently these days, and remained plagued by thoughts of his dead brother's wife.

The organist played the first sombre bars of the death march to which George was to make his last journey. With furrowed brow, the vicar followed the pallbearers. Disapproving of the Albinoni Adagio, he had tried to persuade the third Mrs Marchant against it. And had got nowhere. Bossily righteous and confident that she would defer to his own sense of what was and was not appropriate, he had found his advice pleasantly but definitely rejected, and when he had still pursued it she had become positively steely, and he had been disagreeably reminded of an earlier set-to with the first Mrs Marchant concerning the spiritual healer Mrs Seed, when he had again got nowhere. Furthermore he had had the distinct feeling that she had been laughing at him, though what he based this on he wasn't altogether sure since she had listened to him with a great show of deference before more or less telling him (very charmingly, though) that it was none of his business.

The mourners filed out of the church behind the family. George was to be buried beside Osbert, where they had all so recently stood, with the exception of Camilla, enacting the same play but with a different principal. In spite of herself, as the coffin was lowered into the ground, Sarah moved forward to put a consoling hand on Camilla's arm. As she did so, she looked across the grass to where those who had come from the village to pay their respects were standing at a discreet distance, and caught sight of someone she had never seen before. Tall and thin, the stranger was wearing a belted mackintosh which seemed to Sarah's English eye to have a distinctly American look about it. Dark blond hair waving thickly back from a high forehead crowned a visage both ascetic and hard, whose pale, bleached tan put her in mind of desert landscapes. Wherever he had come from and whoever he was, he looked extraordinarily unlikely standing among the homely crowd from the village.

Sarah felt rather than saw Camilla's tension. As with a hunted animal there was a heightening of awareness which was almost tangible, a tautening of both mind and body ready for any action which might be required. This must be the person she had been looking for in the church. Having caught her attention, the man bowed to Camilla, and Camilla, in return, almost imperceptibly inclined her head. That was all. So tightly was she clutching the bunch of snowdrops, Sarah noticed that her sharp fingernails digging into the stalks had severed some and bruised the rest. After a brief hesitation George's widow threw the flowers onto the coffin, where they lay on the dark wood, fresh and white and delicately veined with green, the living destined to lie with the dead.

The early promise of the day had not been fulfilled and it was under a livid sky that the small subdued family group made its way back to Marchants, followed at a distance by the rest. The rear was brought up by the foreigner who spoke to no one and loped rather than walked. On the gravel, in front of the house, he stood looking up at the façade and then turned around and surveyed the park through which he had just come, before entering.

Inside, in the dining room, Mrs Melbury had prepared refreshments including wine. It was at this point that Camilla introduced the outsider, for so the family, zealous guardians of the privacy of their grief, already regarded him. Jake Weston. An old friend, so she said, of hers and George's, from Rome. Jake, who was nothing like as young as Sarah had thought at a distance, had a face which had worn well, but she now could see that the skin stretched tightly over the bones was covered by a web of fine lines, many of which were round the eyes and pos-

sibly were indicative of a life spent squinting into
hot suns. It was a dried out face. He was, perhaps, a
well-preserved forty-five, Sarah guessed. And he
was…here she searched for the word and came up
with one which sounded old-fashioned but nevertheless summed him up, an adventurer. Not for the first
time she queried her own instant verdict and still
could not disagree with it. The required commisera-
tions and pleasantries were delivered in a voice
which was classless but had a faint twang of something which might have been American, and might
have simply been affectation. With misgiving, Sarah
watched his gaze flick around the room, finally coming to rest on the painting they all called the Gainsborough, School of. *He looks as though he is taking
a mental inventory,* she thought.

'Jake will be staying here for a while,' announced
Camilla. It was a flatly delivered statement, notable
for its lack of enthusiasm. Really? The family all
looked at Jake and all saw something different. Or
maybe it was just that there was something in Jake
for everyone. With a stirring of interest, Diana saw
a handsome and personable distraction from her
withdrawal symptoms after the long love affair with
Tom. Tom saw a rival, and instinctively felt that Jake
had been, and possibly still was, more than just a
friend of Camilla's. Otherwise why was he here?
Any other friends she and George might have collected in Rome were conspicuous by their absence.

Camilla was now circulating the room, talking, thanking, being sympathized with. *The perfect widow*, thought Diana bitterly. All the time Jake's light eyes followed her progress as he talked to Marcus and Sarah. There was, decided Sarah, eyeing him, something distinctly predatory about Jake.

Noticing that the vicar was apparently about to take his leave Sarah excused herself and moved off in the direction of the Reverend William Gilbey, leaving Marcus talking to Camilla's house guest.

'How long are you going to be in England?' Marcus asked him, having already ascertained that Jake had flown into Gatwick from Maputo two days before. Jake was vague. He really couldn't say. It depended how a certain business deal he was trying to put together worked out. So unspecific was he that Marcus, whose next conversational gambit would have been to enquire about the nature of Jake's profession sensed a reluctance to talk about it, and asked something else instead. Jake himself had no such inhibitions and framed a great many questions, mainly concerning the size and profitability of the estate. It was at this point that Diana decided to join them.

In ones and twos and threes the village contingent was beginning to leave. Lowryesque in best suits and black polished shoes they could be seen drifting off across the lawns and down the drive. Jake's expressionless eye rested on Camilla's sister-in-law. He thought her attractive in an obvious sort of way, but that was all. His gaze veered away from her and ranged around the room until it once more lit on Camilla. Watching him lose interest, Diana was piqued. Determined to secure his attention, she began to ask him about himself, in her experience a subject few men could resist. Rather surprisingly it seemed that he could resist it. Reluctantly Jake refocused on her upturned face. Without, in fact, answering the question she had just asked him, he asked one of his own instead.

'Where's the boy?'

Momentarily at a loss for words, Diana said, 'Do you mean Anthony?'

Well of course he meant Anthony, thought Jake, irritably. Who the fuck else would he mean?

'Camilla wrote and told him about George's death, but she didn't want him to come to the funeral. She thought it would be too upsetting for him. He suffers from asthma, you know.'

'I do know,' answered Jake shortly.

For some reason it had never occurred to Diana that Jake would know Anthony. He must predate George by quite a long time in Camilla's life, she thought. A very old friend then. Just briefly, watching him, she had a sudden disconcerting sense of *déjà vu*, a feeling that she had seen this man before, although, of course, she couldn't have.

She saw with relief that the last guests were leaving, which provided her with a good excuse for quitting Jake's graceless company. She went to say her farewells to the Fordyces and the Kirkpatricks. Jake stood where she had left him, an isolated, foreign figure. He made no effort to talk to anyone else. Entirely unembarrassed by his own separateness, he continued his survey of the surroundings in which he found himself. Camilla had done well here, he thought. The pickings would be rich. It would be worth staying around for a while. He caught her eye and held it. Camilla gave him a blank stare back and was the first to look away.

9

In the days following the funeral, Tom found himself unable to think of anything else but Camilla. Love, he decided in despair, was like some dreadful incurable illness. He hoped to God he never had another attack. That is, if he ever recovered from this one. In vain he had waited for a summons to her bed, or even some sign that she still cared for him. Nothing. And the sight of Jake, for whom Camilla seemed currently to be reserving all her confidences, was almost more than he could bear. It was not that Camilla was unkind to him, quite the reverse, but the absent-minded brand of attention she did deign to give him humiliated him and made him feel like a rather vapid lapdog. With Jake, on the other hand, she spent an immense amount of time, and Tom found himself wondering what on earth they talked about. Consumed as he was with jealousy, there was very little he could do about it since finding her alone, without Jake in the offing, seemed an impossibility. Except, presumably, in bed at night. *At night!* That was it. He would go to her room when everyone else had retired and the ubiquitous Jake was safely out of the way.

Owing to the fact that old Mr Greenhill, the family solicitor and other half of Canford and Greenhill, had been indisposed and was insisting on handling the whole thing himself, the reading of the will had been postponed. Money, or rather the lack of it, was another of Tom's preoccupations. It was tacitly assumed by everyone that Marchants and the estate would have been left in trust for George's child, with Camilla allowed to live in the house and off the income for life if she so wished. It all depended on whether George, having learnt his wife was pregnant, had immediately revised his will. On the whole, Tom thought he would have. George had always been very efficient about that sort of thing. Either way it didn't help Tom's financial situation. Unless…he suddenly had a brilliant idea. *Unless he, Tom, married his brother's widow.* It would, after all, be the perfect solution. She had the house and the money. He already lived in the house and needed the money. The tidiness of it quite overcame him. He congratulated himself. They would have to wait a decent interval, of course, and then there would be a certain amount of gossip, no doubt. Tom had been scandalous all his life, and had never given a toss about what other people thought of his behaviour, and Camilla's attitude, he was willing to bet, would be more or less the same.

Not for the first time, Tom wondered when Jake proposed to leave. The friendship between the fellow and Camilla intrigued him. The two of them were as thick as thieves, but there was a certain formality, almost a businesslike quality about the way they talked together, and though Tom had no idea what the subject of their conversation was, watching them he received an impression of negotiation. One thing he was now sure of was that they were not lovers. Whatever it was that bound them so closely together it was not that.

Diana, on the other hand, had plainly fallen for Jake. After his initial offhand behaviour on the day of the funeral, he had since made an effort, and it appeared that he could, when he felt like it, turn on the same sort of spurious charm as Tom. Tom, used to being the centre of attention where Diana was concerned, found the way she hung around the man nauseating. Not wanting her himself, it was still difficult for his *amour-propre* to come to terms with the fact that she might incline to someone else, and so soon too.

The reasons for Jake's change of attitude were not immediately apparent. Perhaps he had simply been out of sorts that day. Whatever the cause, it now appeared that a complete change of heart had taken place. The two of them even went riding together. None of this seemed to affect Camilla, and made Tom certain that his instinct concerning the platonic nature of the relationship between her and Jake had been correct. However, the fact that Jake and Diana had begun to spend a certain amount of time *à deux* did nothing to help Tom realize his ambition to speak to Camilla alone, for whenever the other two went off together, she simply disappeared. In a house the size of Marchants this was easy to do and because almost every room had two doors, it was possible for Camilla to avoid him very successfully. And he had now come to the conclusion that she *was* deliberately avoiding him. Never one to suffer from a lack of self-confidence where women were concerned, and forgetting that he had seriously under-estimated Camilla twice before, Tom reasoned that she would come round. He knew her own mind better than she did. He would persuade her. It was only a question of time.

Without knowing it, he had already made one wrong assumption, which was that Diana was infatuated with Jake. Certainly she found him attractive in a dangerous sort of way, but the love affair with Tom had been Diana's *raison d'être* for too long to be quite so lightly replaced by another. Forming a relationship with Jake was, Diana forlornly felt, perhaps her last chance to rekindle Tom's old passion. Flirting with Jake was facilitated by the fact that Marcus was currently abroad, and Diana had every intention of making the most of this.

The desire to rehabilitate her marriage in the wake

of Tom's betrayal had evaporated. The gulf between the two of them had become too great, and Diana had no heart for the task of bridging it. So that was that. Watching things drift on, Sarah privately wondered what Marcus really thought about it all. Up until now she had felt that if Marcus could have brought himself to be a little sterner with his wayward wife, the situation just might have improved radically. But once or twice lately it had crossed her mind that he had quite simply lost interest in his marriage, and she had noticed a barbed sarcasm creeping into his dealings with Diana. He had always been a dark horse, and, for the first time, she considered the fact that he might be seeing somebody else, though so far she thought, his loyalty to his wife had never been open to question. As it was, they were as far apart now as they had ever been, with the additional element of Jake complicating matters, and observing Diana and Tom separately moping, she wondered if things hadn't been better the way they were. At least there had been a certain equilibrium where now there was only deprivation. Still grieving for George, and saddened by the discord within Marchants, Sarah was extremely glad to be out of it all. It now only remained for the will to be read, and never having been surprised once by George all his life, with the sole exception of his atypical marriage, she wasn't anticipating anything unexpected from that quarter either.

It was two nights later that Tom decided to put his plan into operation. They were all sitting in the drawing room after dinner. Jake and Diana were playing cards. Camilla, who had been reading, stood up and announced her intention of retiring to bed. Was it his imagination, or did her gaze linger rather longer than usual on Tom as she said this? It suited him to think that it did. She went. He let half an hour elapse, and then made his way up the staircase towards her room. The room where George had died. He knocked softly, and, in answer to her barely audible invitation, opened the door and entered.

Camilla, who had apparently been removing her makeup, stood up and faced him. She appeared to be wearing only the grey silk wrap and framed by the nebulous darkness of her hair her face was white and pinched. She looked strained.

Turning back to her dressing-table mirror, she said, 'How can I help you, Tom?'

He could hardly believe his ears. He felt himself to be treated like some slight but tiresome acquaintance rather than her lover.

'Camilla, I must speak to you.' Listening to himself he knew that this was no good. He sounded plaintive. She wasn't the sort to respond to being beseeched. Thoroughly put off his stroke now, there seemed nothing for it but to continue or to retire in disarray looking like a gauche idiot. What on earth had happened to him? He decided to go on.

'I've hardly seen you lately. You've been so remote. If you only knew how miserable I've been. I
love you and I can't live without you.'

He took a step towards her. Camilla recoiled. He
felt in a state bordering on panic. Whatever had happened to the suave rehearsed speech?

'I want to marry you!'

She stood and stared at him. He later decided that
it was this very silence and immobility that had undone him. Wanting to rescue the situation, for she
still made no move, he caught her in his arms. Body
inert, eyes closed she let him kiss her but did not in
any way respond. Receiving no encouragement, Tom
eventually stopped and, when he did so, Camilla disengaged herself and, turning towards the cheval mirror said to his reflection in the spotted old glass,
'Well I don't want to marry *you*. I would rather die
than marry you. I don't even like you.'

The way this speech was delivered left no room
for doubt. Her face was pointed, its expression ven-
omous. The words themselves were delivered in a
small, poisonous voice. He would not have been surprised to hear her hiss.

Frustrated and furious and unable to take any
more, Tom spun Camilla round and hit her hard. As
he did so, in the middle of the turmoil, he noticed
that she had had the angel repaired. The angel which
had been beheaded the day George had died. In an
excess of rage and humiliation he swung out at that

as well, badly bruising his hand as he did so, and it toppled and fell. This time the head remained in place (it must have been a good repair), and the angel lay sightlessly on its back, its fleshy lip curled.

Camilla, who had also been knocked to the ground by Tom's onslaught, got painfully to her feet. She did not reproach him or weep or call for help the way any other woman might have done, but made her way slowly towards the bathroom. When she reached it, without turning round she said in a small, expressionless voice, 'Get out of my bedroom. Tomorrow I want you to leave this house. Don't ever come back. If you do come back I shall call the police.'

She went in, shutting the door. So great was her contempt for him that she did not even trouble to lock it.

It had been an unmitigated catastrophe. There was nothing left to do but leave.

Once back in his own room he threw himself on his bed and burst into tears of shame, drumming his fists on the pillow very much the way he had as a boy when his will had been balked and he felt the world to be generally unfair.

At breakfast the next morning it was noticed that Camilla's face was swollen and bruised. No explanation for this phenomenon was forthcoming and no one liked to ask what had happened. Jake had break-

fasted hurriedly and left for a meeting in London.
Alone with her, Mrs Melbury gave her mistress a
curious look. She recalled, as she did so, seeing Mr
Tom leaving early that morning before the rest of the
house was up, with two large suitcases and several
boxes. He had, with difficulty, fitted all these into the
back of his sports car and driven away. Suitcases the
size of those indicated a long stay somewhere else,
a fact which surprised Mrs Melbury since the reading
of Mr George's will was due to take place that day
and she would have expected him to wait for that
before departing on what she assumed was a holiday.
And then there was the state of Madam's face. Black
and blue it was. Unable to come up with any explanation for what seemed an odd combination of
events, she decided to keep her own counsel, and put
the whole thing to the back of her mind as she went
about her tasks.

The appointment at the offices of Canford and
Greenhill was for five o'clock in the afternoon. Marcus was due to return from his trip round about
lunchtime that day, and it had been tentatively arranged that they would travel into Compton in two
cars. Tom's and Marcus's, collecting Sarah en route.
There was, however, no sign of Tom or his car, Diana noticed. Putting two and two together and mindful of Camilla's face, she guessed that the two of
them must have had some sort of violent quarrel.

Obeying a sudden impulse, she climbed the stairs

to Tom's room and, trembling, knocked on the door. As she had expected, there was no response. All the same she felt it was as well to be sure before walking in. When she finally entered she discovered it to be quite empty. All his possessions had gone including Icarus, who had sat in the same place on top of the chest of drawers for as long as Diana could remember, and whose removal had left a polished gap in the thick dust. She crossed the floor and looked out of the window. The day was sunny and windy, and mare's-tails flowed gracefully across the pellucid blue of the sky. The park was filled with the green vibrancy of spring and, looking at such plentitude, Diana felt impoverished. Spring had come and soon would be gone, and she felt herself to be stranded in a perpetual winter of the spirit. She thought she would never be happy again and now understood for the first time that, whatever the state of affairs between Camilla and Tom, this was immaterial where her own situation was concerned because he would never come back to her. She retraced her steps, conscious as she did so of the faint echo that all empty rooms acquire. She went out and mentally shut the door on the last thirty-two years of her life.

10

Sitting on an old leather armchair in the office belonging to Peter Greenhill, who had been the Marchant family solicitor for decades, Miles Canford being a rather more recent addition to the partnership, Camilla tried not to think about her aching face and jaw. On first arriving she had felt dizzy and sick. Mind over matter on her part had caused this sensation of general malaise to ebb a little, but she was now suffering from low backache, no doubt brought about by the venerable and overstuffed armchair on which she balanced. Also present were Marcus, Sarah and Diana. Tom had not put in an appearance as yet and Camilla very much doubted that he would. Here she was proved wrong, for as a harassed Mr Greenhill entered the room, apologizing for being all of thirty seconds late, Tom arrived behind him. Thin mouth turned down, expression thunderous, he brought his own atmosphere with him. Mr Greenhill clucked. He had, in the course of his long professional life, done many such ritualistic will readings, and it was his experience that, by the end, almost never was everyone happy. Now he was doing one where, before he had read a word of it, deep discontent was being manifested. He looked over his gold half-moon spectacles at the assembled company. His gaze rested for a startled, speculative moment on the widowed Mrs Marchant's vivid cheek. Whatever had she done to her face? Collecting himself, he cleared his throat and began.

After the usual preliminaries (*We are gathered here today to read the last will and testament of George St John Marchant dated 12 March 1987,* and so on) which he delivered in a sonorous, rather biblical voice, nobody spoke, but Mr Greenhill's finely honed legal antennae detected a heightening of interest when he announced the date. He himself had been surprised, not so much by the revision since certain clients were always tinkering with their wills, usually vengefully, but because of the urgency and secrecy which had attended this event. Just as well, though, in the light of what had happened next.

Launching into it, he dealt first with various small bequests. He always conducted things in this order, mainly to keep the suspense up since, once the fireworks were over, an air of general somnolence usually stole over his listeners, accompanied by foot shuffling and fidgeting, and, on one notable occasion, heavy sighing. Plus the fact that if there was going to be a fight it made sense to get the more mundane matters over first and then wind things up quickly, pending litigation if the disputatious person or persons concerned felt sore enough. It also had to be said that Mr Greenhill had a strongly developed taste for the dramatic, possibly inherited from an aunt who had been a moderately successful actress, and, as a country solicitor, will reading was the only chance he really got to indulge it, which was why he still insisted on this quaintly old-fashioned procedure.

His voice droned on. Sarah was surprised and deeply touched to learn that her eldest son had bequeathed her the painting of Venus and cherubs. She slid a sidelong glance at her daughter-in-law to see how she reacted to this news, but Camilla appeared oblivious to it, her attention apparently focused on the portrait of the founder of the firm, which presided crustily over the proceedings in its ornate gilt frame.

Tom sat leaning forwards with his head on his hands. Peter Greenhill was now on to larger pecuniary bequests. Both his brothers and Diana, whom George had always regarded as a sister, had been left generous sums of money on top of the usual crop of sentimental bequests, as had Sarah. This news appeared to cheer Tom up not at all. It was, his mother suspected, perhaps a droplet when set beside the vast ocean of his debt.

Mr Greenhill took a sip of water, paused, and then looking over his glasses said, '*And to my stepson, Anthony James Vane, I bequeath such monies as shall be needed to pay for his education until such time as he shall leave University. The said money shall be in the form of a trust fund which shall be administered by my wife, Camilla Eleanor Marchant, and my brother Marcus John Marchant.'* Sarah, who had been idly speculating on why they all called Miles Canford 'Miles' yet Mr Greenhill always 'Mr Greenhill', never Peter, although they had known him much longer, was suddenly alerted by this. It was interesting that he had not given his wife carte blanche where Anthony's money was concerned. Apart from their eventual inheritance of the estate, similar educational provision had been made for George's own child or children but here three trustees were appointed, Miles Canford's name being added to those of Camilla and Marcus. Although he was the elder twin, Tom's name was conspicuous in its absence. By now, an expectant silence pervaded the room. Camilla shifted her gaze from a badly foxed set of stipple engravings entitled *Cries of London* which hung above Mr Greenhill, and directed it at the old man himself. She wished he would get on with it. Eventually, after a suitably long pause for maximum dramatic effect, he did.

'In the event that she survives me, to my beloved wife, Camilla Eleanor Marchant, I bequeath the house called Marchants together with its estate, and the income therefrom, in trust for any children we may have, on condition that she spends at least ten months of each calendar year living in the aforesaid house. Should she marry again, it shall be assumed

that her husband will henceforward support her, and the aforesaid income shall revert to the Marchants estate.'

Nobody made a sound. There was no doubt that he had their full attention. Thoroughly enjoying himself by now, he elaborated on the subject of the trust, finally continuing, *'In the event of the failure of this trust, Marchants, the estate and the income therefrom shall revert to the Marchant family. It is my wish that Camilla Eleanor Marchant, Marcus John Marchant and Miles Roderick Canford shall administer the aforesaid trust.'*

Tom began to laugh. They all looked at him, aghast. Peter Greenhill, who was quite used to bizarre scenes such as this one, patiently waited until he had finished.

'That is all.' He took off his spectacles with a flourish, carefully folded them up, put them away in their case and began to gather up his papers.

'Now, can I offer anyone a glass of sherry?'

They all refused. With great presence of mind, considering the chagrin she must be feeling, Camilla rose and held out her hand to the solicitor.

'I'd like to thank you for your time and trouble, Mr Greenhill. It has been a very sad time for us all, as you know.' She shot a malevolent look at Tom.

Mr Greenhill bowed. 'My pleasure, Mrs Marchant, my pleasure,' he murmured.

Watching this little scene, Sarah had to admire

Camilla's self-possession and sheer nerve. They all did. Somewhere along the line George had plainly seen some sort of light where his wife and money were concerned. Otherwise, surely, he would not have imposed such stringent conditions concerning its use. They all stood up. Perhaps, thought Sarah, he had written this will intending to change it if the marriage looked like being an enduring success. There was, after all, a lot of money at stake, and George had always had a strong sense of family and family property. Still, it was a great humiliation for Camilla, leaving her very little room to manoeuvre on the grand scale she normally favoured.

Out in the street, Sarah failed to persuade Tom to return with her to the Dower House for dinner, probably because Marcus and Diana were going too. Camilla had also refused her invitation, and had brought her own car in order to retain her independence. They went their separate ways.

Head throbbing, Camilla drove back to Marchants through the lapis-blue evening. She felt as though every bone in her body ached. It was quite obvious to her that something in particular must have caused George to frame his will the way he had. But what? It was true to say that the ball had been an extravagance, but in the end he had given her a generous allowance for it, and, as far as he knew, she had operated within this. It occurred to her that when she arrived back she might go through the contents of George's desk, something she had intended to do anyway. As she pulled up outside, she noticed that Jake's hired Mercedes was not there, meaning that he was probably not back from London, which was a relief since it gave her the opportunity to sift through George's papers without interruption, and this she did.

George, she discovered, had been quite meticulous about paying his bills and it was in his in-tray that she found her answer. The dressmaker who had made her Renaissance costume had tired of sending invoice after invoice to Camilla herself, and had sent a solicitor's letter straight to George, threatening to sue if the money was not immediately forthcoming. Camilla swore under her breath. She crumpled up the statement and the letter. Why on earth hadn't George confronted her? She picked up the bill from the floor and flattened it out. It was dated a week before her husband's death, and she supposed he must have been waiting for an appropriate moment to bring it up. He had lost no opportunity to update his will, though. And here she was. Pregnant with a child she did not want, shackled to a country house she did not like and very thoroughly deprived of the financial killing she had hoped to make. The only consolation, she thought, viciously stabbing George's mahogany desk with his paperknife, was that the vulture Jake would have to go without as well. Desultorily she went through the rest of his correspondence but there was nothing else of note. Only a few bills of recent date to be settled.

The low backache which had been affecting her ever since the early afternoon suddenly became acute. Camilla went to the bathroom and swallowed two Nurofen. Maybe something to eat would help. She went from there to the kitchen, left immaculate by Mrs Melbury, and made herself a snack. The only other occupant was Frescobaldi alias Frisky, whom Camilla had completely forgotten about. He eyed her with an unemotional yellow orb and she eyed him briefly back. She supposed Mrs Melbury must feed him. Picking up her tray with one hand and a glass of wine with the other, she made her way into the dining room and sat down at one end of the long rosewood table. The pain felt marginally better. Her gaze wandered around the room, and finally came to rest on what the family referred to as the Gainsborough, School of. She felt depleted and very tired. Amazing, she thought, that the eighteenth-century Marchants looked very like today's lot. The group consisted of Thomas Marchant, faintly untidy and distinctly countrified in a brown frock coat, knee breeches and buckled shoes, with his gun and his dog, Ranter, at his feet. The ruddiness of his complexion bore witness to the better summers they apparently regularly enjoyed then. Flanking him, their exquisite daintiness and grace emphasizing his own rumpled air, were his wife and daughters, his only son not yet having been born. With long pointed bodices, and panniers, fragility personified in palest pink, white and blue silk, and clutching beribboned straw hats which were *de rigueur* against the sun, they gravely faced the painter with clear, unclouded brows. Set as it was in an English country landscape, presumably in the grounds of Marchants, the scene exuded the air of certainty and placidity endemic to the lives of the eighteenth-century rich. Camilla, who had what antique dealers call a naturally good eye, had always felt that this painting was better than the Marchant family knew. She wondered who had evaluated it as a Gainsborough, School of, rather than just a Gainsborough. On the spur of the moment she decided to get it reassessed, together with another rather dingy canvas which hung in one of the passages, and which Camilla thought might just possibly be worth something too. This one, which depicted a water spaniel, or possibly two, would benefit from a clean anyway. She was still in the dining room, though by now on the chaise longue, when Jake returned.

Naturally a quiet mover, he appeared soundlessly in the doorway and stood there for a minute or two looking at her. Camilla was lying full length with a cushion in the small of her back. Her head was thrown back and the bloodless face with its livid bruise was in startling contrast to her hair, which spread darkly all around it. Pregnancy did not become her as it enhanced certain other women.

Noiselessly he moved forward on the thick pile of the carpet, and, when he reached her, he picked up her hand which felt ice-cold and kissed it.

Camilla, who had sensed rather than heard or seen his presence, opened her eyes without turning her head and said, 'Oh, it's you.'

'It's me,' he rejoined. 'What happened?'

'You don't beat about the bush much do you, Jake?'

'We've known each other too long for that,' he said. 'What happened, Camilla?'

'Oh, he left me money all right, only he didn't leave me enough. It's all tied up, Jake, and I don't get a penny of it unless I go on living in this fucking house with his fucking family. If I marry again I lose everything. I seriously underestimated my loving husband. Not such a soft touch after all. Anyway, the bottom line is that I've lost and you've lost too, darling.' The last sentence was delivered with vituperation. She closed her eyes again.

Jake said in a voice of quiet menace, 'I don't believe you. I came here for money and I intend to have it.'

'Since there isn't any money that I can lay my hands on, I'm thinking of cutting my losses and leaving. At that point you really have no further hold over me.'

She sounded inexpressibly weary.

'What about the baby?'

'*What* about the baby?' She really didn't sound very interested.

What a hard bitch she was. At the same time he loathed her and was fascinated by her. There was something almost irresistible in her sheer indifference to him. He stared at her for some time in silence and then said, 'I don't believe you.'

'Believe what you like.'

He suppressed a strong desire to strike her. Furiously he said, 'You can cut the crap, Camilla. I'm not going to go away. Get used to that. There's a stack of cash here, and it's up to you to settle my bill. Sell something. I don't care what you do or how you do it. And while we're on the subject, I've got plenty on you and don't forget it!'

''How do I know you would leave me alone if I do pay what you euphemistically call your bill?'

'You have my word.'

Camilla laughed. 'There's no honour among thieves, you know,' was her parting shot as he left the room.

Sell something.

She looked thoughtfully at the nonGainsborough, and resolved that she would organize at least one expert opinion and maybe two, on its origins and possible worth. She wondered if the sort of person she had in mind would come to her. Camilla was extremely anxious that no one should find out about her activities in this direction, especially Jake. She recalled that he was due to go to London for a couple of days the following week and decided to try and arrange viewing appointments for then. In the meantime, she would trawl the attics again, and the rest of the house. Since she would probably end up paying the expenses of whoever did come down, she might as well get as much out of the whole exercise as she could.

As she stood up, she was aware that the ache in her back had now extended itself to her stomach where the pain had become rhythmic. It would seem, thought Camilla, who was a noncomplainer on this sort of issue, that more Nurofen were needed.

She took two and went to bed.

Since she very seldom thought of the baby except as an inconvenience, it never occurred to her that she might be having a miscarriage. In the morning Mrs Melbury, who arrived with the breakfast tray and the morning paper, was shocked by Mrs Marchant's pallor and listlessness, and, on being informed that her mistress was suffering from intermittent back and stomach pain, took it upon herself to ring Dr Kirkpatrick. Later that day, in hospital, Camilla miscarried George's son.

11

When Camilla was once again back at Marchants, it was with very mixed feelings that Sarah went to visit her daughter-in-law. She noticed with appreciation that the rhododendrons which grew along the drive were beginning to flower and the massed army of buds indicated that it would be a superb year for them. The crimson Cornubia was well into bloom, foiled to great effect by the ivory and pale pink of Unique. After these two, which were always early, the rest would swiftly advance in drifts of purple, scarlet and ivory, sheathed in the glassy bottle-green of their leaves. Planted by the Victorian Marchants in specially imported peat, many of them stood as high as twenty feet and for the duration of their dramatic flowering they regally dominated the drive and the rides around the grounds.

There was no sign of Camilla in the drawing room, where Sarah admired a pair of tall Chinese blue and white vases which stood on either side of the fireplace, filled with huge, cerise blooms. She had never seen these before and wondered if Camilla had exhumed them from the attic. One had a small chip in the top, she noticed, which was probably why they had been put away in the first place. As she had indicated she might be, Camilla was in fact in her bedroom, but was up and dressed and lying on the day bed. The two women kissed without warmth.

It was the second time Sarah had seen Camilla since the miscarriage, and she noticed immediately the striking improvement in her general appearance. It was paradoxical, she reflected, that while most women were radiantly pregnant, Camilla was radiantly unpregnant. Still, she reminded herself, losing a baby was probably much more traumatic than one realized at the time of its actual happening. It was amazing, though, the amount of stamina Camilla seemed to have considering how slim she was.

'How are you, Camilla?'

'Getting better with every day that passes, but how kind of you to ask. What can I do for you?'

Stung by the question which rather inferred that her visit was holding up certain other more important proceedings, and would she please get on with it, Sarah said crisply, 'You can't help me. I thought I might be able to help you. It was, in fact, concerning Anthony that I wanted to speak to you.'

'Oh?'

'As I'm sure you are aware he has a holiday coming up, the Easter one, and I wondered if you were thinking of having his chum Ned Pemberton to stay.'

'Well, what if I am?'

Like Sisyphus, Sarah felt as though she was trying to push a very large stone uphill.

'Well, *if* you are,' she responded on an acerbic note, 'assuming they both want to ride, then I shall have to arrange to borrow another pony, probably from the Canfords. However, I should have to make enquiries about that. But, on the other hand, if you want to entertain both boys yourself, I shall quite understand.' *Touché. That's the last thing she'll want.*

It was.

'No, no, on balance I think that's a good idea,' said Camilla graciously. 'Let me just check my diary. Where are we?' She leafed through it. 'Yes, here we are.' She studied it. 'Ah! It doesn't, in fact, arise as I see Anthony is going skiing with the school this time around, and', she leafed on, 'half term is being spent with the Pembertons who are taking him to Cornwall with them. So that lets us off organizing anything for the foreseeable future.'

Mentally watching the stone roll down again, Sarah thought, *Lets us off! That absolutely encapsulates her attitude. Poor little Anthony.* She knew for a fact that Camilla had informed Anthony of his stepfather's death by letter, and found such heartlessness shocking. Well, she had quite decided that whenever possible she would be *in loco parentis* to the little boy, and would endeavour to make up for the thin emotional time he had had as much as she

could. In a way she felt it was the least she could do
for her own son and since Anthony had gone back
to school she had herself written to him regularly.
She decided not to prolong the interview. It was plain
that her daughter-in-law's mind was elsewhere.

'Oh, you still haven't got the Venus,' said Camilla
almost absent-mindedly. 'I'll make sure it is sent
over to the Dower House.'

Here was a surprise, a welcome one, since in spite
of George's unequivocal wishes as stated in his will,
Sarah had assumed that dislodging the painting from
the wall of the bedroom in which they sat would
prove practically impossible.

'Thank you,' she said, getting up to go, 'and you
will let me know if there is anything I can do to help
you.' A barren formula, as they both knew. There
would never be any way in which these two could
help each other.

Camilla nodded and bared her teeth in a smile. She
very much wished Sarah would leave. She was anxious to get on with the business of evaluating the
paintings. Most of all she wanted to rid herself of
Jake's unwelcome presence, and, if she could combine that with lining her own designer pockets at the
same time, so much the better. She began to make a
list of all the things she had to do.

Riding through the grounds with Jake, she on the
bay mare, Jemima, and he on Othello, Diana thought

her lover seemed preoccupied. For he was now her lover, if such a civilized word could be applied to someone as feral as Jake. This had been quite a revelation to Diana, accustomed only to Marcus and Tom. Together with the sort of expertise which must give pleasure, there was a controlled ferocity about him which both excited and frightened her. She sensed him to be capable of almost anything and this added a dicey dimension to their love-making which gingered her up, at the same time, making her neurotic so that she became prone to bouts of solitary, nervy weeping. It was probably precisely because of this dangerous quality, and because she knew herself to be expendable as far as he was concerned, that she, who had cynically hoped to use Jake for her own ends, fell masochistically in love with him instead. Diana, it seemed, was destined for enslavement not politics.

That day there was a reverberation of thunder in the air, and the lowering sky behind the dense brilliance of the rhododendrons promised heavy rain. The horses, who disliked the still closeness with its inherent threat of storm, were fidgety and restless. Riding being a warm sport, neither Jake nor Diana was wearing a coat, and as the first drops began to fall they turned in the direction of home and ten minutes later clattered into the stable yard. By chance, the girl from the village who groomed and mucked out and who came once a day at her own convenience, happened to be there and offered to untack and put away both horses for them.

Impulsively, Diana said to Jake, 'Let's go to the summerhouse and watch the storm from there.' Without waiting for his reply, she set off back across the yard through the shining, sheeting rain. Cursing, Jake, who had never seen the summerhouse and had no particular wish to, followed her. This turned out to be a white, clapboard structure with a verandah which faced a small lake. Inside were two rooms, the one at the front containing two shelves of dog-eared paperback books, a couple of shabby cane chairs and a table, and the back room a bed and bentwood chair. It was obvious that it was some time since anyone had used it.

Jake's legs being longer than Diana's, they arrived wet through and both together as forked lightning shot a serpentine tongue across the sky. Such was the tropical violence of the cloudburst that, pitted with the force of its fall, the lake had become opaque like a great grey stone and the park on the other side was hidden from view by its silvery density. Standing watching the spectacular display, Diana had the odd feeling that the rest of the world no longer existed and that they and the summerhouse hung, encapsulated by water, rather like the inhabitants of a diving bell in the depths of the ocean.

Water began to drip through the ceiling. Against the staccato rattle of the rain, Diana said dreamily, 'I

used to come here a lot when I was a little girl. I
looked upon it as a refuge from the rest of the world.'
She might have added that she and Tom at the height
of their affair had used it as a refuge too, often after
riding, with the horses tied to the verandah outside,
but she did not.

Fed up with this girlish chatter, Jake roughly
caught hold of her. He pulled off her hat and, as he
did so, her long blonde hair unwound itself and
slipped down her back. He undid his riding breeches.

'Take off your clothes,' he said peremptorily.

'Let's use the bed,' suggested Diana, mindful of
the uncarpeted boards.

'I'm not interested in the bed,' said Jake, whose
wish it was to take her right there on the floor. And,
reflecting that this was a not unpleasant way of passing his time until he and Camilla reached a satisfactory settlement, he did.

12

The foray to the attic turned out to be more than a little productive. Luckily, this did not have to be reached by means of a stepladder since a narrow staircase concealed behind a door normally kept locked, ran up to it. It had been in Sarah's mind for years to purge the attics, which rambled all over the top of the house, but in the event she had never got round to what probably would have proved a mammoth task. Camilla had already carried out one superficial raid but had not been searching for paintings then. As with all such storage places there was a great deal of rubbish not quite rubbishy enough to have been thrown out. There were also, however, many objects which had not been considered fashionable in the twenties and thirties and these had been carefully packed away and apparently forgotten about. Camilla knew that pretty things with no real intrinsic value of their own often looked ten times better than they really were when juxtaposed with really good pieces. They were what she called inspired junk, the inspiration coming from her. Antique *trompe-l'oeil*—of this sort of stuff there was a veritable treasuretrove, and another day she would enjoy going through it.

Today the quest was for canvasses. An initial investigation produced nothing, and she settled down to go through the heaps painstakingly bit by bit. One and a half hours later she was just about to concede defeat, for the moment anyway, and decamp for lunch, when she found a collection of half a dozen or so stacked behind an old white painted chest of drawers which, in its turn, was concealed by a ping pong table. Camilla was ready to bet that no one in the family knew they were there.

It would have been much easier to ask one of the gardeners to help her carry them down, but since secrecy was of the essence she decided to move them one by one herself. Once she had got the little collection onto her bedroom floor, she shut and locked the door to the attic staircase, replaced the key on its usual hook, and then went back to have a look at them. Three she put immediately to one side, designating them as rightly having been hidden for the last few decades. The remaining three were more interesting. One appeared to be a painting of the ubiquitous Ranter, or a hound very much like him, one showed a couple sitting in a phaeton drawn by a pair of greys and the third was of a horse apparently being held by a groom. Two were framed and all were badly in need of a clean. Not a bad haul, she decided. There was nothing she could see which indicated who the painter was, but when one considered how filthy they all were with what could have been the accumulated dinge of at least a century, this was hardly surprising.

A week or so after all this took place, Mr Waterhouse of Jessops auction house travelled down from London without, it must be said, any inflated ideas of what he might find at Marchants when he got there. Many were the paintings he had been asked to assess in the course of his professional career, and of these, only two had turned out to be in what he privately thought of as the top league. He arrived on the dot of eleven o'clock, and was shown into the drawing room by Mrs Melbury, who had no idea what he was there for. Here he was found by Camilla, holding a cup of coffee and admiring a burr walnut bureau, which, he thought, was probably William and Mary. Since furniture was not his speciality he could not, however, be sure. Whatever the date, it was without doubt a very fine piece. He said as much to Mrs Marchant.

Camilla said with a shrug, 'There is some valuable furniture here but there is quite a lot of mundane stuff as well. The same goes for the paintings, which is why I've asked for a valuation. We need to know for insurance purposes, you know.'

They all said that, he reflected as he followed her

into the dining room, noting as he entered the very impressive D-end table (George III?).

'Ah yes,' he said as Mrs Marchant indicated the conversation piece. Between them they lifted it carefully down. He inspected it thoroughly. Disappointing. From her description he had thought it might be exciting. In fact, as he then explained to Camilla, it was a very attractive portrait but nothing special, he thought. She was, of course, welcome to get a second opinion but he was pretty certain that he was right. It was, he said, worth a bit, and was of course an enhancement to any room, but definitely not a Gainsborough by any manner of means. This was a blow, a major blow, in fact. Mr Waterhouse, who had had a lot of experience of this sort of thing, sensed her extreme disappointment and said kindly, 'Let's look at the rest. There have been some spectacular finds made in attics, after all.'

Including the water spaniel, there were four canvasses. Mr Waterhouse propped them up against the wall and stood back. He was conscious of a sudden heightening of interest. His own words reverberated within his head: ...*some spectacular finds have been made in attics.* He could, of course, be wrong, but nevertheless... Opening his case, he extracted a powerful torch, and carefully scrutinized the paintings one by one paying particular attention to the bottom right and left of each. All were covered in thick, grey surface dirt. Normally he preferred to sell paintings as they were, but in this case he felt very light cleaning would probably be necessary. The frames looked as though they were the originals.

At last he turned back to Camilla who had been watching him closely. Trying to conceal his elation, he said, 'I'm not sure, but I think we may have something here. Would you allow me to take them to London with me for further examination? I shall give you a receipt naturally.'

'Yes, all right,' replied Camilla, 'but may I ask who you think the artist is?'

Mr Waterhouse refused to be drawn.

'Impossible to say that until I've had a more detailed look,' he responded cagily. 'We must cross our fingers, Mrs Marchant, cross our fingers. Now have you anything in which I could wrap these treasures up? Individually, I think, don't you?'

When he had gone Camilla sat for some minutes thinking over the whole interview. Then, selecting the better of two amateur Marchant daubs, which she had initially, rightly, rejected as worthless, she hung it up in the passage where the water spaniel had been, fairly certain that no one would notice the exchange. It occurred to her that if one or all of the canvasses were worth anything, by which she meant anything like serious money, it would be comparatively easy to sell them quietly and pocket the spoils. And there would be no need to tell Jake either, for Jake was greedy. No, she would simply give him the amount he had asked for, less if she could get away with it, and hope he kept his word and left. She went upstairs humming. She felt that her luck might be about to change.

These days Sarah found herself seeing less and less of her family. Diana dropped around occasionally, but, on the whole, kept her distance, mainly, Sarah guessed, because of the liaison with Jake Weston. Marcus, on the other hand, was a regular visitor, especially in the evenings when he seemed to be at a particularly loose end, and in Sarah's eyes this only served to point up the gulf which had opened up between him and his wife. Diana's depression after the defection of Tom had now lifted, but had been replaced by a sort of brittle vivacity which Sarah found very hard to take.

Where Marcus was concerned she was less sure what was happening. Once or twice she had thought he was on the brink of telling her something but in the event he did not and she knew better than to push him. With determination and competence he had always got on with his own life, unencumbered by all the *Sturm und Drang* which seemed to attend Tom's every move, and had been known to take major decisions from a very young age without consulting anybody and, on the whole, they had been good decisions. Osbert had had the same trait. He had thought things through and then, when confident that he had viewed every angle, had made up his mind. Probably the only truly emotional gamble he had taken had been to get engaged to her. It was interesting that since logic usually does not go hand in hand with falling in love, it was the one decision which her cerebral son Marcus had got wrong.

His twin had simply not reappeared since the extraordinary behaviour at the reading of the will, nor had he even communicated by telephone. Sarah had no idea where he was. For the Nth time she wondered where she had gone wrong with Tom. So far as she was aware she had brought up all three of her sons to observe the same high standards of integrity, and yet one had turned into a moral maverick. Why? Was it something she had done or not done, or was Tom genetically simply a bad apple? As usual she found her own question unanswerable. Unquiet in mind, she restlessly got up and walked to the window. From the Dower House the tall chimneys of Marchants were visible through the trees, and, in the park, the purple grandeur of the last rhododendrons was just beginning to fade. She turned away just as the racing green Jaguar slid past with Camilla at the wheel.

Two hours later with the car placed as had been arranged in the directors' car park, she sat in Mr Waterhouse's comfortable, old-fashioned office. Unable to keep all the elation out of his voice, he had been tantalizing, even arch on the telephone, refusing to illuminate further until he saw her, and had insisted on a London meeting at his office. Faintly annoyed by what she saw as his absurd prevarication, but still filled with a keen sense of anticipation as he had intended she should be, she flicked through a catalogue while waiting for him to arrive. When he finally did turn up having been detained at a previous meeting, he wasted no time on apologies.

'Come with me, Mrs Marchant,' he invited mysteriously beckoning and leading the way into another much smaller room, putting her in mind more than somewhat of the spider and the fly. Resting on a table, and propped against the wall beside which it stood, were the four paintings.

'We may disregard these two,' he said dismissively, gesturing towards the third and the fourth. The two indicated, it transpired, were poor old Ranter whose liquid eye appeared to veer sadly in the direction of Mr Waterhouse, and the water spaniel. She made a mental note to reconsign this to its old position in the dark passage by the bootroom. With crooked finger Mr Waterhouse indicated that Camilla must come forward. Feeling that his conspiratorial manner was now getting distinctly on her nerves, but mindful of the fact that he might be about to tell her something to her advantage, she approached.

Reverently picking up the painting of Thomas and Juliana Marchant sitting in the phaeton, he invited her to inspect it. It had been partially cleaned.

'Look at the bottom right-hand corner,' instructed Mr Waterhouse who by now could scarcely contain his glee. Any minute, thought Camilla, he would begin to rub his hands together. She looked. And looked again. The painting was inscribed with the words *Geo: Stubbs pinxit*. There was no date.

In spite of herself, her hands shook a little. Turning to Mr Waterhouse, she said, 'Are you sure it's authentic?'

'Quite sure,' he replied, 'but this, this is the star,' pointing to the horse and groom which had also been partially cleaned revealing the legend *Lord Compton's, Dash*, and was signed and dated 1766. Camilla looked questioningly at Mr Waterhouse.

'Dash was a celebrated racehorse, which won at Huntingdon and York and had a particularly famous victory at Newmarket. There is, in fact, another painting of this stallion in existence also by George Stubbs with the jockey Jerome Tyndall up, which is owned by an American collector. Yours, which as you know, is on canvas has not been cleaned before, so it is in prime condition. Quite simply it is a fabulous find, and worth a very great deal of money.'

'How much would you say at a guess?'

Mr Waterhouse named a sum. He wondered if she was considering selling. He said, 'Of course, at auction you would probably realize rather more.'

More! The first sum had sounded astronomical and now he was talking about more. What a pity she would have to give some of it to Jake. Mr Waterhouse watched her. She was, he thought, a very cool customer indeed. Most people being faced with the news that such an important, not to say lucrative, discovery had been made in their house betrayed some emotion at least.

'Why would two paintings such as this have been consigned to the attic, do you think? And how do you suppose that Dash ended up at Marchants?'

He shrugged. 'You have to understand that Stubbs was by no means as highly regarded in his own day as he is now. At one point he was merely referred to as Mr Stubbs the horse painter. We know that when his racing days were over Dash was eventually sold to a country neighbour of Lord Compton for stud and, as sometimes happened then, it appears that the portrait was sold with him.'

'What about the other one? Doesn't it seem almost too good to be true that two should turn up together?'

'In one sense yes, but in another why not? After all, Stubbs was asked to execute at least two paintings for Lord Compton, who, if I'm not mistaken, was a near neighbour of Marchants. And though your ancestor didn't commission this one, he may have liked it enough to ask Stubbs to paint himself and his wife. Who knows? Anyway, be that as it may, I can assure you that both are genuine.'

The implications were almost too great for her to grasp. Finally, after some thought, Camilla said, 'I want this to be completely confidential for the time being. No publicity of any sort.'

'I quite understand, but, should you want to put them on the market, it won't be so easy. This is, after all, a sensational find and there is bound to be a great deal of interest and excitement.'

'Presumably I could sell them anonymously?'

'Yes, you could certainly do that.' A long pause ensued. The possibilities seemed endless.

'Let's have lunch,' finally suggested Camilla, suddenly realizing that it was nearly 1.30. 'It seems to me that we have a great deal to talk about.'

Driving home later, after this most momentous of meetings, Camilla reflected that it did seem that fortune was favouring her at last. Paying off Jake was not the least of her problems, since this would have to be achieved in such a way that he thought he had extracted the maximum possible from her and would therefore leave her alone in future. She did not relish the thought of being bled white for the rest of her life. Mr Waterhouse had reckoned that cleaning would take at least six weeks, and since Stubbs could be complicated he was keen to commission a certain Miss Reid, whom he had used extensively and whom he knew to be highly competent, for this purpose. Camilla felt she could safely leave all that to him. Jake was, she knew, departing for Africa in a week's time in order to sort out his business affairs, and had indicated that he would be away for a few weeks. He had also indicated that on his return he wanted his cut. Well, he might have to wait rather longer than that. She would just have to fob him off.

By now she was off the motorway and driving along the country lanes. Turning a corner at speed, she almost ran into a herd of cows which were being shepherded along the road interminably slowly by a youth with a stick. Hoping that they were not going all the way to Marchants, she changed down to their pace, her mind still exploring all the possibilities.

Trickiest of all would be organizing herself and her loot back to Italy, for Camilla had no intention of remaining entombed in the English countryside a second longer than she had to. By doing this she would, under the terms of her late husband's will, forfeit her interest in the Marchants estate. This bothered her not one jot, she decided, since the stakes for which she was now gambling were suddenly so much higher.

The cows, who appeared to know the way, now turned right, forcing her to stop altogether, and, mooing brainlessly, began to amble through a miniature swamp into a farmyard, their hooves making loud sucking noises. Leaning against a post, the cowman watched them displaying no sense of urgency whatsoever. When the last one had plodded through he pulled the gate shut, preparing to squelch after them and then, apparently noticing the green Jaguar for the first time shouted, 'Thanks, Missus.'

Only just deigning to acknowledge him, Camilla put her foot on the accelerator again, and three corners further on found herself stuck behind a tractor, which was moving only marginally faster than the heifers. *I loathe the country,* thought Camilla, sighing with frustration. *It wouldn't bother me if I never saw another cow ever again.* And, hopefully, she wouldn't have to. It was all to play for. Freedom and money were her goals and it now appeared that both were within her grasp. Anthony, as usual, never entered her calculations.

On her return Jake was there. He had been wondering where she had been all day, and, knowing her as well as he did, one look at her was sufficient to tell him that something was up. She had an air that was both secretive and at the same time smug, as of one who enjoys a hugely amusing private joke, probably, he thought, at someone else's expense. His perhaps. He noticed that she was carrying two largish rectangular parcels but when, with a rare display of good manners, he offered to take them off her, she refused, saying that she had been shopping in London and would take them up to her room herself, and did. When she came down again they sat without speaking in the library, she sifting through the *Daily Telegraph* which she had not had time to read as yet that day, and he looking morosely out of the window.

He thought she appeared more relaxed than he had seen her since the reading of the will. He knew there was absolutely no point in quizzing her about this change and, recognizing the need to remain on top of the situation, wondered if he should put off the African trip. He did not trust her one inch. On the other hand, he had now been in England for some time and certain of his business affairs did need his urgent attention. On the whole, he decided it was better to go now, and rely on the hope that putting into operation whatever she had in mind would take longer than his absence. She raised the newspaper so that he could no longer see her. Pointedly excluded in this way, Jake rose and began to pace up and down. Conscious of the fact that her absorption in the *Telegraph* was irritating him, Camilla continued to peruse every column inch minutely. When she finally looked up, having first carefully folded the newspaper prior to placing it in the canterbury by her chair, it was to discover that he had silently left the room.

Let him go, thought Camilla. *Let him go to hell, in fact.* She smiled to herself and rang for tea.

13

Rather to Sarah's surprise, it was Camilla who went to pick up Anthony and his friend from school at the end of the Summer Term. Up until now she had usually been quite content to let her mother-in-law do this. Cognizant of the fact that a large part of the summer holiday was to be spent with Sarah, Anthony felt that he could just about cope with his mother, given that he assumed that he was going to see very little of her. Sarah had written to say that she had been able to organize another pony for Ned, and he looked forward joyfully to riding Blue again. Blue had become the one certain thing in his life, a living creature on which all his stifled love could focus, and the knowledge that the old pony belonged to him and would be there waiting for him on his return to Marchants, sustained Anthony after the crushing news of his step-father's death. Owing to the school skiing trip at Easter, followed by the half-term exeat spent with the Pembertons, this was the first meeting with his mother since then, and it was a measure of his increased self-confidence that he found himself able to face it more or less without a tremor.

She arrived suitably and chicly dressed in a tailored black light-weight suit with pearls (for tears). To her son's enormous surprise she was all smiles, and there was no trace of the usual boredom and impatience normally on display on this sort of occasion. Covertly watching her greet Ned Pemberton in a positively friendly manner, even remembering his name, Anthony was filled with astonishment. What on earth could have happened? George had died, the baby had died, and yet here she was in the best mood he had seen for years. Collecting his things together he decided that he would never understand his mother.

Once in the car, Anthony, who liked pop music, resigned himself of two hours of Vivaldi. To his further amazement Camilla seemed to want to talk to him instead. Hopelessly out of practice on this front he tried to comply and discovered that, after all the years of her indifference to everything he thought and felt, he could find little to say to his unfathomable parent. Here Ned, who was uninhibited by Anthony's fear of saying something asinine, and who had had plenty of practice in talking to his own more accessible mother, was invaluable, for when one of the frequent silences occurred, he effortlessly chattered. In this, for Anthony anyway, stilted and uneasy way they passed the journey to Marchants. Still, the spectacle of Mummy as affable as this was one not to be missed, he reflected. It might after all never happen again.

To his delight, and as he had hoped she might be because he had a present for her, Sarah was at Marchants waiting for them. Putting down his bag in the hall, Anthony delved into it while she greeted Ned, eventually extracting a heavy object wrapped in an old copy of *Football Monthly*.

'This is for you,' he said with pride, handing it to her. 'I made it myself.' Relieved that Camilla was putting the car away, for tact dictated that he should have given his present to his mother rather than herself, Sarah opened it watched by both boys. It was a very sturdy pot, which he probably hadn't properly centred on the wheel thereby explaining its pronounced list. She had a cupboard full of such lopsided artefacts which had travelled home with relentless regularity from the school art room.

'Is this really for me? Anthony, you are a sweetheart. I absolutely love it.'

Pink with pleasure, Anthony said, 'Do you really like it? I mean *really* like it?'

'It's smashing. Thank you, darling.' She kissed him.

Noting her enthusiasm, Ned said, 'I've got one for my mother too.' He got out another anomalous vessel and proudly exhibited it. Clearly the hand of the potter had shaken here as well. Sarah, who had had plenty of practice at this sort of thing said, 'I think you've both done brilliantly! Wrap that up carefully, Ned, so that it doesn't get broken before it reaches your mama. If I may, Anthony, I'll take mine back to the Dower House with me now, and perhaps both of you would like to come and have lunch with me there tomorrow. If Mummy agrees.'

'She does,' said her daughter-in-law who had entered the hall at that moment.

'Good, then that's fixed.'

Camilla's sunny mood continued for the rest of the week and Jake in particular was disturbed by it. Something was in the air. But what? His business trip was imminent and he was loath to put the whole thing off. Watching her tranquillity, he speculated endlessly on the reasons for this but came up with nothing. There was something alerting in the way she looked at him, as though she was enjoying herself at his expense. In the end he decided to go anyway, taking the view that, whatever she was stirring up, the hold he had over her was sufficient to enable him to make her drop her spoon should this prove necessary. It was a pity that she and Diana were not close for then he might have learnt something. On the whole Camilla did not have female friends, partly because she despised her own sex, and partly because she posed too much of a predatory threat where men were concerned, being totally uninfluenced by anything as mundane and inconvenient as loyalty to a sister. Although it was now years since he and she had been romantically involved, he surmised that he was closer to her, in thought anyway, than anyone else. He understood the coldness and amorality of her character and rather admired it. For such as the two of them, who had started life with no real material advantages, except for good looks and an ambition to live well (and easily) at someone else's expense, there was no room for sentimentality.

A trip to Paris in the heat of August, where Marcus had insisted she accompany him, did nothing to relieve Diana's unhappiness. Sitting in the Musée d'Orsay while Marcus attended a meeting with a client, she forced herself to address certain facts which she would rather not have confronted at all, the first and most unpalatable being that Jake almost certainly regarded her as a temporary interlude during his sojourn at Marchants. She still had no idea why he was there either. The only attempt she had ever made to discuss the matter had provoked freezing displeasure and she had never tried to raise the subject again. For all that he obviously enjoyed her body, there was a quality of detachment about him that chilled and depressed her. It was, she reflected, her tragedy to fall in love with those who, at the end of the day, took her and left her. She had lost the initiative with Tom in the early days and now exactly the same thing had happened with Jake. How to regain it was not the issue, since she recognized that Jake was not, *au fond,* so much interested in her as an individual as in her as a carnal diversion. Facing up to this was not easy, and, as well as being painful, did not advance her very far since nothing seemed to blunt her feelings however much she reiterated to herself the unpalatable truth. She had become besotted with the man.

Damage limitation was then the name of this particular game, for remembering the awful desolation of spirit which had descended on her after Tom had left her, Diana was by no means sure that she could cope with that again without going mad. And then there was the question of whether it was Jake with whom she was obsessed or whether he was merely a physical substitute for the unobtainable Tom. A surrogate lover.

Where does infatuation end and love begin, and what is love anyway, she asked, mentally addressing Manet's Olympia, who stared back with the hauteur of perfect, naked self-possession. The painting reminded Diana of her sister-in-law. A younger version, yes, but the imprint of Camilla was all there, even, she noticed, down to the thin black ribbon cutting the white throat in two, and Manet's version of Frescobaldi at her feet, receiving just about as much attention from Olympia. The eyes of Olympia met those of Diana who felt herself to be appraised and found wanting. The look was not one of disdain but one totally devoid of interest. Magnificently *au na-*

turel, her self-absorption total, Olympia held court
alone and Camilla, she reflected, was very much the
same. Existing only for her own pleasure, it seemed
to Diana that she shone darkly, and like a malign star
emitting a deceptive radiance, poisoned the lives of
all those unlucky enough to stray within her orbit.
With a sudden insight, Diana realized that, whereas
she had come to terms a long time ago with the fact
that she disliked Camilla, the truth was that she hated
her sister-in-law. The recognition of this generated in
her a destructive purpose, providing a focal point for
all her disappointment and pain, something into
which she could sink her entire emotional capital.
She resolved at the very least to see Camilla off, and,
if possible, ultimately to destroy her.

It was over a very good dinner that evening that
Marcus, without any warning at all that she had noticed, said to Diana, 'I think we should separate.'

She could not have heard him correctly.

'What?'

Patiently he said, 'Separate. Live apart, with a
view to getting divorced.'

This was truly a bolt from the blue. Certainly she
had vaguely noticed a degree of withdrawal on his
part, but obsessed with her own problems and taking
completely for granted his total support as she always
had in the past, she had neither made any effort to

reach out to him nor even bothered to ask him about his obvious distraction.

Shocked, she stated, 'This is why you wanted me to come to Paris with you!'

'Correct. I wanted to get you out of the family orbit so that we could have an adult discussion about the situation without any interference.'

'But I don't want a divorce.' Her voice began to rise. 'I want things to go on as they are.'

'Yes, I expect you do but I'm afraid I don't. And just so that there can be no misunderstanding, I'm not merely suggesting a separation, I've already made my mind up that that is what is going to happen. So, you see, what you want has no bearing on the matter.'

Oh Christ, she was going to cry. A tear fell and was followed by another.

'Why are you being so unkind? I don't recognize you. Why do you want to desert me like this?'

'*You* deserted me long ago.' Silence. She hung her head. These 'little girl' habits which had once induced tenderness in Marcus now repelled him. 'Well, didn't you?'

Panicking and sick at heart, Diana thought, *this must be what it feels like to be in the witness box.* Already condemned, on the grounds that she might incriminate herself even further she did not answer.

Inexorably he went on, 'You know as well as I do that we have been drifting apart for ages to the point where I can no longer see any advantage for either of us in perpetuating this hollow sham which is our marriage.' He underlined it. 'There is quite simply, for me anyway, nothing left. Hasn't been for years.'

His voice framing its awful words, though it had remained even, was stern, and this convinced her as nothing else could that he really meant what he was saying. Any minute now he would confront her with his knowledge of her long affair with Tom, and then the current liaison with Jake Weston. She had an absurd desire to put her hands over her ears like a five-year-old child. Surprisingly, he did not do this. Perhaps, after all, he had no knowledge of the colossal betrayal of his trust over the years with his own brother, or that she had been, and still was, Jake Weston's mistress. In fact, he had considered and then rejected the idea of confronting her with her own adultery. Since there was to be no negotiation concerning what happened next, he had seen no point in humiliating her more than necessary, besides which he himself had not been faithful either.

The waiter brought their second course, and noticed with concern the tears pouring down Madame's face. Her companion appeared to be immune to this affecting sight. They had both stopped speaking while he was there.

When he eventually reluctantly moved away, Diana said in a low, desperate voice, 'Please, *please*, don't leave me, Marcus, I'll change. I'll be a good wife to you. I *can* change. Let's begin again, please let's begin again.'

The abyss of being alone opened up in front of her. She shook her hair in front of her face to conceal, as well as she could, her emotional disarray from the other diners. To her intense distress she could not move him.

'Diana, my indifference has grown out of yours. There is no going back now. I entertained a brief hope a few months ago that we might have been able to begin again. It was unrealistic and absurd.'

'Are you saying that you no longer love me at all?'

'Of course I still love you. After all, we've been together for a long time. But I am no longer in love with you.' He could have added that he no longer liked her very much either, but felt that this would have been gratuitous.

Then she saw it. Only one thing could have severed him from her quite so completely. There must be someone else. The realization of this fact suddenly made him much more desirable. He was like Tom and yet not like Tom, and too late the confusion which had beset her for years clarified.

'You've been having an affair with someone else! *I* love you. How could you?'

Amazed by how badly she had reacted to what he had to say, considering that most of the time she barely seemed to notice whether he was there or not, Marcus had decided against revealing this fact at this particular moment. Now she had asked him outright there was nothing for it but to confirm it.

Regarding her expressionlessly and thinking, *she has no self-knowledge at all,* he said, 'Yes, I have, and no, you don't.'

Diana did not deign to ask who the other woman was. Picking up her wine glass, which was very nearly full, she drained it, replacing it very carefully on the table, and then, with great dignity, she rose and walked a little unsteadily to the door. Running after her, the waiter presented her with the single long-stemmed red rose that this particular restaurant habitually awarded to its prettier female customers.

Marcus did not attempt to follow her. *What a mess,* he thought. There was, however, no going back. When he had married her he had been in love with her. Knowing this she had used him, and betrayed him, and he had been forced to watch her doing it. As a result, he had begun to spend more time in London, where he had enjoyed the odd casual sexual encounter. Even so, after the arrival of Camilla, he had been inclined to give it one more shot. A non-starter, he soon recognized. Why on earth he had wanted to do this he now couldn't imagine. Habit, probably. It had been after this latest revelation on his emotional road to Damascus that he had finally decided to cut loose. The flirtatious friendship he had conducted for some time with Jane Prior had long since ignited into a very physical affair, though he no longer expected ever to fall in love again with quite the same intensity as he had the first time around. The experience of his marriage had made Marcus cynical on the subject of romantic love and its durability.

He asked for his bill.

Holding the rose, Diana walked along the street. She had no idea where she was going. Eventually she turned right and then crossed the boulevard. By now, the tears had dried on her cheeks but a thin yet penetrating drizzle had begun to fall and had made her face wet with rain instead. She felt more than a little drunk. He loved her, he loved her not. Although she needed him, she knew she had never loved her husband and had married him only to retain her proximity to Marchants and to Tom. It had been said that the art of successful marriage lay in choosing the person you could live with rather than the person you couldn't live without. Well, she, it seemed had succeeded in doing neither. As she walked she reflected how ironic it was that, at the end of the day, he was not leaving her because of her spectacular infidelity with Tom, about which he appeared not to know, but simply because for years she had not taken enough notice of him.

She walked and walked. By now she was at the river and opposite the Ile de la Cité where the massive medieval bulk of Notre Dame loomed, black against the midnight sky. She pressed on. During the course of her long tramp the rain had drenched her, and the slim high-heeled evening shoes she wore squelched with water and one had lost its diamanté buckle. Her wet hair clung mermaidlike in flat tendrils to her cheeks and forehead. She must have come a long way, for by now she had reached a virtually deserted part of the river bank. She sat down at last on a cast-iron bench. Outrage had been replaced by exhaustion and despair, and she found herself left only with a burning sense of shame coupled with a sort of amazement at the recklessness of her own behaviour. What, she asked herself, had been the point of it all? Where had it got her? The answers were no point and nowhere. Diana began to sob again. On impulse she stood up, dropped her bag, kicked off her shoes and pulled herself up so that she was now sitting on the broad, slippery wetness of the low balustrade which snaked along this part of the Seine. A solitary student walking home from a party saw her swing her legs from one side to the other but was too late to stop her as, after a fractional hesitation, she launched herself, arms outstretched as though to embrace it, towards the sluggish, unreflecting water below.

In her pleasant sitting room in the Dower House Sarah sat writing her letters. The desk at which she worked was one which had come with her from Marchants and so this Monday morning which was devoted to her correspondence, as they all were, was reminiscent of many such throughout the years. At one time when they were all much younger, the bulk of the administration she was currently engaged on would have revolved around the boys and Diana. School fees, foreign exchanges, music lessons, extra tuition and so on, all had passed across this desk in their time. Marcus had been one of those sensible children who from a comparatively early age had organized his own affairs. George had too. Tom had not. He had not even tried to, relying on her to sort him out. Countless were the times she had driven across the country because on the eve of some school trip abroad he, as usual, in spite of all her reminders had left his passport behind. Sometimes she wondered if he didn't do it deliberately. This sort of thing had still been going on when Tom was sixteen. Of course, Marcus hadn't always been easy, and because he was a clever, thoughtful child had been very prone at one stage to arguing about everything. This in its way had been almost as exasperating as the recurring passport crisis and almost as time consuming. Once, she recalled, amused by the memory of it, she and Marcus, who must have been all of five years old at the time, had had a falling out—she could no longer remember what about—and he had announced his firm intention of leaving home. Unable to dissuade him, 'But darling,' she had finally protested, 'you haven't any money.'

'Yes, I have,' he loftily replied. Knowing that Osbert was at the main gate supervising the felling of a rotten tree, Sarah had let him go, and had watched his lonely little figure setting off down the drive, with a battered brown cardboard case in one hand. Eventually father and son had returned together, Osbert having a man-to-man talk with Marcus.

'But Mummy was being very difficult,' she heard Marcus say, to which her husband's traitorous reply had been, 'Women *are* very difficult, old boy, you just have to get used to it.' Later on, opening the brown case, she found it to contain a pound note, his teddy and a dog-eared copy of the *Beano*.

Ned and Anthony ran past the window shouting to one another. Why was it that where small boys were concerned every exchange had to be at top decibels? Seeing them reminded her that she had promised both a riding lesson that afternoon, and this in turn reminded her of George, Tom, Marcus and Diana on their ponies in the park.

All these trips down memory lane, reflected Sarah wryly. *I really must be getting very old.*

Diana had had a grey called Lavender which specialized in spectacular bucks, meaning that in the early days, until she learnt to sit them, Diana had spent a fair amount of her time being deposited on the ground. As they all grew up, ponies had come and gone, and the only one she had retained had been Blue. Luckily as it now turned out.

Her thoughts turned to her other daughter-in-law who had kept an uncharacteristically low profile lately. Like Jake she suspected Camilla of some sort of nefarious activity but she too could not begin to guess what that might be. Interestingly, no further progress had been made in the redecoration of Marchants, almost as though its current chatelaine had lost her impetus on this particular project. Camilla's situation was an odd one altogether in Sarah's view, and the idea of trying to dislodge her by means of a payoff had more than once occurred to her. Obviously, had George's child been born, there would have been no question over her position as mistress of Marchants but, as things stood, there was no child and no George, but only Camilla queening it over an inheritance which should rightly have gone to Tom in default of a legitimate heir. And although Tom, she knew, might prove as much of a liability as Camilla albeit in a different way, at least he was family. There was also the question of whether they could afford whatever price Camilla might choose to exact for leaving. On the whole, Sarah thought, probably not. She sighed.

Her gaze rested on the blue and white Chinese ginger jar full of garden flowers which stood on the desk. What a pity Marcus had not been born the elder of the twins. It had to be said that the prospect of a battle with Camilla, and the ensuing scandal in the county if the issue went to law, palled at the prospect of the profligate Tom taking over at the end of it all. Just thinking about the confrontation which possibly lay ahead made her back begin to ache.

She decided to make an appointment with a sharp London solicitor to try to work out the legal position *vis-à-vis* future occupancy of Marchants. After that, depending on what advice was given, there should clearly be a family conference to decide whether they did something or nothing. She feared that because of the way the will had been drawn up, the family would have no redress, since for obvious reasons George could not have foreseen the imminence of his own death nor that Camilla would lose his child, and so no stipulations had been made in case both these events should occur together. She pulled a notepad and pen towards her with the intention of making a list. As she did so the telephone rang. Picking up the receiver, she found herself talking to Marcus in Paris.

Lying in a narrow and lumpy bed in the hospital was almost as uncomfortable as being immersed in the oily Seine. Later Diana was to admit that the cold slap of the water as it hit her brought her to a realization that whatever the starkness of the immediate outlook, she wanted above all to live. Normally an adequate swimmer but never having tried to stay afloat encumbered by clothes before, she lost her nerve. The skirt of her dress began to wind itself around her like a shroud, inhibiting movement, and stinking black water was everywhere. It was in her mouth and in her eyes and it drummed in her ears. She tried to scream but could not. The rose, which for some reason she had hung on to, floated away down the Seine. Weighed down by her sopping coat and physical exhaustion, the thrashing of her arms began to lessen, and she felt herself to be about to give up the struggle. It was probably because of this that the student who had been so fortuitously passing and had seen her jump was able to get her to the side without losing his own life in the process.

When she regained consciousness in the hospital, suitably stomach pumped and purified, the first sight to meet her eyes was that of a tight-lipped and furious Marcus. *I nearly died and he is angry with me!* Tears of misery and self-pity welled up and traced their familiar path down her cheeks. She seemed to cry all the time just lately. She saw with awful clarity that in spite of what he had said not only was he no longer in love with her but he no longer cared about her at all. Every coin in that particular treasury had been spent and there was quite literally nothing left.

The hospital staff did all that was necessary for her but were equally unsympathetic and very French in their attitude. Would-be suicides wasted the time which should have been spent on those chronically sick through no fault of their own, the cool looks and responses seemed to imply. During his second visit she forced herself to try to overcome the leaden tiredness which seemed to have seeped into her very being, along with the river water, and tried to listen to what her husband was saying to her. For he was still her husband.

'The hospital want to discharge you tomorrow.' He felt like adding, *because they need the bed for somebody who is really ill,* but refrained. 'I've booked a flight which leaves at four o'clock. Mother is expecting you to stay with her for as long as it takes you to get back on your feet again.'

'Oh, no, no, no. No, please, no!

The cry, never actually uttered aloud, reverberated inside her poor aching head. One look at his shut face told her that pleading aloud would achieve nothing. The final act of her marriage was to begin immediately. There was to be no appeal, no stay of execution and no chance to make him change his mind. In any case, she had no energy left to fight it. She turned her face away from him and closed her eyes.

'All right,' was all she said.

14

It was now late August and Anthony had gone back to school. At Marchants the garden at least had succeeded to the full richness of its legitimate inheritance. Antirrhinums, phlox, cornflowers and roses among others proliferated, lifting their old-fashioned, pretty heads towards the sun which shone on relentlessly through what had proved to be one of the hottest summers on record. In the stillness which accompanied all this heat, butterflies abounded, often, Camilla noticed with some cynicism, dancing in couples, and the reverberation of humming bees could be heard all over the lawns and meadows.

For Camilla it was a time of waiting. Waiting, she thought lazily, for Mr Waterhouse. It had taken much longer than he had anticipated. He had not wanted to entrust the Stubbs paintings to anyone else, and unfortunately Miss Reid had gone on holiday for six weeks to America, Connecticut to be precise where she had friends, and when she had returned it was to a backlog of work which included some pressing deadlines involving dealers which had been agreed prior to his own appearance with the Stubbses. This meant that his treasures had had to wait until she was able to finish them. It had all been extremely tiresome, but now it looked as though everything was finally under way. With growing irritation Camilla had rung him a couple of times, and had been told that these things couldn't be hurried. Patience, my dear Mrs Marchant, patience. They were, he said, getting there. It shouldn't be long now. She decided there was no point in pursuing him and, basking catlike while halcyon day succeeded halcyon day throughout this most Italianate of summers, Camilla felt that, after all, she could wait with equanimity.

There had been no word from Jake since he left, but she had known him for far too long not to realize that, in his own good time, he would be back, hand outstretched. Well, she could afford to feed him now and, provided he was allowed to feel that he had picked the bones clean, be reasonably certain that he would leave her alone in future. Eventually, when it suited her, she would take off, bearing the secret wealth of Marchants with her. And wouldn't they all be glad to see her go. Camilla was under no illusions as to what the rest of the family thought of her. Since her last meeting with Sarah when the transfer of the Venus from Marchants had been discussed and then arranged, and despite the fact that Anthony had spent most of his latest holiday at the Dower House, there had been no communication between the two women, apart from a couple of telephone calls from

Sarah enquiring after her daughter-in-law's health. Without being exactly rude, but more by means of her generally lacklustre response to these overtures unmistakably indicating that she had better things to do with her time, Camilla had succeeded in offending and alienating the elder Mrs Marchant to the point where Sarah's pride dictated that the next move to preserve this unsatisfactory family relationship would not come from her.

So there was now a standoff, which situation Camilla had done nothing to improve or resolve. Why bother, she thought. Diana, she assumed, must loathe her, for had she not seduced her sister-in-law's lover, only to drop him after a disgracefully short interlude? Camilla smiled to herself at the memory. Though the physical violence had been unfortunate, she could have done with the diversion of someone in her bed from time to time, although the enervating heat of the days and nights, both in the house and outside was enough to curb the most rampant sexual appetite. Although she had not heard anything from Tom since the reading of the will, Camilla was quite sure that if she crooked her little finger he would come. Confident that he was still in thrall the question was did she want him and the answer to this was that probably, on the whole, she did not. With her plans about to reach a critical stage it was of paramount importance that she maintained her concentration and had all her wits about her. Better to leave well alone and not go out to play just now. Eventually, when the thing was concluded, she would have all the lovers she wanted, and on her terms too. No more husbands though. Husbands cramped the style and were not generous enough with money. Camilla was through with marriage, of that she was quite certain.

At the Dower House Sarah, who thought she had never seen anybody weep with quite such dedication, was doing her best to put some backbone into a forlorn and deflated Diana. It was just as well that she had driven Anthony and Ned back to school the day before. Marcus had briefed his mother on the Paris débâcle, deposited his wife with her luggage and abruptly departed. Left alone together, the two women wordlessly embraced. Sarah installed her wilting daughter-in-law on the chaise longue and went to make some very strong coffee. As she did so, she mulled over the situation but came to no conclusions as to what she could usefully do about it. Marcus, it seemed to her, was behaving uncharacteristically cruelly but, maybe, it was the only way he felt he could deal with the end of his marriage. Perhaps he also felt that if he and Diana once again inhabited the same house he would revert to allowing things to go on as before. Old habits were very hard to break, especially now that they were both back in the family orbit. Confronting her own knowledge of the charade that had been the marriage, it was her

private opinion that it should end, freeing them both
to start again. Still, she was surprised and more than
marginally irritated that Marcus was absolutely refusing to take responsibility for his own wife, and
had more or less said that if his mother refused to
take her in, Diana would have to go into a hospital.
Frowning she loaded the tray and carried it into the
drawing room where Diana lay looking listlessly at
her hands which were folded on her lap. She had
removed her wedding ring, Sarah noticed.

She set down the tray, poured out the coffee, and
then walked to the French doors and threw them
open. The heady smell of the garden, a compound of
herbs, scented flowers and new-mown grass filtered
into the room, bringing with it its own qualities of
timelessness and peace. First, thought Sarah, Diana
must talk about this, and then I must talk about it
too, with Marcus. The main thing was that she accepted that the marriage was over. First realism and
then, hopefully, rehabilitation. Like her son, she was
extremely surprised that Diana had taken the demise
of her marriage so hard, for, after all, she hadn't really taken any notice of Marcus for years. On the
other hand, it was one thing to indulge in hopeless
affairs with unreliable lovers with the security of a
husband in the background, but quite another to do
so without it. Clearly the prospect of being without
Marcus's protective carapace had terrified Diana.
Maybe the truth of the matter was that Diana always

had needed her husband more than she realized, and now it was too late. For the first time since her parents had been killed, she would have to face life alone which would not be easy for her. At the advanced age of thirty-two she would have to grow up.

Determined to start the healing process sooner rather than later, Sarah said gently, 'Would you like to talk now or later? Or not at all? It's entirely up to you.'

'If I don't talk to someone, I honestly think I'll go mad.' Diana's voice faltered.

'I do think the time has come to stop crying,' pronounced Sarah, feeling exasperated and trying not to show it. 'I know it's difficult for you but please try.'

It augured well for the future that Diana not only tried but practically succeeded. She had, after all, been brought up within a family by whom the ability to get a grip during times of trial was regarded as an essential virtue.

At the end of a very long, sometimes barely audible monologue, during the course of which Sarah listened intently to its lachrymose narrator but refrained from making any comment, Diana slipped into an exhausted slumber. Unwilling to disturb one who looked as though she had at last achieved some degree of tranquillity for the first time since her arrival, Sarah slipped a cushion under the sleeper's head and spread a blanket over her. Then, in spite of her own tiredness, she poured herself a glass of wine and walked out into the garden.

The scent of summer jasmine was so strong that it made her feel almost light-headed. What had to happen next suddenly became very clear to Sarah. Camilla must be dislodged whatever the cost. So far the carnage had been principally social, but who knew what someone with as few scruples as she appeared to have would do next? She recalled the words of Mrs Seed. And then there was Anthony, another of his mother's casualties, also to be considered. Sipping her drink, Sarah felt a sudden surge of resolution. She drained her glass, went into the drawing room and poured herself another.

When morning came most of the previous night's euphoria had worn off along with the wine, but the certainty remained. Sitting having her breakfast in the kitchen, Sarah decided to defer a family conference on the matter until Diana had begun to present a rather more resilient front. In the meantime she would combine lunch in London with Marcus and a visit at last to the solicitor. She couldn't say that she felt very optimistic about the outcome of such an interview, but, on the other hand, the family might as well know where it stood.

Drinking her coffee, she considered Tom. There had been no communication from him for weeks and it occurred to Sarah to wonder if even Marcus knew where he was. Among other things it struck her as important that her feckless elder son should be apprised of the breakdown of his twin's marriage. She was now certain that Marcus had known all along about his brother's long love affair with Diana, and for reasons best known to himself had let it run. Marcus had always been a dark horse, though how dark she had never fully recognized until lately. Even so, better not to bring it all out into the open if another family ruction was to be avoided. Sarah felt that she would have to retire to a retreat for a month if she had to cope with another one of those. Replacing her cup in its saucer, she went upstairs and dialled Marcus's office number.

'Of course, you realize they'll try to get you out of here, don't you?' The speaker was Jake Weston. A week had passed since Marcus and Diana's return from France, and, typically, he had turned up at Marchants one day unannounced. Since the goodwill of the rest of the family was obviously important to Camilla given her present anomalous position, he was surprised by her attitude, especially since she was usually very sound on the politics of getting her own way. There was also the little matter of his payoff which might be in jeopardy if she carried on with this policy of alienating everyone.

'I'm aware that you don't give a fuck for any of them,' he persevered, in the face of her apparent indifference, 'but don't you think it would be wise not to alienate them more than you have to?'

Not knowing that her intention was to decamp anyway, he couldn't fathom her behaviour.

'Maybe,' she agreed absently. Darting a sly look at him from beneath iridescent eyelids, she said, 'Worried about your money, are you, darling?'

'Yes, I am,' he frankly admitted. 'Look, I want to leave and you want to be shot of me. I don't care how you extract the cash from the estate, but do it. And then I'll go.'

Changing the subject, she said, 'What do you intend to do about my languishing sister-in-law?'

'Nothing,' he replied, surprised. 'Why, what would you expect me to do?' If the truth be told he had rather forgotten about Diana, whom he had always seen as only an amusement anyway. On the other hand, since his stay at Marchants looked as though it might have to be prolonged for a while, he may as well enjoy himself for some of the time.

Aloud he said, 'You know I don't give a shit about her.'

'Gracefully put, but perhaps you could see your way to cheering her up while I get to work on the others.'

This was more like it. She was at last showing some appreciation of her position and of what needed to be done. He wondered if the family had ever contemplated simply paying her off. So long as he got his cut he didn't really care. He found the current atmosphere at Marchants poisonous, and would be glad to get away.

Eyeing Camilla, he remembered how close they had once been. In so far as he was capable of the emotion, she was the only woman with whom he had ever been in love. No feeling of the tenderer sort remained now but he retained a great admiration for the efficient way in which she operated, when she was operating, that was. He could not account for her current inertia and felt disquieted by it. Clearly he was not ahead of the game, and instinct told him that all was not as it was being presented to him.

Coiled within the circle of light shed by the lamp, for it was now early evening, her hair pulled back into a chignon because of the heat, and wearing a tubular dress of some fluid, silvery material, there was a cold-blooded, snakish quality about Camilla's beauty.

The closeness of the room in which they were sitting suddenly became intolerable to Jake, who, in any case, liked open spaces. This night was promising to be as hot and humid as the last. Finishing his whisky, he stood up and made for the door. Once there he paused, hand on the knob, and said, 'I'm going to stroll over to the Dower House later. What time is Mrs Melbury serving dinner?'

'Eight-thirty. Don't you think you should telephone first?'

There was no reply. He had gone. Camilla raised her eyebrows and began to leaf through a magazine. Manners had never been Jake's strong suit.

He arrived to find Sarah out and Diana sitting in the garden, a book which she must have been reading upturned on the seat beside her. Moving with his usual stealth, he was practically upon her before she even realized he was there. The touch of his hand on her shoulder made her start violently. Jake was surprised to see how thin she had become though she was still young enough for the results of this to be attractive. Deeply shadowed by a series of sleepless nights, her eyes looked huge and lambent in the fading light and her cheekbones projected smoothly white like two stones worn by the tide. Looking at her, it seemed to Jake that her unhappiness had refined her, and given her a sort of precarious dignity which she had never had before. He began to kiss her, and passively Diana let him. She felt herself to be a blank page on which others wrote whatever they liked, with no reference to her and her desires at all.

'Let's get away from here,' said Jake.

Her arm through his, they moved off towards the end of the Dower House garden, climbed the stile which separated it from the meadow beyond and continued through the long flowered grass. There was no wind at all, and the moon, which was not quite full, rode high in the violet sky. Eventually they reached the bank of the small stream which divided the next field in two and there they sat down. Jake lifted Diana's loose shift over her head. Beneath it she was now so slim that her body looked like that of a young girl. Ordinarily Jake preferred his women with more flesh on them, but had to admit to himself that this one still looked very seductive. He ran a brown hand down her slender frame as far as her thighs, noticing as he did so that her shoulder blades were sharply pointed, like embryonic angel's wings, and kissing her breasts, slid her silk knickers down. Moving away, he quickly took off all his own clothes and then, drawing her towards him, slipped inside her. At Marchants Camilla dined alone. Under the clustered stars, Jake made love to Diana not once but twice.

Walking back to the Dower House, Diana glanced sideways at her lover, if someone as remote as Jake could be termed a lover. Many people are aware of being looked at, even when their attention is engaged elsewhere. Jake, however, was not one of these and appeared oblivious to the light pressure of her gaze. Staring ahead, he ran his fingers through his hair appearing deeply preoccupied, though what the subject of his thoughts was she could not begin to guess. Once again she experienced a small, unnerving vibration of recognition. She felt that she had encountered this man or some part of him somewhere else, and it troubled her that she could not pin down the source of this elusive familiarity.

15

Sarah was thinking over the week's events. Lunch with Marcus had been a sober affair and on the subject of his wife he was quite inflexible and announced his intention of moving out of their cottage, so that when Diana was well enough to leave the Dower House she could go there. Sarah felt this was all very well on the practical front for him but not so very practical on the emotional front for her and his wife. Plainly it would be quite some time before Diana felt up to living alone, and since Marcus had firmly said that he was not prepared to carry her any longer, it would be left to Sarah to do so. Exasperated, it occurred to her to wonder what he would do if she suddenly announced that she was going abroad for six months, and what did *he* propose to do about it? And then he wanted her to meet someone called Jane Prior, with whom he was apparently having an affair. Out of loyalty to Diana, Sarah had categorically refused to do this for the time being anyway. Later on, perhaps, when things had settled down, but for the moment it was quite out of the question.

Feeling that she had had enough of Marcus's mar-

riage for the time being, Sarah decided to raise the
question of Camilla's position as queen of Marchants. Not entirely to her surprise he came down
unequivocally on the side of getting rid of his exotic
sister-in-law. His cutting edge, always well-honed,
seemed to have been sharpened up still further by his
decision to abandon his wife. Maybe, because he was
now thinking in terms of marriage with children,
rather than the sort of one-sided teenage romance
which he and Diana had perpetuated between them
for years, his inheritance had now become important
to him. Over and over again she regretted the fact
that, should they succeed in dislodging Camilla, Tom
would inherit simply because of the accidental fact
that he had been born minutes before Marcus. Still,
if Tom never married, then it might all go to his twin
eventually, and they had all witnessed the fragility
of life over the past months. George had seemed indestructible and now George was dead, and so was
his son and heir. Definitely from Marcus's point of
view she could see that there was everything to play
for.

Aloud Sarah said, 'I'm interested to hear your
views because I'm consulting a solicitor about the
legal position this afternoon.'

She named the firm. Marcus, who had heard of
them, approved.

He said, 'Well, they certainly are famous for playing hard ball, and if there's a way of getting her out,

they'll tell you what that is. But the problem is that
George made no provision for any of this in the will.
And, of course, you'll have to get old Greenhill in
on the act.'

'I know that but I'm unwilling to go public in any
way until I know whether there's a ghost of a chance
of succeeding. If their advice is positive, then I think
we should have a family summit to discuss the whole
thing. Actually I think we should do that anyway,
because the other option would be to pay her off.'

'Pay her off!' Marcus was sceptical. 'She would
clean us out.'

'Yes, I dare say she would. But then the lawyers
will probably do that anyway,' Sarah said. 'Litigation
doesn't come cheap.'

'So what's to be done?'

'Not sure. We may be stuck with her.'

Stuck with her! What a cross. As this depressing
scenario passed through Sarah's head, another possibility struck her. It was so revolutionary from her
point of view, and yet so simple that she decided to
say nothing about it for the moment.

Looking at her watch, she said, 'I'll have to go.
I'm due there in half an hour.'

'Let me know how you get on,' said her son, settling the bill and at the same time asking the waiter
to organize a taxi for her. Ten minutes later, as he
installed her in the cab, he thought, *she has an air*

*of resolution about her, and whatever the lawyers
say she is not going to give up lightly.*

Pausing in the hall, ostensibly to pick up his post,
Jake was, in fact, trying to listen to Camilla's telephone conversation.

'At last!' he heard her say. 'That's marvellous
news, absolutely marvellous. So what happens next?'

Silence. The voice at the other end must be answering. To whatever it said, Camilla replied, 'The
sooner the better. No publicity though, you understand.'

Another pause during the course of which the
other person was presumably speaking again. At the
end of it, her voice vibrant with excitement, Camilla
said, 'I agree. We had better meet and talk about the
arrangements. What about lunch? Could you hang on
a second while I get my diary out?' Leaning forward,
hoping to catch the venue and time of the proposed
lunch, all pretence of reading the day's mail abandoned, Jake suddenly found himself under the disapproving scrutiny of Mrs Melbury who had arrived
at the drawing room door with the four o'clock tea
tray. Mrs Melbury did not particularly like her new
mistress and liked Jake Weston even less. She
thought the whole situation highly irregular. Leaving
Marchants where she had worked for so many years
had more than once crossed her mind, but finding
another post such as this at her age might not be easy,

and after much weighing up of the pros and cons she had eventually decided, reluctantly, to stay.

Pointedly ignoring the hovering Jake, she knocked.

Inside the drawing room the telephone conversation which had just begun again with the location of Camilla's diary, abruptly ceased. He thought he heard her arranging to ring them back, whoever they were. Expertly bearing her burden in one hand, Mrs Melbury entered the room and firmly closed the door behind her. Tantalized and furious, Jake gathered up his letters and went upstairs.

Quite often these days, when Sarah arrived back at the Dower House from some expedition or other, it was to find Diana sitting in the garden with Jake. This was one of the problems of having house guests, palatable and otherwise, and was rendered acute in this instance since Diana's stay looked like being of indefinite length. For Sarah, Jake Weston fell without question into the unpalatable category. She greeted him without warmth. He was, she noted, drinking a generous tumbler of her malt whisky, which would not normally have bothered Sarah who was not a mean woman, but did now because she could not stand the man. His presence today was doubly annoying since she was anxious to discuss the matter of Camilla with Diana and obviously that was out of the question with him here.

Upstairs in her bedroom, running a comb through her hair, she went over the interview with the solicitor Gervase Hanson. He had not been optimistic about the chances of dislodging the third Mrs Marchant, assuming that was, that she fulfilled the terms of the will. The family could, if they wanted to, take Learned Counsel's advice, but the whole exercise might prove long and drawn out, and extremely costly. And, he had added, shrewdly appraising his client as he did so, though there was a possibility of success, he was by no means confident of this. Sarah felt this was all lawyer-speak for forget it. That left bribing Camilla to go or putting into play her last idea. Twisting her wedding ring around her finger, Sarah wished that Osbert was there to advise her. Having no one to talk problems over with was one of the most isolating aspects of widowhood. They had discussed most things and although she had not always agreed with his advice, she had always valued it and, more often than not, had taken it. She determined to use Diana as a sounding board once her dislikeable friend had departed. Having finished by repairing her lipstick, she went downstairs and poured herself a dry sherry. Diana, she noted with approval, was not drinking anything, which, since she was on tranquilisers, was as it should be.

In the garden Sarah turned the sprinkler on and the aromatic smell of flowers and damp, scorched earth, distilled and sharpened by the falling water, rose through the warm evening air. For Sarah this was the very essence of summer, and she breathed it in with delight, wondering how long it would be before a hosepipe ban was imposed upon these parched country gardens. Eventually she went and sat down with Jake and Diana and braced herself to be pleasant. By now even Diana wished Jake would go. She felt embarrassed to have been found apparently dispensing Sarah's drinks (Jake had, in fact, simply helped himself on arrival) without her hostess being present, and felt the atmosphere to be glacial. Jake was not impervious to the drop in temperature either, but didn't give a damn whether he was welcome at the Dower House or not, and decided to put them through another thirty minutes of his company before he strolled back to Marchants for dinner.

When he had finally taken himself off, Sarah said, 'I simply cannot bear that man.'

'No, I know. I'm sorry. I'll meet him elsewhere in future.'

'Might be better,' Sarah said, feeling rather hard-hearted but deciding that if Diana was to be in situ for quite a while longer certain markers would have to be put down if they were to coexist harmoniously.

'Anyway, listen, never mind about him for the moment. There's something else I particularly want to talk to you about, concerning the whole current Marchants setup.'

Immediately alerted, Diana put down the vegetable knife with which she was slicing courgettes.

'You want to get rid of her.' It was a statement not a question. 'Of course you do. Well, so do I. You must know I absolutely hate her and I'm really not exaggerating when I say I wish she was dead.'

'Oh, come now, let's not be *too* dramatic,' responded Sarah, who was getting more than a little tired of Diana's histrionics. 'No, it simply seems to me that without George and without George's child, there is no earthly reason why Camilla should remain at Marchants. And anybody but her would have been honourable enough to suggest sorting out what is clearly an oversight of the will long before, rather than just sitting it out.'

Diana thought suddenly of Jake, and wondered why *he* was sitting it out. The odd unsettling sense of being familiar with him in some other context entirely returned to her. It bothered her that she could not make this particular connection. Pushing this to the back of her mind for the time being, she replied, 'The whole family dislikes her so much that any acrimony which may arise shouldn't be too hard to stomach, should it?'

'I've taken London legal advice and the opinion is that the will as it stands would be very hard to contest and that we probably wouldn't succeed anyway, never mind the horrendous publicity which could easily ensue,' Sarah continued. 'It seems to me that we have two options open to us. The first is to buy her out, and the second,' and here she took a deep breath, for the whole idea was not only alien but repugnant to her, 'is to employ somebody, an agency or whatever, to look into her past. I know it's a long shot, but when you think how little we know about her *(and,* she thought, *how little George was allowed to know about her and she was his wife)* it just might be that she does have something to hide. Does that sound ridiculous to you?'

A disgraceful past? Diana would not be in the least surprised. On the whole she thought it was a good idea.

'What we need,' Sarah went on, 'is a lever of some sort. A means of persuading her to go quietly, so that the whole thing can be contained within the family.'

'Yes, I can see that. But have you considered the fact that, under the terms of the will, she has to spend ten months of the year at Marchants, and, divining as we do that the country isn't exactly her first choice, isn't there just a chance that she may decide to decamp of her own accord?'

'I think not. My own theory is that she is chronically short of money.' Even as she framed these words, a sudden flash of insight concerning the presence of Weston illuminated everything for Sarah. That there was a simmering hostility between him and Camilla, a feeling of battle lines being drawn up, was undeniable. So, this being the case, why should she tolerate him in her own house? She suddenly saw there could only be one answer to that. Sarah wondered why she had not seen it before, why this particular mental click had taken so long to happen. Probably because blackmail was the last thing one expected to encounter in the rural and respectable world of Marchants. Sarah imparted none of this revelation to Diana. There was no need for a family conference, she decided. She would simply go ahead on her own.

'What about Anthony throughout all this?' asked Diana.

'Look, Camilla doesn't care about him. She sees him as an encumbrance. He may as well be somebody else's child for all the notice she takes of him. George was very fond of Anthony, and I'm quite prepared to treat him as my own grandson. And, if you think about it, under the terms of the will, his school fees, which are considerable, will be paid by the estate, which gives Marcus a veto if she tries to vary the existing arrangement. Even if she was spiteful enough to try something on, which I doubt because, *au fond,* she isn't interested in her son, it's very unlikely that she would succeed in getting away with it. At the end of the day I think you'll find that Anthony will simply go on regarding Marchants as home, and us as his family.'

Listening to this speech, Diana felt revitalized. The dragging lassitude which had beset her ever since the

Paris débâcle lifted, and the prospect of revenge and some sort of redress for the humiliations she had suffered at the hands of Camilla invigorated her. At that moment anything seemed possible.

Aloud she said, 'When this is all over, I'm going to tell Marcus he can have his divorce. And then,' she added vaguely, 'I think I'll get a job.'

A job! Really? What sort of a job? Sarah wondered with some scepticism. Diana had, after all, done nothing practically all her life. Still, a positive attitude, even if it was unrealistic, was much to be commended. For the first time in weeks she looked animated and interested in her own future again. Maybe she would get to a point where she could confront her problems with honesty and energy. If so it would be a triumph of hope over experience.

As she began to set out the cutlery for dinner, Sarah said, 'You really should try to distance yourself from Jake, Diana. I wouldn't exactly say he was mad, but he's probably bad and almost certainly dangerous to know. Think about it.'

Diana knew this to be good advice, but nevertheless did not intend to take it, for with her very slow recovery from the shock of Marcus's defection went the need for sexual reassurance and that meant a man in her bed on a more or less regular basis. *Faute de mieux,* Jake was currently cast in this role and, she thought, she would rather have him than nobody at all. Lowering her eyes and resuming work on the courgettes, she said nothing.

16

By dint of saying that she had found Mr Weston just outside the door, and would Madam like her to bring him some tea as well, Mrs Melbury, without exactly telling tales, managed to convey that Jake had been eavesdropping. Camilla's brows drew together and, tigerish, her eyes narrowed.

'No, thank you, Mrs Melbury,' was all she said.

Mrs Melbury was not deceived by the lack of comment and went back to the kitchen fully satisfied that the point had been taken. Sitting drinking soothing Lapsang Souchong, Camilla let her mind range back over the Waterhouse telephone call, and was fairly sure that Jake could have gleaned no clue from it as to what she was up to. Mrs Melbury's timely arrival with the tray had prevented any appointment being made. All the same he was now watchful and she would have to be very, very careful. Really, she thought, the sooner she was able to tie the whole thing up the better. Deciding that even Jake would not want to be caught lurking in the same doorway listening to her private conversation twice in one day, Camilla seized the telephone, rang Mr Waterhouse back, and arranged to meet him in his office early the following afternoon.

Sipping on, she thought about living in Rome again, about contacting old friends and about having plenty of money. She pictured the collective Marchant astonishment when she informed the family that she had nobly decided to relinquish any claim she might have on the estate, and to leave England for good.

The thought of Anthony only entered her head peripherally, since his situation would not change. She would simply leave him where he was, at school, in the country. Anthony, she remembered, was due to come home again towards the end of October for half term. Well, he would have to look after himself. She would have too much on her mind to have any time to spare for him. It occurred to her that if she invited Ned Pemberton too, the two boys would occupy each other. Mrs Melbury could look after them, and she assumed that Sarah would organize some riding in the same way as last time. Her mother-in-law's antipathy to herself did not extend itself to Anthony.

She looked at the latest school photograph of her son which Sarah had propped up on top of her desk, having exhumed it from the bottom of his trunk during the course of a ritual dirty clothes muck-out. The face had lost the babyish roundness of childhood, and was showing signs of the much leaner good looks which were to be Anthony's lot in later life. For the first time, Camilla felt a sudden slight stirring of interest in her child. Although, because he was dark, he was beginning to look strikingly like her she could also perceive a similarity to his father which might grow more pronounced as he matured. The time would come when she would take up Anthony again and supervise his social education herself, but not yet. Manipulative and selfish as she was, Camilla did not ever consider that one day her son might castigate her as heartless and unnatural, and even totally reject her. On the contrary, it was her view that, whatever her past shortcomings, she would have something to offer him and, simply because it was there, he would take it. In Camilla's world taking was a way of life. Giving was for the gullible and stupid. Anyway, that was all some way off and, just like that, Anthony slipped out of her mind again, filed away for future reference.

Going back instead to Mr Waterhouse and the paintings which were, she hoped, to make her fortune, there were many practicalities to be considered, not the least of which was organizing the money out of the country. Camilla still had a bank account in Rome, but where a sum such as this looked like being was concerned, inclined to the idea of opening another in Switzerland. She was going to have to organize herself some expert and very discreet professional advice quite quickly. And then there was the whole question of secrecy. She had considered

the idea of simply selling privately without resorting
to auction, but on Mr Waterhouse advising her that
she would probably make herself a lot more by going
for the second option, she had decided to chance it.
She, of course, would not attend the sale in person
but he had assured her that whoever acted for her on
the day would be on the telephone throughout keeping her abreast of events minute by minute and receiving any instructions she might care to give. This
could have posed a problem with all the telephone
extensions dotted around Marchants except for the
fact that the phone on George's study desk had been
his own private line. She would ensconce herself
there for the duration of the auction. Once the news
got out that two hitherto unknown paintings by
Stubbs were to go under the hammer the sensation
in the art world would, Mr Waterhouse assured her,
be considerable. Off hand he had been able to predict
several private buyers who would be interested, plus
some leading galleries here and in the States. Putting
down her teacup, the china of which was so thin she
could practically see her fingers through it, Camilla
rang for Mrs Melbury. On her way to her desk to
make a list of all the things she must ask during the
course of tomorrow's meeting, she paused in front of
a gilt mirror, one of a fine nineteenth-century pair
which hung on either side of the fireplace. Her own
face looked back at her, no longer youthful but not
middle-aged either. It could be said that she was in

her prime, her unusual beauty underscored rather than diminished by the years. How long this would last was anybody's guess. Already, beneath the eyes, the odd line, fine as a cobweb, could just be discerned and where the dark mass of her hair sprang back from her widow's peak she noticed a solitary silver thread. Fishing a pair of eyebrow tweezers out of the little crocodile handbag, Camilla removed it, and noticing another as she did so, removed that too. All this could be corrected for quite some time to come with make-up, and the artifice of a good hairdresser. The money would come in time for her to enjoy it together with her looks. Later perhaps she would invest in a facial nip and tuck. Not at all dissatisfied with what she saw, Camilla turned away to her desk. Picking up her pen, she began to write.

Although a late lunch at Tante Claire was on offer, Camilla declined and said she would prefer to settle for a sandwich in Mr Waterhouse's office. This surprised him. Never had he known a client turn down this particular restaurant. In fact there was nothing Camilla would have liked more than to have talked business over some exquisite food, but caution dictated that it would be prudent to avoid anywhere quite so public. When she arrived, it was to find both paintings on display. The transformation brought about by even the lightest of cleaning was amazing. From beneath the grime of two centuries had emerged pristine colour, and all sorts of detail not apparent before, including, Camilla noticed with considerable annoyance, Marchants itself in the distance behind the phaeton.

This was a very unwelcome revelation. Watching her obvious displeasure as she leant forward to study the offending detail more closely, Mr Waterhouse wondered, not for the first time, what it was that motivated Mrs Marchant. Clearly intelligent, and undeniably handsome, there was nevertheless a hollowness about her, which was a pity. No centre of gravity, he thought, that was it. The fact that she was perturbed by the revelation of the building in the background must be because she feared that someone would recognize it. But why? There was, so far as he could see, no doubt that she was the mistress of the country house in which they had first met. Therefore the painting, which had emerged from years of incarceration in the attics of the said house, must be hers to sell. Though he himself was acting in good faith, he was unable to banish from his thoughts a strong feeling that all was not as it appeared. This gave Mr Waterhouse, who was nothing if not a model of old-fashioned rectitude, pause for thought.

'Have you reached a decision concerning auction as opposed to private sale?' he enquired, more to break a long silence than anything else. Camilla decided to chance it.

'Auction, I think, don't you?' was her answer.

Without waiting for his response she went on, 'That
being the decision, let's get this show on the road,
shall we?'

It had been Marcus's suggestion that the civilized
approach to the Camilla problem would be to convene a family meeting and to try to persuade her to
leave Marchants by dint of negotiation. Normally this
would have been his mother's instinct too but her
distrust of her daughter-in-law inclined her to do her
research first, even if it was expensive and even if
she never had to produce the results, whatever they
might turn out to be. Forewarned was, after all, fore-
armed. If possible, Sarah wanted the forthcoming
confrontation to be a conclusive battle, not merely a
preliminary skirmish.

The next problem to confront her was how on
earth one went about finding a private investigator.
Nobody in her experience had ever had occasion to
use such a thing. It suddenly occurred to her to look
in the Yellow Pages. Redirected from Private Inves-
tigators to Detective Agencies, she was intrigued to
discover half a page of them. In the end, because the
firm was in Compton and because she liked the
name, she settled on Golightly and Golightly. *Tracing of missing persons, matrimonial enquiries, fraud,
insurance investigations, bona fides of individuals
and businesses investigated,* Sarah read. Bona fides
of individuals. She picked up the telephone receiver

and dialled the number. After a second or two, a woman's voice answered. Assuming this to be a secretary, Sarah said, 'Could I please speak to Mr Golightly?'

'I am Harriet Golightly, his daughter and partner. How can I help you?'

There was a perceptible pause which was ended by Miss Golightly saying, 'You are surprised to find a woman doing a job like this. I shall quite understand if you would prefer to see my father.' This speech was delivered in a professional voice, without pique. 'Depending on the nature of the problem, people sometimes prefer to deal with a woman rather than a man.'

'I think I would like to see both of you, if possible,' said Sarah.

'Certainly,' replied the efficient voice of Miss Golightly. 'When would you like to come in?'

They settled on a time the following afternoon. After she had replaced the receiver, Sarah sat for some minutes, immobile, reflecting on the curious course her life had taken. She was quite determined to see it through now, though. Pulling a pad across her desk she began to jot down the few facts she had at her disposal concerning Camilla. She wondered if Anthony's birth had been registered in England or in Italy. Assuming they agreed to take the case on, she would be fascinated to see what Golightly and Golightly succeeded in unearthing.

Diana entered the drawing room. That evening she was going to see a film with Jake, and then out to dinner afterwards. Because of this, Sarah had felt able to summon Tom (it had emerged, he was staying in London), to the Dower House to alert him to what was going on. It was understood that he was to leave before 11.30 and Diana's return. By the time he arrived, she had finished preparing supper and was sitting down doing *The Times* crossword.

She kissed him because he was her son, but as always, when she did so, she wished she liked him more. Because he had lost weight he looked even taller than usual, and it crossed her mind to wonder why he was wearing a city suit since, as far as she was aware, he was still suspended from his job.

'Let me get you a drink, darling. Whisky?'

'Yes, please. I gather from Marcus that you want to talk to me about my sister-in-law.'

'About Camilla, yes. But before we get on to that I have something to say concerning Diana. Although I'm pretty certain that Marcus has always known that you and she were lovers, I want your word of honour, Tom, that you won't raise the subject. It's all too delicate.

'Of course I won't Mother.' Tom was faintly irritated by her assumption that he might do that. On the other hand, he couldn't see that it really mattered. He himself had always rather thought that Marcus knew all about it, and always had, and had simply assumed the role of complaisant husband. Why his brother should have elected to do this, Tom had no idea.

'You know, do you, that Marcus wants a divorce?'

'Yes, he told me.'

'And you also know that Diana has had a nervous breakdown?'

She looked him straight in the eye. Her inference was obvious. Shame being an emotion entirely foreign to Tom meant that he was able to stare back, but only just. The force of Sarah's look when displeased was well known. He decided to get off the prickly subject of Diana as quickly as he could. Leaning back in his chair he raised an expensively shod right foot and elegantly positioned it on his left knee. Then he took off his jacket and loosened his tie. Loose-limbed and apparently absolutely relaxed, he exuded a certain sort of upper-class English insolence that Sarah found very hard to take. She felt like slapping him.

'You want to dislodge Camilla.'

Controlling her temper, she said, 'Yes, that's right. Obviously if George's child had lived, things would have been quite different, though I'm bound to admit I don't think I could ever have liked her.'

Tom considered for a moment whether or not to make his next remark and then couldn't resist it and went ahead anyway.

'I asked her to marry me, you know.'

Well, no, she hadn't known. Frankly appalled, Sarah waited to hear what he would say next. He swallowed some whisky. Then, almost as an after-thought, added, 'She turned me down, though.'

In spite of his air of easy nonchalance, Tom was aware that he had made a bad mistake. Mother on her high horse always made him want to shock, and this time he had said more than he intended. There was nothing left to do but to brazen it out.

'She's rotten,' he said defensively, 'a bad apple. I was obsessed with her.'

It takes one to know one, thought Sarah. *Those two really deserve each other.* Remembering that Tom and Camilla had both been present the day George died, she opened her mouth to ask him when the affair with Camilla had begun, for affair it must surely have been, and then couldn't frame the words. The implications of such a question and its possible answer were too much to contemplate.

It was gall and wormwood to her that she was fighting for the family inheritance, and, at the end of the day, if she succeeded in her endeavours it would go to this amoral creep, her son. The only good thing to be said about him was that he was a family creep and not an interloping adventuress.

Finally she said, 'I don't think I feel like eating. Let's just conclude this conversation, and then I suggest you go.'

I suggest you go. It took him back to their early

confrontations. It was a grown-up version of being sent to his room. Displaying no offence at her last remark, for, after all, he might have much to gain from her activities, he said, 'Naturally I shall join the family front. If I can't marry my inheritance then this is the only way to get it.'

She was furious. His composure in the face of her arctic displeasure took her in her turn back to his intractable childhood. He had even then been absolutely impervious to the deleterious effects of his actions on others. Memorably, in the course of one of their frequent rows, when she had been standing at the top of the staircase and he halfway up it, he had suddenly picked up a valuable and much-loved Minton bowl of hers, which for years had sat on the turn of the stairs, and, with one eye on her expression as he did so, had rolled it down the rest of the flight where it had smashed to smithereens at the bottom in a fragrant cloud of potpourri. It had been just before he went to his prep school. He must have been almost eight. And then there had been the cheating, which had upset Osbert more than anything else. He appeared to have been born with no moral dimension of any kind, and in spite of all her efforts, she had been unable to instill one into him. It really was a notable defeat, the consequences of which were going to impinge on them all. He would never change.

Given that fact, she wearily decided not to deny them both dinner. They were locked together in this matter, and since they had a common purpose for once, they might as well discuss how to achieve it. Over supper she briefed him on her forthcoming visit to Golightly and Golightly.

Later, as he was leaving he kissed her on the cheek.

'By the way, Mother dear, I got the sack today,' he said.

17

The office of Golightly and Golightly was just off the market place, all that advertised its existence being a highly polished, discreetly small brass plaque. Climbing the steep stairs, Sarah was aware that her back was beginning to ache. Tension she supposed. She wondered how many people in a moderately sized country town like this ever needed to consult such an agency. Enough to pay the Golightly's rent and overheads, presumably. After a short pause for nerve, she opened the frosted-glass door and walked into the room. As offices go it was surprisingly pleasant. Miss Golightly's influence no doubt. Here, Sarah later discovered, she was entirely wrong.

Miss Golightly, it transpired was a small, rather ferrety-faced woman buttoned into a dateless garment of the type Sarah always mentally referred to as a frock, and could not have been less interested in the colour of the curtains, her own or anybody else's. With her lank hair and long, drooping cardigan she resembled nothing so much as a particularly unsartorial member of the Bloomsbury Group. The voice then came as something of a surprise, being both cultured and deep, so deep in fact that it could almost have belonged to a man. And then there were the eyes. Sarah was a great believer in the eyes being the windows of the soul. These eyes, framed by oval steel spectacles, were luminously intelligent and disconcertingly direct. Coupled with the contralto voice they added an impressive dimension of command to the diminutive Miss Golightly.

The two women shook hands. Miss Golightly's hand felt hard and dry, like a twig.

'My father has been delayed,' she said. 'We can either begin without him, or wait for him to arrive, exactly as you please.'

Sarah, who felt she had summed up the woman opposite to her complete satisfaction, said, 'I think we should get on with it.' Drawing out her notes, she began to outline the nature of the problem.

Almost exactly one hour later she left, having handed over a largish deposit towards the expenses which were likely to be incurred, especially as a trip to Italy was bound to be required. Confident that quite by accident she had landed in a safe pair of hands, the failure of Mr Golightly to appear did not concern her. It now only remained to be seen what could be discovered about Camilla's past, and whether any of it would be germane to dislodging her from Marchants.

An Indian September had given way to a rather cooler October much to everyone's relief, though without a sorely needed monsoon. Since they lived much closer to the school than did the Marchants, Anthony usually spent one-night exeats such as the September one with the Pembertons, but was due to come home again towards the end of October for half term, which was later than usual this year. There was no word from the agency, apart from one brief phone call from Miss Golightly to say that they were following up one or two leads and that as soon as she had something to report she would be back in touch. It was, she said, her intention to fly to Rome during the second half of the month to make some further enquiries there. Based she couldn't quite say on what, Sarah received the distinct impression that some progress had been made, but in the absence of any encouragement to do so decided to ask no questions and to leave them to get on with it for the moment.

Towards the middle of October Camilla announced her intention of spending a few days in London. This gave Diana the chance to spend a night or two comfortably in bed with her lover, an opportunity which did not present itself too often these days. Camilla's mysterious sojourns in the capital annoyed Jake profoundly. He would have put a large sum of money on the fact that she was up to something but had absolutely no idea what it could be. Even a fur-

tive search of her desk which she had very uncharacteristically apparently forgotten to lock one day
produced nothing. Worse, when he next saw her, he
could have sworn that she knew what he had done
and found it amusing. Bitch! She had asked for time
to raise the money; well, time was up. He would put
the screws on. Meanwhile he might as well enjoy
himself. He dialled the number of the Dower House.

Mrs Melbury had been given the Thursday evening and the following day off by Camilla and, as
was her habit, had removed some of her emergency
offerings from the chest freezer and had left one on
the kitchen table for whoever should be eating in.
This was fortunate, for Jake liked his food and Diana
was no cook. She put it in the microwave while he
went down to the cellar and selected two of George's
better bottles which he stood on the Aga warming
plate to bring them up to some semblance of room
temperature.

Diana was standing with her back to him topping
and tailing green beans, more or less the height of
her ambition when it came to culinary activity. Eyeing her pert bottom currently clad in blue jeans, Jake
had a sudden desire to make love to her where she
stood. Moving up behind her with his stealthy jungle
tread he cupped her breasts with his thin, brown
hands. He liked to catch people off their guard. It
gave him the initiative. Turning her round, he began

to unbutton her shirt, all the time kissing her roughly. Diana put up only a token resistance as he made love to her standing up against Mrs Melbury's Belfast sink. Excited and enjoying it in spite of herself, she nevertheless had at the same time felt cheap. Meaning it, she said, 'You make me feel like a whore.'

Jake laughed. 'Let's eat,' was all he said.

It was when sitting watching him over dinner, which they ate by candlelight sitting at one end of the long dining room table under the Gainsborough, School of, that Diana suddenly recognized where it was that she had seen her lover before. The shock was so powerful, and had such implications for them all, that it left her breathless and trembling. Jake himself, whose mind was on Camilla and all her machinations, did not notice her discomposure. It had been the way he had run his hand through his hair with a slight shake of his head while looking towards the window, frowning and distracted. Suddenly she realized that she had been on the wrong tack all along, for it was not Jake himself that she had encountered before but his indelible stamp on another.

Hands shaking, she stood up and began to clear away the plates. She had an overpowering need to get away and think and was all of a sudden aware that the wind had risen considerably outside. In her present turmoil of spirit the idea of a storm-buffeted walk home appealed to her. She said, 'I don't think I'll stay tonight after all.'

'Why not?' asked Jake, his attention caught by this atypical statement of intent. Her voice had a tremor in it. He hoped she wasn't about to make a scene. Looking down at the table top, she did not answer. Jake decided not to pursue it. He had, it is true, been looking forward to fucking her again, but couldn't be bothered to insist.

Rather hoping she wouldn't accept, he said, 'I'll drive you back to the Dower House.'

'No. No, I'd really rather walk, thanks all the same.' Draining his wine glass he looked at her curiously. Something had changed, but what? Maybe he hadn't been paying her enough attention. Well, too bad. He rose, went and got her jacket for her and saw her to the hall. He was bending to kiss her, when the wind whipped the heavy open front door out of his hand and slammed it shut again with a crash which shook the whole house. The sheer elemental force which must have been needed to do this astonished Jake.

'Are you really sure you want to go?' he queried.

Diana did not answer, but set off down the drive leaning against the wind. Luckily it was not raining but the night was still a wild one. Jake picked up the torch which lived on the windowsill and ran after her with it.

'Here, take this. You'll need it.'

Wordlessly she did as he said and pressed on. Shrugging his shoulders, Jake battled his way back to the house. When he reached its sanctuary he stood for a moment looking after her. Even during this brief space of time the gale seemed to have escalated. Clouds raced hectically across a convulsed and ragged sky, affording only the odd glimpse of an all but extinguished moon. Jake watched the erratic light of the torch until it finally vanished. He wondered if she would have the common sense to cut across the fields which would probably be safer in this wind than the tree-lined road.

Diana had, in fact, done just that. She became aware as she stumbled along of groaning and cracking noises which could be discerned above the shriek of the wind. Owing to the sheer force of the gusts, walking had now become only intermittently possible and she felt herself in imminent danger of being blown right over. There was a sudden roll of thunder, so loud that it must have been right overhead, and very heavy rain began to fall. Drenched and gasping, she fell to her knees and pulled herself along the ground to the hedgerow which allowed some respite though not much, from the relentless battering she was being forced to endure. The noise of the wind had risen to a scream interrupted by sounds of rending and crashing which seemed to be coming from all around her. Focusing the beam of her torch as far as it would reach into the middle distance Diana was awed to see a mature tree bend like a sapling before the onslaught and then topple, massive roots shooting into the air. The primeval ferocity of it all frightened her beyond measure. Staggering, crawling and keeping as much as she could to open ground she eventually gained the safety of the Dower House and collapsed at the front door.

Friday morning came clear and still after a night during which Diana had eventually fallen into a fitful sleep at four o'clock while the whole house was being shaken to its foundations to the dreadful tearing and cracking accompaniment which sounded to her in the throes of her dreadful dreams like the birth agony of the world. When she woke she lay for several minutes reconstructing the events of the night before, and made a decision to phone Sarah who was away overnight. Getting out of bed, she walked to the window and drew back the curtains. The scene which greeted her was one of destruction. The lawn was paved with slates and the enormous old chestnut, beneath whose branches she had been obliged to pass last night on the final stage of her journey, had literally snapped in two. In the field beyond the devastated garden, which seemed to have been mostly blown away, three massive old trees had fallen in a row, rather as though a chorus line had tripped, vast extraordinarily shallow roots wrenched out of the ground.

Already in a precarious mental state, Diana felt thoroughly rattled. She had always taken trees for

granted, now she wondered how many of the grand
old giants of the park were still standing. Fearfully,
she picked up the telephone receiver and dialled the
number where she knew Sarah to be staying the night
in London. Unobtainable. She supposed that the lines
must be down. She rang Marchants to be greeted by
the same. Switching on the radio she listened trans-
fixed to its story of casualty and disaster. The gale
had been rechristened the hurricane. Diana got
dressed. The most important task was somehow to
contact Sarah. This might be possible either from the
village or failing that, from the town. Neither, it transpired, was possible, for when Diana opened the
front door she discovered that the lime tree had collapsed onto her car, flattening it and the outhouse
beside which the Fiat had been parked. The alternative, she suddenly thought, was to ride over to the
village. She went back indoors, changed into jodhpurs and started to walk to Marchants. On the way
she mulled over the revelation she had had concerning Jake. Last night she had agonized over what she
should do. This morning it was all obvious. She must
tell the family what she had seen and instinctively
knew to be true.

Since she had no desire to encounter Jake then, or,
indeed, ever again if she could help it, for what she
was about to do would conclusively end their affair
anyway, Diana took a rather more circuitous route
than usual to the stables. Although she had to do a

certain amount of climbing under and over the debris to achieve her objective, the hurricane seemed to have circled the area immediately surrounding the house, and Marchants itself appeared virtually unscathed.

There was no sign of Jake's car at the back which was where he usually parked it. Perhaps he too had gone to try to telephone or maybe to try to find her. It no longer mattered any more.

She found Othello both restless and bad-tempered. Inspection of their boxes revealed that none of the horses had been fed or watered, which presumably meant that the girl who normally did this had been unable to get through. Prior to tacking up and mounting the gelding, Diana gave them all a drink, and fed Jemima and Blue. Othello would have to wait until they got back. Then she and Othello made their way through the stable yard and on, out into the park. The storm had rendered the main drive impassable. Trees had fallen to right and left and, since all were still in leaf, they formed an impenetrable barrier. Diana and Othello had no choice other than to set off towards the back gates which meant going through the grounds. Still in a lather as a result of the high winds of the previous night, the horse began to jog, a habit Diana detested and she smacked him on the shoulder with the whip. They arrived at one of the long, wide rides between the rhododendrons where she frequently let him have his head, and in an effort to stop his fractious fidgeting she stepped him up to a canter. Anticipating the gallop, he speeded up again. Her mind still exercised by the astounding realization that Jake Weston was Anthony's father, and forgetting the cardinal rule of looking where she was going, Diana saw too late that a large branch had half fallen across the path. Moving by now very fast, Othello passed beneath it. His rider was not so lucky. It caught her beneath the chin, sweeping her out of the saddle and as she hit the ground, there was a brittle click like the snapping of a carnation stalk.

18

In the chaos which ensued after the storm, it was not until Othello came home alone to Marchants that anyone realized Diana had ridden him out of the stables. By this time Jake, who had managed to reach the village via the back gates, was back, and, due to the fact that the capricious course of the hurricane had largely missed the road to London, so were Sarah and Camilla. Both were at the main house, differences having been set aside in the face of what was, for once, a natural disaster confronting them all. Without a word, Jake caught the horse and led him at a run towards the stable block. Once there, he swiftly ran up both stirrups, put Othello in his box and looped the reins behind one stirrup leather. The horse sorted out for the moment, he sprinted back towards the women.

Alarmed, Sarah said, 'All the trees are down along the main drive. She must have gone in the direction of the back gates.' The calm and shining day which had followed the uproar of the night had suddenly acquired a hard, flat, brightness whose metallic menace frightened her.

Searching, they came to a fork in the path where horse and rider could have gone either way. Camilla said, 'You go that way, Jake; Sarah and I will look down here.'

It was Jake who found her. He took in what had happened straight away. Without calling immediately for the other two, he knelt down beside where she had fallen among the flowerless rhododendrons and tried her pulse. She was still alive, though unconscious, and was lucky not to have broken her neck, though one arm was twisted at an odd angle. Jake knew better than to move her, or even to attempt to ease off her riding hat. He got up and stood for several seconds looking down at her, where she lay among the dark green leaves as though asleep, and then swiftly went in the direction of the others.

Diana, apart from being badly concussed, had broken her arm in two places and had dislocated her shoulder as well as injuring her back. The extent of this damage was presently unclear. Currently in Compton General Hospital, when she finally recovered consciousness it was discovered that she had no short-term memory. Possibly this would return, pronounced the consultant, but possibly not. Because of her fragility, both physical and mental, on Desmond Kirkpatrick's advice they decided to send her to a private clinic to recuperate as soon as she was well enough to be moved.

The aftermath of the great storm and Diana's fall
temporarily brought the whole family together again,
possibly, thought Sarah, for the last time unless the
Golightlys turned something up. Marcus seemed to
have taken it better than Tom, who looked drawn,
and who, his mother noticed, was beginning to go
grey. She wondered what he was doing for money.
Marcus, on the other hand, seemed, she searched for
a phrase, *politely,* solicitous, almost as though Diana
were somebody else's wife. Which to all intents and
purposes, Sarah thought, she had been. She wondered
at what point absolute love had turned into absolute
indifference. Longer ago than anyone else had realized. Not surprisingly, Tom seemed more affected
than Marcus by the shock of Diana's accident. For
the time being some sort of truce seemed to be in
operation between him and Camilla, but, whereas her
composure was complete, Tom's edginess seemed
infinitely combustible. Jake kept out of everyone's
way, and eventually took himself off to London for
a few days.

Marcus and Camilla spent some time together deciding how best to clear up the ravages of the storm.
The damage had been extensive though not everywhere since, judging by the aerial photograph taken
by the local paper, the hurricane had pursued a capricious, spiralling course of destruction, outside
which very little seemed to have fallen. The white
clapboard summerhouse by the small lake had been

entirely demolished. There would be no more lovers' meetings there. However, since there were no more lovers left at Marchants, this hardly mattered.

As Diana's hospital stay looked like being indefinite, once back at the Dower House, Sarah decided to sort out her room. Marcus, significantly, wanted nothing to do with it and gave his mother carte blanche where this was concerned. It was not a job she looked forward to and when she picked up the small silver-backed hand mirror, part of a dressing-table set she and Osbert had given Diana for her twenty-first birthday, and thought of all the times it had reflected the charming face of its owner in happier days, she felt suddenly bleak. Diana occupied the place of the daughter she had never had, and was loved as such.

Reapplying herself, Sarah turned her attention to the small collection of odds and ends on the bedside table. Among these was a notebook on which Diana had apparently begun to write a list. About to put it in the wastepaper basket, Sarah suddenly noticed a drawing at the foot of the page. Peering at this more closely, she managed to decipher Jake's name, though the hand of the writer had apparently been shaking quite badly and, to complicate matters more, the pen itself, which presumably was the battered biro lying beside the pad, looked as though it had been about to run out. On impulse Sarah tore the sheet off and put it to one side, intending to look at it later when she had more time. Consulting her watch she saw that it was nearly six. Tired though she was she decided to push on, not relishing the idea of restarting this particular task tomorrow and, by the end of two more hours, had completed it. As must always happen in these instances there was a small, poignant collection of personal things which, Sarah felt, did not merit being sent to the clinic. These included a half-used Lancôme lipstick, one delicate gold earring which seemed to have become separated from its twin and a droplet of Diana's favourite and very expensive scent. In the end Sarah gathered them up and put them carefully in the top left-hand drawer of the chest. There they could remain, together with the silver set, until their owner should be well enough to claim them, though the drawer itself would retain the evocative fragrance of Cabochard for years after that.

The idea of getting rid of Camilla had become something of a fixation with Tom. Finally, conclusively, without a job, short of money, a state of affairs which was becoming acute, and—as things stood at the moment anyway, without any hope of getting his hands on what he felt to be his rightful inheritance unless he married it, which was out of the question, because of what he saw as her intransigence—he felt baffled and frustrated. All of this made Tom feel dangerously adrift, for it seemed to him that any hopes he might have entertained of sal-

vation were receding rapidly. It never, of course, occurred to him to economize, and so the handmade
shoes were reordered together with the cashmere
socks and the Bond Street shirts and the overdraft
mounted and with it the pressure, though he had a
feeing that the overdraft was about to be cut off in
its prime since a letter from his bank had followed
hard on the heels of his last statement. Obscurely
feeling that what he did not open could not affect
him, Tom had done just that, and it sat on the mantelpiece of the single room he rented from a friend
in London. Sometime after that another had arrived
and he had not opened that either, but was beginning
to live in fear of the public embarrassment of
bounced cheques. He wondered if there was any
point in asking Mother for a loan and, on the whole,
thought there wasn't. All the same, remembering the
detective agency, he decided to go and see her.

On her arrival back from the London trip, Camilla
found herself with a great deal to think about. Her
principal reason for going had been to see Mr Waterhouse and generally to sort out where they went
next.

The meeting had ended not so much in a contre-
temps as a lecture. Elbows on his desk, he had carefully placed both long, thin hands together, thumb to
thumb, finger to finger so that they formed a point.

'With a find of this importance, the paintings must

go on view prior to the sale, and they must also be illustrated in the catalogue. No question about it. Furthermore, since in my opinion such notable American collections as the Met, the Paul Mellon Collection and the Yale Center for British Art, among others, are bound to be interested, it is highly desirable that both paintings should go on show in New York as well as London.'

Camilla appreciated what he was saying, but, nevertheless, in her opinion this was all getting out of hand.

'With all this publicity how can you guarantee that my name won't get out?'

'Your anonymity as the seller will be scrupulously protected but there is bound to be a great deal of interest among both collectors and museums, not to mention the press, popular and otherwise, and you must brace yourself for this.'

Once again he wondered about her reluctance. Mrs Marchant struck him as being neither shy nor reclusive, quite the opposite in fact, and yet she seemed to have a pathological fear of publicity of any kind, a complicating factor when one considered the sort of sensation the unveiling of two previously unknown Stubbs paintings was about to cause. There would be envy in the auction world, thought Mr Waterhouse, with no little satisfaction.

Regarding Camilla severely he decided to lay it on the line.

'I strongly advise you to consider your position, Mrs Marchant,' he said, 'and to be quite sure that selling at auction is what you really want to do. I have to say that you seem more than a little ambivalent to me. After all, should you so desire, it would be perfectly possible to effect a private sale. Why don't you go away and think about it and let me know?'

Caution and greed fought for supremacy as Camilla listened to this speech. She found it impossible to make her mind up. Regretfully, for he keenly anticipated a sale as important as this one would be, he decided that she would probably go for the other option. He had encountered clients who wanted to be anonymous before, many times, in fact, but never one who wanted to keep the actual painting or paintings under wraps until the last minute as well. How was he supposed to generate interest in something nobody was allowed to see? No, no, it really wouldn't do. Outwardly expressionless, inwardly very undecided, Camilla eventually decided to take his advice and to go away and sleep on it. She rose and so did he. Helping her on with her coat, a truly magnificent fur, he noted her preoccupation. All at once she looked rather older than he had at first thought. When she had gone he sat at his desk thinking about her but came no nearer to cracking her code.

Driving herself home, listening to *The Coronation*

of Poppea, Camilla put the pros and cons to herself. Obviously if one of the Marchant family recognized either of the paintings the game would be up. However, that was unlikely since they had been incarcerated in the attic for heaven knew how long. No, the real risk was that someone would recognize either Thomas and Juliana or, even more likely, the house in the background. She tried to think whether any of them had ever expressed any interest in paintings being sold at auction or indeed in art at all, and could not remember a single instance. Sarah very seldom went to London, Tom Camilla knew to be something of a Philistine, and then there was Marcus. Aware that she had never quite fathomed Marcus, she had absolutely no idea what he did during his days in the City. For all she knew he strolled around Jessops once a week. And then, of course, she thought, it wasn't just immediate family who were a risk but also London friends of Tom and Marcus. Tom in particular had many, a large proportion of whom had visited Marchants and, quite apart from knowing the house itself which had changed little outwardly since Stubbs' day, had no doubt admired the group of Marchants in the Gainsborough, School of. On balance, though it went against her grain, she felt in this particular case discretion to be the better part of valour. By the time she turned the car through the gates of Marchants to find the drive blocked, she had virtually taken her decision.

The first person she met on eventually entering the house was Jake. Deliberately ignoring him, Camilla picked up her post and began to go through it. Not prepared to put up with this treatment, Jake caught hold of her.

'I want to talk to you.'

'Well, I don't want to talk to *you*,' replied Camilla. 'Can't you see I'm doing something else at the moment?'

'That can wait. What I've got to say is more important.'

'That's a matter of opinion, and *my* opinion is that we have nothing whatever to say to one another, and now, if you would excuse me...'

Jake gave her a murderous look. *One day,* he thought, *someone* will *kill her, cold castrating cow that she is.* Aware of the fact that Mrs Melbury had her day off today, and that they were alone in the house, he was not prepared to take any nonsense. She wrenched her arm away from his restraining hand and prepared to leave. Unceremoniously, Jake picked her up and slung her over one shoulder, surprised at how light she was, like balsa wood, he thought. Once in the drawing room he dropped her on one of the sofas, where she lay still wrapped in the fur coat, watched by an interested Frescobaldi who was reclining on the window seat.

'Now, listen and listen well, Camilla,' he said. 'You owe me money and I'm going to have it.

What's more, after the way you have fucked me about, I'm going to have it with interest, and the longer you take to cough up the more it's going to cost you.'

He waited for the stream of vituperation, which, to his bemusement, didn't come. She simply lay there giving him an attentive yet opaque look. Any other woman would have screamed or cried or even tried to cajole him out of it, but she did none of those things.

'What if I can't lay my hands on that much?'

'You will, because if you don't I'll put a stop to all your little games, and I mean *all*.'

She stared back at him without speaking. How she despised him. Shifting her gaze to the leaping yellow flames of the fire she thought, he's taken the decision for me. In order to afford him and his demands I'll have to take the chance of going to auction otherwise it won't be worth the candle. The main thing is that he doesn't know where the money comes from or how much of it there actually is but thinks he has got as much as he can out of the estate.

Frescobaldi had settled down in the luxury of the fur. Locking on to his dispassionate amber gaze, and absently stroking his black head, after a long silence, she finally spoke. 'Okay,' was all she said.

'When?'

'Oh, for God's sake! When I can.'

For the first time, Sarah met Jane. Jane was hand-some, sensible and sunny. She was quite different from Diana with an uncomplicated vitality which, be-cause it bore no relation to Marcus's own subtlety and depth, would add a new dimension to him. He would be able to wear her lightly, like a fresh garden flower in his buttonhole. She was, in short, the girl he always should have married. She was also, Sarah suspected, the sort of girl who would have run Mar-chants admirably, whereas Tom…

By dint of one of those odd mental coincidences as she was thinking of him, he was telephoning her. He wanted, he said, to talk over The Situation and also to hear the latest news of the Golightlys.

'There isn't any as yet,' said Sarah crisply, 'and, anyway, I can't talk to you now, I've got Marcus and Jane here.'

'Who? Marcus and who?'

It was immediately obvious that Tom did not know about Jane and she saw at the same time that it was a measure of the coming of age of Marcus that he had neither introduced her to his twin, nor even told Tom of her existence.

'Jane. She's a close friend of Marcus's. I'm sur-prised you haven't already met her.'

Not deceived by the euphemism 'friend' and cu-rious as a cat, Tom said, 'Do you mind if I drop round?'

'Not at all. They aren't leaving until six.'

He strolled in an hour later. Watching him and Jane shake hands, appraising each other as they did so, Sarah was aware that each had found the other wanting. Women, or rather, a certain type of woman, usually fell over themselves to charm her elder son. Jane, it seemed, was not so easily impressed which augured well for her and Marcus. On the other hand, as far as Tom was concerned, she was quite simply not beautiful enough, and therefore merited only the minimum amount of attention that good manners demanded. This was made pointedly obvious by the way in which he immediately turned away from her and began to talk exclusively to his mother.

Coming back into the room at that moment, and sensing a distinct chill in the air, Marcus slipped a protective arm around Jane's shoulders, and rather to his own surprise, announced, 'Tom, I think you should know that as soon as a decent interval has elapsed, Jane and I intend to be married.'

It was obvious to Sarah from Jane's expression that this was an unscheduled speech which had greatly embarrassed her. There was a short awkward silence which she was about to break by congratulating them both, when Tom got there before her and said, cruelly, 'There couldn't be a long enough interval before making that sort of mistake.'

Jane flushed.

'Thomas!' ejaculated Sarah, outraged. 'You *shit*.'

Momentarily taken aback by his mother's uncharacteristic language, Tom was opening his mouth, probably to compound his rudeness, when Marcus stepped forward and hit his twin very hard indeed on the nose. It was impossible in the light of what had been said, to object to this action, and nobody did. Tom, his air of superiority instantly dissipated, lost his balance and fell backwards, taking with him one of a pair of fine walnut torchères and a fern, which showered him with damp earth as its blue and white jardinière exploded on impact with the fireplace. Recalling the spectacular end of the Minton bowl, Sarah thought, *he really is death to porcelain.*

He lay there for at least a minute. After the pain, his main emotion was one of amazement. Realizing that his nose was pouring with blood, he tried to staunch the flow with a silk handkerchief, and then, feeling rather dizzy, attempted to lurch to his feet. There was no helping hand.

Marcus said with biting contempt, 'Mother's right. You are a shit and you've always been a shit. A lazy, womanizing, dishonest shit. I should have done that years ago, and if I had I would have been doing you a favour. And Diana.'

The silence was profound. So he had always known, and bound by the twin loyalties of blood and, at the beginning anyway, love, had kept that knowledge to himself. His emotional growth had been stunted for years by the ingrown and incestuous habits of his childhood, which had been nurtured in their turn by the enclosed order of life at Marchants, and not even public school had broken such allegiances. At the end of the day it had been the witch Camilla who had stepped inside this magic circle and penetrated its apparently perfect defences. Jane's uncomplicated love, Sarah saw with certainty, would be Marcus's salvation.

Stonily, she said to Tom, 'I think you'd better go.' She seemed to have spent most of her life telling him either to go to his room or, latterly, since he had allegedly grown up, to leave her house. He went without a word. There was, after all, nothing left to say. They heard the door slam and then the receding crunch of footsteps on the gravel.

Sometime after this scene took place, Sarah went to visit Diana, who was convalescing in Cherry Garth, a private nursing home which had been recommended by Desmond Kirkpatrick, and who was now deemed well enough to receive visitors. The invalid was sitting in a chair by the window and when her mother-in-law entered the pale, thin face lit up.

'Sarah! I'm so glad you've come. They didn't tell me to expect anyone.'

'Before I sit down, I have to tell you that my instructions from Sister, who is fearsome as I'm sure you're aware, are that I am not to stay too long in case I tire you out, and that you are not to be over-excited.'

'Yes, I'm sure. I do get absolutely exhausted. I don't really understand it. After all, I have fallen off horses all my life. Remember Lavender?' They both laughed.

'I do! Funnily enough I was just thinking about you and that beastly grey pony the other day. This is rather different though, isn't it? You really are lucky to be alive. When Jake found you he thought at first you had broken your neck.'

Jake Weston. Diana frowned. Of course she remembered all about Jake, or thought she did, but still could not rid herself of an uneasy feeling that there was something else. Something that she meant to tell Sarah. It was no good. She had tried and tried to remember and finally had had to accept that it was hopeless.

'Did you know that Marcus has been to see me?'

'No, I didn't. I'm amazed that your consultant sanctioned that in your delicate state!'

'I wanted it.'

'Did you?'

'Yes. I wanted him to know that he can have his divorce as soon as he likes. Canford and Greenhill are working out the financial details now. I want it all sorted out as quickly as possible so that I can start afresh. Did you know that I've been having psychiatric help while I've been here? It really has straightened me out on a lot of fronts. Dr Gresham is wonderful. I'm expecting him this afternoon as a matter of fact.' A tinge of colour stained her wan cheeks. Sarah was intrigued.

'Oh, I almost forgot, I brought you these. Yellow roses. They used to be your favourite.'

'Still are! Do you mind asking Sister for a vase?'

'Of course not.' Going along the corridor she almost bumped into a fair-haired man of medium height. She paused long enough to watch him knock on Diana's door and then pursued her search for Sister. He must be Dr Gresham. Having found a vase, she filled it with water and made her way back to Diana's room. Dr Gresham was sitting in the chair she had just vacated and rose when she entered. He was introduced as Philip, not Dr Gresham, Sarah noticed. Solemnly he shook hands with her. *Is it my imagination, or is he hostile?* wondered Sarah. *Whatever it is, his air of gravitas is perfectly absurd.* In contrast, Diana had become animated and talkative. For the first time she looked almost pretty again. Watching her as she arranged the roses, Sarah thought, *She's infatuated with Gresham. That's why she is happy to let Marcus go. Off with the old on with the new. But it's the best thing, no doubt about that. And he probably blames us for her current condition. On the other hand, if her current condition wasn't what it is, they would never have met.*

Noting the time and anyway feeling *de trop*, she stood up. 'I must go. I promised Sister I wouldn't stay longer than half an hour.'

'Oh no, oh, must you?' It sounded faintly insincere.

She does want to be left alone with Gresham. Sarah kissed Diana. 'I'll visit again very soon, I promise. Goodbye, Dr Gresham. Look after my daughter-in-law, won't you?' This time he did smile, though distantly, and bowed slightly but did not answer. Diana, she saw, was staring at him with spaniel-like devotion. Digesting this as she left, Sarah thought, *such a cliché! I do believe she has actually fallen in love with her psychiatrist.*

19

Camilla rang Mr Waterhouse and told him that the auction was on. This made his day, and the next morning he hummed as he spread his Cooper's marmalade thickly on his toast, and anticipated the treats to come.

Sarah rang the Golightlys and was told that Miss Golightly was still in Italy but that they hoped to be able to start compiling a report on her return.

Tom, when his face had stopped aching and he felt able to do so, rang Marcus and apologized. He felt he could not bring himself to apologize to Jane, however. Since this was the first time in a long history of their relationship that such a thing had happened, Marcus graciously accepted on condition that his brother also expressed similar contrition personally to Jane. Tom did. If he was going to grovel, he reasoned, he might as well grovel all round while he was at it. Jane was almost offhand. It did not seem to Tom that she had accepted his sorrow in the right spirit at all, the miserable bitch. Marcus did not apologize to Tom.

Since the visit to Mrs Seed which had taken place

before George's death, Sarah had not made another appointment, even though her back had been troubling her. It had been in her mind to take Anthony along again but since the last time his asthma had been much better and anyway his latest exeat had been spent with the Pembertons who had taken both boys on a sailing weekend. In fact she was reluctant to expose herself to the possibility of another unnerving session of the healer's clairvoyance. Still the back pain persisted though some days it was worse than others. In the end she compromised and got herself added to Mrs Seed's absent healing list. Maybe that would do the trick. If not, she decided she would combine a visit to Shangri-la with the Golightly appointment.

At Marchants Sarah, Camilla and Marcus collaborated in the daunting task of sorting out the aftermath of the storm and debating how best to do it. Standing in the park, surveying the devastation, Marcus observed, 'According to Richard Harrington, some of the trees are veneer oaks, which means we could make some money by selling them. We might as well salvage all we can from this mess.'

'Obviously that makes sense, but we really ought to get in some expert advice before doing anything. The ash, for instance, might be worth something too.'

'Alas, most of it probably won't be useful for anything except firewood,' was Camilla's contribution, turning a disenchanted eye on the park, and spitefully thinking, *hopefully!* as she voiced this.

'Pity about the limes in the daffodil wood,' said Marcus. 'With one exception, the whole lot have come down.'

'Yes, *such* a shame.' Camilla again. 'Not a wood any more.'

Although this short speech was delivered without any discernible edge, eyeing her as she made it, Marcus thought, *it's my view that she's secretly enjoying all this chaos.*

'But have you ever considered pulling them upright again?'

They were both taken aback at a positive suggestion from a normally negative quarter.

'In order to do that we should have to lop the tops off first. They wouldn't be very pretty.'

Not very pretty at all. So what! Aloud she said, 'They'll bush out again eventually, won't they? And at least that way there will be something there until replanting gets under way.'

'There's something in that, Marcus.'

'Oh come on, let's just bite the bullet and clear it,' said Marcus, decisively, sweeping aside Camilla's suggestion mainly because of the instinctive distrust he felt for her and anything she might come up with, 'and talking of replanting, the other thing we could do is to enquire whether we are entitled to any sort of grant.'

'Why on earth should Marchants be eligible for a grant?' Feeling that her own idea had been treated in cavalier fashion, Camilla was dismissive.

Disregarding her daughter-in-law's question, and thinking, *I've never met anyone before with such a talent for being so unhelpfully helpful,* Sarah said, 'That is a good idea, I'll undertake to look into it if you like. Unless you'd prefer to do so, Camilla?'

'I'd like to, of course, but I'm afraid I can't. I'm much too busy on something else at the moment.'

What, Sarah wondered, *can that be? She doesn't appear to do anything very much these days.*

Marcus trained his binoculars on the far reaches of the estate. 'We are going to need one hell of a lot of hands to cope with the tidying up.'

'Anthony can join in,' volunteered his mother, who had decided that she would be long on ideas but short on actually doing anything herself, 'and I'm sure there won't be a dearth of local woodcutters and their daughters, if they are allowed to keep some of it in return.'

'With trees down all over the country, I'm not sure you're right.'

That evening, writing her weekly letter to Anthony, Sarah described what had happened in the wake of the hurricane, and told him what they were proposing to do about it. He would soon be back for half term and she found herself counting the days.

Given the scale of the carnage, it was difficult to

know where to begin what was plainly going to be a very long haul, and in the weeks that followed, the grey autumn air reverberated with the deceptively summery buzz of chain saws and would do so for some time to come. Of Tom there was no sign, Camilla having indicated at the end of the brief truce after Diana's accident that he was once again *persona non grata* at Marchants. It was ironic and absolutely typical of him, reflected Sarah, who did not know Camilla had done this, that, while the rest of them did all the work, Tom, who was nowhere to be seen, would be the one who inherited the fruits of their labours if any of her plans matured. Quite often these days she even asked herself whether it was worth ousting Camilla simply to replace her with another bad lot. There was, on the other hand, possibly Marcus and any family he might have to be considered if there was anything left of the estate by the time Tom had finished with it.

Anthony came home for a week and marvelled at the massive fallen trunks which were being systematically denuded of their foliage. When he was not helping with the clearing and the burning, he and Sarah tramped around the grounds together and she photographed him standing on top of the huge upended root balls and jumping into the craters. Recognizing that his existence had gone a long way towards filling the void left by Osbert's death, she said to him one day as they walked, 'I wonder whether you realize, Anthony, how much I enjoy your company.'

Bright-eyed he said, 'Do you really mean that?' He took her hand.

'Yes. It's time there were children here again. Almost as though with the falling down of the old trees and the replanting it is the beginning of a new era for all of us. A time of rebirth, if you like.' Not exactly certain what she meant, but recognizing that now was the time to tell her in return what he felt for her, he did.

'You are the first person I've ever truly loved. I've never had a real family before.'

Putting her arms around him and gathering him to her, her heart full, all she said was, 'I know. I love you too.'

They strode on in companionable silence for a while, and then, changing the subject, he commented, 'I'm surprised Mummy is helping with the trees.'

'Are you? Yes, I suppose it isn't really her thing, is it?'

Camilla's interest in the park puzzled Sarah too, especially since all ideas of redecorating the house seemed to be in abeyance and she would have expected this to be more her daughter-in-law's style than sorting out the grounds.

In fact, Camilla felt bored and restless indoors. Since she hoped to be leaving before too long, it seemed to her there was little point in refurbishing a house in which she fervently wished eventually never to set foot again. She thoroughly resented the pressurizing presence of Jake and avoided him as much as she could. Outside in the park she was able to shake off all that, and feel much more confident in her ability to achieve her freedom and make her fortune with this one throw. Also, as Marcus had suspected, she actively *enjoyed* seeing the fallen, giant trees. Intensely disliking what she regarded as her enforced captivity at Marchants, she felt herself to be in triumphant league with the very elements which had caused such wanton havoc, and rejoiced in their successful strike. Sarah and Marcus were forced to admit that she did have some constructive things to say about the salvage, though this was hardly surprising for intelligence had never been one of Camilla's problems.

Of Anthony at that time she thought hardly at all, for she fully intended to leave him behind when she departed, along with all the detritus of Marchants. These days she fantasized constantly about her own future, looking forward to the time when she would be able to do as she pleased and not as others pleased. Heartlessly she would glitter, a powerful star in the firmament of Roman society, taking lovers when it suited her, and disregarding them for the same reason. Or maybe not in Rome. Maybe somewhere else, to escape from the relentless leeching of Jake, for she was under no illusions there, and knew that if he ever discovered how much money she really had at her disposal she would never be able to rid herself of his unwelcome attention.

Jake too found the measured pace of the English countryside insupportable. It was not so much that he liked bright lights and cities, but rather that he thrived on wider, emptier, harsher landscapes. Solitude bothered him not at all and the bourgeois rural cosiness that he was having to endure at the moment in the interests of furthering his own interests, made him feel both caged and infuriated. As with an animal this made his mood unpredictable and sometimes dangerous. He felt himself to be trifled with and did not like it. He could, of course, have left, but the smell of money was quite simply too much for him and brought out an innate competitiveness where Camilla was concerned. He could not bear to see her win.

Sensing his impatience ripening into frustration and from that into positive menace, Camilla avoided being alone with him as much as she could. There was, she learnt, nothing she could do to push things along. An auction as important to the art world as this was likely to be had its own ritualistic dance which could not be hurried. As things stood it was due to take place at the end of January, and the advent of this momentous event, and how to contain Jake occupied most of Camilla's thoughts. In the end she decided to tell him that she would be in a position to pay him the full amount by the end of February, on the principle that if he had something definite to look forward to he might leave her alone, might even, she hoped, decide to go away for a while.

In the event this was exactly what he did do. The thought of an English Christmas rendered him even more misanthropic than usual. In case she felt tempted to trump him during his absence, he decided not to inform her when he was going, or where, or when he was coming back. So he simply disappeared one day, and only the clothes left hanging in the wardrobe in his room gave any indication that he might be returning. Camilla knew him too well to indulge in the idea that he might have got tired of waiting and finally decamped, but still luxuriated in the relief afforded by his absence.

Christmas, unlike last year, was to be a low-key affair at Marchants, and Anthony came home (as he now thought of it) once again to a house that looked much the same as at any other time. His mother seemed remote and preoccupied but this bothered him much less than it would have done. Lately Anthony operated from a different emotional power-base, which was fuelled by the love and encouragement Sarah gave him, and with his new-found confidence felt himself able to cope with even Camilla's sarcasm which he had once dreaded.

He noticed that Sarah very seldom went to Marchants these days and wondered why. He supposed that she and Mummy might have disagreed about something, but whatever the cause, his mother raised no objections when he spent the majority of his time at the Dower House. Still in many ways a watchful child as a result of his neglected and nerve-racked early years, and with a wisdom well beyond his age, he knew that she was relieved to be rid of him. This knowledge which for so long had crushed his spirit, no longer had the same power to do so, for he now evaluated himself in Sarah's terms rather than his mother's. So the tuck box and most of his clothes were gradually transported to the Dower House where a Christmas tree had been erected and, apart from dinner at Marchants every day which Sarah insisted he attend in the interests of tact and good manners, he spent the greater part of his time away.

As a result of his attendance at the evening meals, he saw a certain amount of Jake, that was until Jake departed on some sort of mysterious journey. Without really knowing why, Anthony was wary of his mother's friend. He had never shown any interest in the boy, though once or twice Anthony had been conscious of Jake studying him intently for a longer period than he found comfortable. This made him uneasy and caused him to run his fingers self-consciously through his hair with a slight shake of the head, which shared gesture had made Diana recognize Jake in him, and him in Jake, before blushing and looking away. When he thought about it, the nature of the friendship between Jake Weston and his mother puzzled Anthony, for it seemed to him that they only communicated with each other when strictly necessary, and then there was no warmth or animation about their exchanges. Mummy, on the other hand, as Anthony had known to his cost for years, was not a very warm person. Even taking that into consideration, he wondered why she allowed Jake to remain as a permanent house guest when she apparently had so little time for him. He would, he decided, never understand his mother.

20

That December there was some snow, but not the heavy falls of the year before. In the park the earliest rhododendron bloomed, its buds an arresting scarlet in a frosty monochrome landscape. The cold made the horses keen and although Anthony rode out a certain amount with Sarah, this and the memory of Diana's accident made him nervous. Sarah did not push him. Othello had been sold, not because what had happened had been in any way the fault of the horse, but because his presence reminded them all of what could have been a tragedy. When they did hack out, therefore, Sarah rode the mare, and Anthony, as usual, sat on Blue. On the arrival of Ned Pemberton, riding at Marchants stopped altogether for the duration of his visit, a fact which bothered Sarah not at all since she had a great deal on her mind one way and another.

A meeting with the Golightlys was scheduled for the following week in their office, and promised to be interesting since a report on their investigation was now being compiled and would be complete by then. The other happening currently exercising her

mind was the presence of her elder son at the Dower
House. With his financial situation by now in dire
straits, Tom had been unable to keep up even the
nominal rent on his London bedroom and had eventually been politely asked to leave. It would have
been out of the question for Sarah to have refused
his request for sanctuary with her until he could get
on his feet again, and in the days when she was chatelaine of Marchants, when the whole family and, to
a lesser degree, friends, passed through constantly
she would not have thought twice about it. Now,
however, she felt more and more like her own company. It must be a symptom of age, she thought,
though if she was perfectly honest with herself, in
Tom's case this was compounded by the fact that she
didn't really like her elder son very much and if he
had not been her own flesh and blood, probably
would not have bothered with him or his problems
at all.

Naturally, there were no signs of him straightening
out his affairs in any way. He seemed at a loss as to
what to do without a pay cheque magically adjusting
his balance at regular intervals, and therefore did not
do anything. The Dower House, though still substantial, was nothing like the size of Marchants, and
Sarah found the spectacle of a loafing Tom in her
drawing room every day exasperating. He seemed,
she thought, to take up a great deal of space, both
physical, and, in a curious way she couldn't put her

finger on, mental, and she began to feel edged out of her own home. Living together in smaller houses, she discovered, not entirely to her surprise, required more tact and precision on the part of everyone. Anthony she noted, possessed both these qualities, no doubt cultivated over years of keeping out of the way of Camilla and striving not to irritate her when they did meet. The Marchant children, on the other hand, had been brought up rather like puppies, lolling and frolicking, often unsupervised, all over the place, and Sarah suddenly found that life in what amounted to a large kennel no longer suited her. She decided to tackle Tom. Eyeing him over spectacles one afternoon as he sprawled on the sofa, reading the *Financial Times,* she decided that now was the time. Accordingly, she put down her own paper, and cleared her throat. As she did so, Tom, receiving and interpreting correctly all the warning signals of a lecture, rose to his feet and, without appearing to hurry, in fact made quite fast for the door. Sarah, who was sitting closer to it than he was, got there before him.

'Sit down,' she ordered.

There was no gainsaying his mother when she spoke in that tone. He sat down.

Deciding not to mince words she said, 'What do you intend to do next?'

It occurred to him to say, *leave the room as soon as you'll let me,* but catching sight of her unamused aspect he decided against it. The truth was that he

had absolutely no idea. He couldn't go on sponging
off Mother for ever, and anyway it was obvious from
her stern mien that she wouldn't put up with things
as they were for very much longer. At the end of an
extremely silent silence, it seemed to her that she had
no option but to resume.

'You ought to be looking for a job. Why aren't
you?'

Tom had already asked himself this. Demands for
money were beginning to shower down like large
confetti, and a collection of unpaid bills and, horror
of horrors, one writ sat in an untidy and growing pile
on the chest of drawers in his room, presided over
by Icarus. Doubtless, he thought, she had seen them.
Here he was wrong, for Sarah had never even entered
his room since he moved into the Dower House, and
in any case was not in the habit of reading other
people's correspondence.

The fact of the matter was that his dismissal from
his lucrative job, with no prospect in the circumstances of getting another had shaken him to the core.
He really had not expected it to come to that. A slap
on the wrist perhaps, a reprimand, but not permanent
exile from this particularly desirable club. At night,
lately quite often in his cups, he looked at the heap
of demands for money with mounting desperation
but by the time morning came creeping inertia set in
once again, and yet another day passed without either
the requisite letters being written or the necessary

phone calls being made. He supposed he must be in shock, and felt it had to be said that life had let him down badly. Typically he failed to examine his own part in this turn of events, putting down his present straitened circumstances to a run of spectacularly bad luck. When this improved something would turn up. There was no need for him to change. With difficulty he forced his attention away from his own thoughts and back to Sarah's interrogation. He said, 'If you want me to go I'll go, though Christ knows where to.'

For a moment he looked beaten and suddenly much older, and then the habits of a lifetime took over, and the old insouciance seemed to reassert itself. Sarah was not fooled.

Rather more gently she said, 'I don't want you to move out, Tom, at least, not yet, but I do want you to *do* something, not simply drift into the habit of being unemployed and sorry for yourself.'

To her amazement, his response to this was to put his head in his hands, and then begin to sob. He could have defied her authoritarian manner but her kindness undid him. In an instinctive urge to comfort, Sarah moved towards him but he jumped to his feet and, pushing her to one side, gained the door. Once through it she had no idea where he went, but he did not return to the Dower House until after midnight, when she heard him letting himself in and softly closing the door behind him, prior to falling noisily over something in the dark. He must be drunk.

Sarah, who had recognized a long time ago that she would never stop worrying about Tom, sighed and went back to *The Times*. Reading in bed had always been her way of getting to sleep. She was just about to fold up the newspaper and put it away, when a small news item caught her eye. It informed her that two paintings by George Stubbs had been discovered in a country house attic in the county, and were to be shortly auctioned. It did not say which house, or who had found them, since the owner apparently wished to remain incognito. Pretty sure that she knew almost everyone around likely to have such treasures in their attic, Sarah was intrigued. She read on. The find was an important one. The paintings were in excellent condition and one in particular was tipped to fetch a small fortune at auction. A great deal of interest and speculation, said *The Times*, had been generated by what was described as one of the most exciting art finds for some time. She could imagine. She let her eye run down the column, found that the auction was to take place at Jessops towards the end of January, and made a mental note to mention it to Marcus. Presumably the paintings would be on view beforehand, and it might be amusing to combine a trip to London with a look at them. By now

it was one o'clock in the morning. She put out her
light.

Camilla had read that day's *Daily Telegraph*
where it was also briefly reported and was extremely
displeased with what she found. What incurred her
wrath was the mention of the paintings' county of
origin. She rang Mr Waterhouse the next day and
said so. Mr Waterhouse was reaching the point where
he felt he could have too much of Mrs Marchant,
major art find or not. What on earth was the matter
with the woman?

'I hardly think, Mrs Marchant,' he said starchily,
'given the size of the county you live in, that anyone
is going to connect the paintings with you.'

'When we agreed to go ahead with the auction,
Mr Waterhouse, I stipulated that I wanted complete
anonymity, and I meant just that. I wish no clue to
my identity to be given to the press or to anyone else
for that matter. Is that clear?'

'Quite clear, and now, if you will excuse me I have
other things to attend to.'

Having put the phone down, Mr Waterhouse sat
at his desk for a few moments feeling ruffled and
distinctly upset. Nobody had spoken to him like that
since he was thirteen. Really, she had treated him as
though he was the office boy, and after the amount
he had done on her behalf too. The sneaking feeling
that things were not as they should be surfaced again,

and was quelled immediately by Mr Waterhouse's
professionalism. Whatever her problems were, it was
not his business. His business was the auction of two
superlative examples of the work of George Stubbs.
He let his eye rest appreciatively on them for a few
minutes. That was all.

Christmas came and went very quietly. As mysteriously as he had vanished, Jake Weston remater-
ialized. Mrs Melbury, who was working in the
kitchen at the time, saw Mrs Marchant arrive back
from Compton and stand for a moment staring at his
car, a scowl on her face, before fishing about in the
crocodile handbag for her keys and letting herself
into the house.

Arriving in the drawing room a few minutes later
Camilla found Jake, hands in pockets, standing in
front of the log fire and staring appreciatively at the
oil paintings above it for all the world as though he
had never been away.

He said pleasantly, 'I've just rung for tea. Perhaps
you'd care to join me?'

Without a word, Camilla rang the bell a second
time. When Mrs Melbury appeared, she said, 'We
shan't be requiring tea after all, Mrs Melbury, thank
you.'

'Very well, Madam,' said the housekeeper, and
withdrew to enjoy Mr Weston's Indian tea herself in
the unfraught atmosphere of the kitchen.

Camilla, who was parched but determined not to allow Jake to be master in her domain, felt correspondingly ill-tempered.

'Aren't you going to welcome me back?' he enquired, refusing to let her see that he was in any way put out by her rescindment of his order.

'No, I wasn't planning to,' she said. 'Where have you been, anyway?'

'Checking up on your activities, sweetheart,' came the not altogether unexpected but nevertheless alerting reply. It was a bluff, of course, but one look at her wary face convinced him that his guess was indeed correct, and that she was engaged on some nefarious plan to her own advantage and therefore, it went without saying, not to his.

'Activities? I haven't the faintest idea what you mean,' said Camilla crossly, turning to face her tormenter across a tealess room. In the absence of any other beverage, Jake went and helped himself to a stiff whisky and soda. He did not offer to make one for her.

'I think you do.'

Camilla rang the bell again. On the arrival of an expressionless Mrs Melbury for the third time, she said, 'I think I will have tea after all. Mr Weston won't be requiring any however.'

Eyeing the whisky with disapproval for it was, after all, only 4.30 in the afternoon, Mrs Melbury said,

'Very good, Madam,' and departed to make some more.

As the door closed on her, Camilla said, 'Aren't you going to elucidate, Jake?' She sounded calmer than she felt. If he really had worked out what she was doing, and the game was up, since his greed matched her own she would end up with next to nothing. When he didn't immediately answer, she shot him a triumphant look.

'I think,' she said sweetly, 'that you are guessing. Well guess away if it makes you happy. I don't, of course, expect you to believe me when I tell you that there is absolutely nothing going on and that you, my dear, are wasting your time. And, incidentally, and much more importantly, mine.'

Unable to reply to this riposte, because she was quite right, there was nothing for Jake to do but look inscrutable and hope that the tea would arrive and create a diversion.

Fairly confident that she had won the skirmish, but not entirely sure, and not about to underestimate him either, Camilla knew that she must maintain her guard. She would have to be extra vigilant from now on. The culmination of her schemes was so close that keeping her nerve was of paramount importance. Of course, she thought, he would be suspicious. After all he had known her for years, but that he had any concrete knowledge on which to base his suspicions, she very much doubted. Still, she decided to bring the dialogue to an end before she either made a mistake, or gave away more than she intended. Rising to her feet, she announced that she felt a little tired and intended to have a rest before dinner. With Mrs Melbury in the offing there was not much Jake could have done to detain her, even if he had wanted to. In the fullness of time the tea arrived and, in the event, it was he who drank it, unusually combined with the large Scotch.

Jane and Marcus arrived at eight o'clock for dinner with Sarah at the Dower House. In spite of Tom's conciliatory behaviour, they tended to visit when Tom was not there. If Marcus did indeed marry Jane, as Sarah was certain he would, the brotherly bond would never be what it had been for years ever again. Which was as it should be. Sarah suddenly saw that misguided loyalties had played almost as great a part in the family disintegration as the cataclysmic arrival of Camilla. It now appeared that Marcus at least had succeeded in coming of age. If only Tom could do the same and achieve some sort of centre of gravity then there might be hope of salvation for the house, and the united family they had once been. *Unfortunately,* she thought, *Tom is the dark side of Marcus and it is highly unlikely that he will ever change.*

Pouring her son a gin and tonic, Sarah said, 'Did you see that piece in *The Times* about the Stubbs paintings?'

'Yes, I did,' said Jane. 'Or, rather, no, I didn't, I saw it in the *Telegraph*. Do you have any idea who the owner might be? I only ask because apparently it's a house in this county.'

'Ice and lemon? I know, and the answer is no, I don't. Fascinating though, isn't it?'

'Do I gather that both paintings are going to be on view for a few days before the auction? If so, I should be extremely interested in going along to see them.' Jane, it transpired, had a degree in Art History.

Marcus said, 'I'll come with you. We'll combine it with lunch. Why don't you join us, Mother?'

'I'd like to very much,' replied Sarah, 'though it rather depends on what I've got on here. Could I possibly let you know?'

They adjourned to the sitting room and sat down. Talk turned to the subject of Camilla, and Sarah's imminent appointment with the Golightly Agency. Jane, who had never met Camilla, was fascinated by all this.

'What sort of things are you expecting them to find out?'

'Oh, family background, recent history and whether there are any skeletons in her particular cupboard of the sort which would enable us to persuade her to relinquish her grasp on Marchants,' replied Marcus. 'It's a long shot, but anything's worth trying.'

'What sort of a person is she? Why would you think she might have a past?'

'Because she's all present and no past. If you met her you would know immediately. She's beautiful, stylish and clever and, in my view, quite heartless. She has an eleven-year-old son at boarding school in England whom she barely saw until she married and came to live here. And I'm willing to bet she only took as much notice of Anthony as she did lately at George's insistence. Moreover, she appears to have come from nowhere. In short, she's an adventuress.'

'Mother!' scoffed Marcus.

'All right, let's put it a modern way and say she is blatantly on the make. Same difference.'

'So how does Jake Weston fit in?'

'In my view,' Sarah answered shortly, 'he's the same.' After a pause she went on. 'My impression is that Camilla would like to see him off, but, for one reason or another, feels unable to do so, which is where, possibly, the detective agency comes in. We shall see.'

Incredulously Jane said, 'You really think he's blackmailing her?'

Sarah shrugged. 'It's a possibility.'

'So if you achieve your aim of dislodging her, Tom stands to inherit.'

'That's right,' said Sarah, with something of a sigh.

It really was tough, reflected Jane, watching the

shadow briefly cross her face, that if they succeeded in persuading Camilla to leave, because of the tradition of primogeniture (in this case consisting of no more than minutes) it was the waster who would inherit. Still, if at the end of Tom's tenure there was anything left, that is presuming he had no children and Marcus outlived him, then it would all go to Marcus. And, should she and he eventually marry, to her and any children they might have. The prospect of this, remote as it appeared to be, did not displease her. She smiled encouragingly at Sarah. They finished their drinks and went in to dinner.

21

Sarah decided in advance of her appointment with the Golightly Agency to drop in to see Mrs Seed. This she did and was surprised to find Shangri-la boarded up and a large For Sale notice outside. The garden had an over-grown and unkempt look such as Honoria would never have countenanced during her tenancy. Further down the street was a man cleaning his car, and having knocked on the door and got no response, Sarah walked along to ask him if he knew where the healer had moved to. Disappointingly, the answer was negative, and in the end she took down the telephone number of the house agent, intending to ring them after she had seen the Golightlys. It had been a long time since her last visit, and, given the number of people who regularly visited Mrs Seed, Sarah saw that informing all of them personally of an impending change of address could prove a vast task. Perhaps Mrs Melbury would know what had happened. Looking at her watch she saw that if she was to be on time for her meeting she would have to get a move on.

It was the middle of lunchtime when she arrived

in Compton, with the result that the market place was comparatively empty and Sarah found a meter almost straight away. Before going in she sat in the car for five minutes marshalling her own thoughts and generally calming herself down. She was amazed by her own nervousness.

Climbing the stairs, she reflected that the most probable outcome to the whole exercise would be nothing at all. Though for Harriet Golightly to have taken so long to unearth no interesting fact of any sort was almost inconceivable. She turned the handle of the office door and went in.

Tom lay on his bed at the Dower House staring at the ceiling. Yesterday, for the first time for weeks, he had gone to London with the express purpose of looking up old and perhaps potentially helpful acquaintances. Although this had not proved particularly fruitful, it had still made a considerable difference to his morale, almost as though, having broken out of the cell of his own inactivity, he could now begin to go forward again. It would be a fresh start. His thoughts turned to Diana, as they often did these days. Because she had left Marchants and, owing to her accident and subsequent incarceration in the nursing home, had become unavailable, he had fallen in love with her now more completely than had ever been the case during their long affair. She would be the yardstick against whom all other women would be measured and found wanting. He considered himself to have loved and lost, and therefore would never love in quite the same way again. Since Tom had never cultivated self-knowledge, nothing about his mournful stance struck him as either hypocritical or perverse, or, even, given the way he had treated her when she was within his immediate orbit, faintly ridiculous. Inconsequentially he noticed that some of the paint was peeling off part of the cornice. It shouldn't be doing that, for hadn't Mother had the whole place redecorated before she moved in? And thinking of Mother, he wondered how her interview with the agency was going. Tom had high hopes of this investigation and much to gain from it. He pictured himself as the squire of Marchants with all the money and social clout that went with it. Although it was worth remembering that George had always said he would have to work if the whole setup was to be kept going in the style to which they had become accustomed. But then, he thought, the very idea of living off capital had always been anathema to George. Not so Tom. His view had ever been that money was there to be spent, preferably by himself. He had, in fact, wanted to go to the meeting at the Golightlys' office with Sarah but mindful of his unpredictable behaviour of late, she had refused to take him. He looked at his watch: 4.40 p.m. She should be back soon. He decided to have a drink in anticipation of the event.

'Would you like a cup of tea or coffee?' asked Harriet Golightly.

'Neither, thank you,' replied Sarah, who was anxious to get on with things.

'Very well then, I'll proceed.' She pulled a fat file towards her and opened it. 'Mrs Marchant seems to have led an interesting life.'

The inflexion given to this simple sentence was such that Sarah knew they had struck lucky.

'Firstly,' said Harriet, 'her family. You were, I think, led to believe that her father was in the diplomatic service and that both her parents are deceased. Not so. Or, rather, half not so. Her father is dead. In life he was a plumber and ran his own small business. Her mother married again after he died, and now lives in Australia with her second husband. She says she has not heard from her daughter for years and has no knowledge of her whereabouts. She also, probably, has no idea that she is a grandmother. According to her they, the parents, scrimped and saved (I quote) to give their daughter a good education and the only thanks they got was a letter through the post one day informing them that she no longer wanted to have anything to do with them. After that, apparently, communication ceased. She says her daughter always had inflated ideas about what the future could hold for her and, even when she was a child, used to fantasize that she was adopted. She wasn't, of course.'

Sarah could see the pattern emerging. She was beginning to feel that nothing she was about to hear would surprise her.

'Was her name Vane?'

'No, it wasn't, it was Lombard and she was, in fact, not christened Camilla but Christine. Doesn't have quite the same ring does it? After leaving school Mrs Marchant attended a London art college, which is where she met her first husband. The first of possibly three, that is. It seems the marriage was a failure from the start and he woke up one morning to find that she had packed her bags and gone.'

Digesting this, Sarah stated, 'So Anthony is the child of that marriage.'

'Well, no, he isn't,' replied Miss Golightly. 'He was born some years after the marriage fell apart, and there is no question of him being the son of the first husband.'

'Does this mean that Anthony is illegitimate, then?'

'We aren't at all sure because here the trail goes cold. She moved to Rome and there was a series of friendships, if you would like to call them that, with older, rather rich, usually married men. Discovering that she was pregnant around this time must have cramped her style more than somewhat.'

'Why on earth didn't she have an abortion in these free and easy days, do you suppose?'

'Mainly, I think, because there was an attempt to

extort money from one of her society lovers by claiming that the child was his. The man in question happened to be married to someone who had long condoned the sort of liaison he had been conducting with Mrs Marchant, and he decided to call her bluff. The upshot was a blood test to settle the matter, and the result of that was that her claim was thrown out. Even in the sort of society in which they moved, the affair caused a ripple. She had broken the rules and was forced to drop out of sight for a while. People we have spoken to who knew her around about then seem to think that there was someone else in the offing throughout this period, and one at least thinks another marriage took place round about then. We haven't so far located any evidence for this but that doesn't mean to say it didn't happen. We are still researching that period of her life.'

'She claims', said Sarah, 'to have been widowed.'

'Well, she claims a lot of things. Still, could be. I have someone out there working on it now. Once we manage to plot the course she took up until the time she met and married your son, we should be in a position to find out.'

Sarah thought about it.

'I think we probably *should* pursue it to the end now. The problem from my point of view is that although your report is very illuminating *vis-à-vis* my daughter-in-law's character, it doesn't provide me with any reason in law for overturning the will.'

'If it isn't there, then I can't find it,' rejoined Harriet. 'All the same, her track record is so dismal I think it's worth pursuing the investigation. After all, what have you got to lose?' She could have added, but didn't, that she had a strong intuition that if they went on looking long enough, they would turn up something.

On balance Sarah thought she was right. She stood up. 'May I take the file?'

'Yes, of course. It's yours, after all, and I have a copy.'

'How long?'

'Could you give us one more week?'

'Go ahead,' said Sarah. They shook hands.

When she got back to the Dower House, she found Tom in the drawing room, talking on the telephone. He looked more businesslike than had been the case for weeks.

'Had any luck today?' she asked when he had put the receiver down.

'In a manner of speaking, yes. It suddenly occurred to me to phone up Michael Hardwick-Smith. Remember him? He was at school with me.'

How, thought Sarah, could she forget. He was the boy who had nearly been thrown out along with Tom over the cannabis smoking incident.

'Anyway he's about to set up his own wine business, and suggested I might be interested in going in as a partner.'

'But, Tom, you haven't any money.'

'He doesn't want me to put in money. The Hardwick-Smiths are rolling in the stuff. No, he wants expertise.'

Really?

Aloud she said, 'I know you know how to drink wine because I've watched you, but I wasn't aware you were a great expert on any other aspect of it.'

Impervious to this sarcastic shaft, Tom said, 'No need. He's got somebody else to advise on all that. What he wants now is a money man to run the financial side.'

It sounded more and more as if Hardwick-Smith was a lamb for the slaughter.

Pursuing it, she said, 'But you haven't seen each other for years. How do you know you'll be able to work together?'

'We don't, yet. I'm going to meet him in London next week for an exploratory discussion.'

Isn't the old boy network wonderful? thought his mother.

Changing the subject totally, she pulled the file out of Osbert's briefcase and handed it to Tom.

'See what you think of that so far.'

She went off to change, leaving him to it.

When she eventually returned, Tom said, 'I simply can't believe it. She's got class and breeding written all over her and this report tells me she's Christine

Lombard, daughter of a plumber.' He seemed inordinately upset. Sarah couldn't help thinking that after
his insinuation that Jane was not good enough for
Marcus, this piece of information thoroughly served
him right.

'She isn't Christine Lombard, plumber's daughter,' observed Sarah. 'She has made herself into
Camilla Marchant, and nothing will change her back.
She's very, very clever. I always knew she was too
astute for George, but she really has fooled us all,
even, Tom, an arch snob like you.'

Tom couldn't claim to like this last remark, but
decided not to follow it up. Instead he said, 'What
do you intend to do next?'

'I intend to give the Golightly Agency another
week to come up with something discreditable
enough to enable us to persuade her to leave Marchants quietly.'

'What if they don't succeed?'

'Then we'll just have to put up with things the
way they are.'

Later, much later, that evening, in their separate
rooms, they each thought about Camilla. Tom pictured his sister-in-law in his mind's eye, the faultless
profile, the perfect taste. He saw her again making
her magnificent entrance to her own party as Lucrezia Borgia, an entirely suitable choice in the light of
what they now knew. How she must have laughed

at them. How she must have laughed at *him*. Tom groaned.

Sarah, brushing her hair, thought of her daughter-in-law too. She could now see a lot was explained by Camilla's past, including, for such an intelligent person, the curious lack of substance. Camilla had literally made herself up. It probably also accounted for the glacial self-possession and the total preoccupation with her own desires and needs. In a world where dress allowances and jewellery depended on the inclination of the latest well-heeled and elderly lover, she had learned to be hard and bright and her high polish had been honed to perfection by a series of affairs with old men who wanted value for their money. She must, thought Sarah, have appeared like a bird of paradise to George, who had fallen violently in love with her. Sarah very much doubted whether Camilla, on the other hand, had ever loved anyone. Men for her were to be manipulated and used and ultimately despised. Where Jake Weston fitted into all of this, she had no idea.

Thinking of Jake suddenly reminded her of the pad with his name upon it which she had found among Diana's belongings. On impulse she rose and got it out, extracting at the same time the silver-handled magnifying glass she used to use for identifying china marks in the days when collecting antique porcelain had been one of her passions. With the pen on the point of running out, Diana had pressed very hard onto the notepad. Considerably aided by the glass, Sarah was able to decipher the imprint of a second name, which was that of Camilla and, eventually, a third name which proved to be Anthony's. A closer look revealed arrows going from Camilla to Anthony, and the next from Anthony to Jake and the last from Jake back to Camilla. All at once she saw it. She saw a lot of things. If she was right, their problems might be almost over.

The next morning Sarah rose early, and was surprised to find Tom already up. He had even put some coffee on. Altogether this was a significant advance and Sarah treated it as such. She did not mention to him her discovery of last night, preferring to wait and see if the Golightlys' investigation confirmed her own suspicions or not. Her first task after her usual frugal breakfast would be to ring them. Afterwards she intended to contact Marcus, to find out whether there was a mutually convenient day on which they could combine lunch with a trip to Jessops to view the recently discovered Stubbses. A day away from Marchants with all its problems would do her good, she felt.

22

After receiving Sarah's telephone call, Harriet Golightly wasted no time. On receipt of the information she was waiting for, and unable to contact her client who had gone to stay with an old friend for a couple of days and had, unusually for her, omitted to tell anyone where she was, she sent a telemessage which read: *We have it! Attend office meeting soonest possible. Harriet Golightly.*

It occurred to Sarah that they should all attend, but, on second thoughts, she decided against this, one of the reasons being that she intended the family solicitor to be present as an independent witness when she passed on whatever news she was about to hear, and it would probably be easier to find a time which suited everybody if a family summit was convened at the Dower House. So she went alone.

Harriet greeted her wearing the same Bloomsbury blue-stocking garb as usual. The large file was produced.

Without elaboration she said, 'The bottom line is that she's still married. She has never legally been Mrs Marchant and is, as you thought, Mrs Weston.

Her son was born before the situation was regular-
ized which is why his surname is Vane. That is all
you really need to know. We have copies of all the
documentation.'

And that, thought Sarah, *is why Jake Weston is
here.* 'I'm absolutely convinced,' she said aloud,
'that Mrs Weston's son has no idea who his father
is, by the way.'

'No, I don't think he has.'

'But why would she keep the identity of his father
secret?'

'One way and another Mrs Weston has always had
a great deal to hide. I think concealment has become
for her a way of life. Besides which, this is another
marriage which was of comparatively short duration.
By the time Anthony was old enough to understand
these things it had all fallen apart, Weston had moved
on unable, apart from anything else, to keep his wife
in the style which she felt was her due. I think,'
Harriet went on, 'you'll find those two had a good
deal in common but not, alas, the vast amount of
money they both craved. Imagine trying to keep up
appearances on the fringes of the seriously wealthy
while in reality living virtually hand to mouth. So
Mrs Weston went back to her old chums and way of
life, always a mistress never a wife, they never bothered to divorce, and Jake Weston went to Africa,
Mozambique, to be exact, to try and make his pile
there. It's quite likely they lost touch for a few years.

And then, of course, she sent Anthony off to school in England as soon as he was old enough, to get him out of her hair.'

Sarah wondered who had paid for Anthony's school fees. Jake, perhaps? On the whole she thought not. They would probably never know.

'But why,' she then asked, mystified, 'marry George? Certainly my son was well off, but could never have been considered seriously rich, as you put it. And why not divorce Weston first?'

'She was heavily in debt. Those in the circles in which she moved knew all about her. Not one of the elderly lovers was about to marry her. Why should they? Then along came your son who knew nothing about her reputation, and who, we have discovered, settled her debts after they married. As far as divorcing Weston was concerned, they had been completely out of touch for some years. She had to take a decision as to whether she should risk letting sleeping dogs lie, or whether she should take the chance of tracing him in order to regularize the situation. We've seen what sort of man he is. I think you'll find that her calculation was that, once he reappeared on the scene, by the time he had finished there would have been no situation left to regularize. According to an old Italian friend of hers we unearthed in Rome, she was absolutely furious when told that they were moving to England, and not even to London, but to the country.' Here Harriet permitted herself a small ironical smile. 'Apparently she was able to get her own way about everything but that. He was immovable.'

'It's amazing to me,' said Sarah, 'that they never discussed something quite so central before they married. After all, George always knew Rome was a temporary incarnation, so to speak, and that he would come back to England when he inherited.'

'Mmm, well people behave atypically when in the throes of a grand passion.'

Sarah looked curiously at Harriet Golightly, wondering if she had ever had a grand passion for anyone. Remembering the brittle clasp of the bony hand, she thought probably not. However she was certainly right about atypical behaviour. She herself remembered remarking at the time about George's vagueness concerning his own wife's antecedents. She thought, *he just didn't want to know, that was it. He didn't want to know in case it broke the spell.*

'But why, when she saw he was determined to leave Rome, didn't she call it a day?'

'She needed him and his money. Simple as that. Besides, Mrs Weston wasn't getting any younger. The life of a professional mistress is, of necessity, a limited one.'

Nicely put, thought Sarah.

'Anyway, from what we can gather, Weston kept spasmodically in touch with certain mutual Roman acquaintances and learnt about the ''marriage'' and the subsequent death of your son. Business, I think you'll find if you looked into it, was not too hot so he came to England on the face of it to look up an old friend, in fact, to blackmail his wife.'

Sarah was silent. Whoever would have thought that darling, dull George would have got embroiled in a hornets' nest such as this?

'What do you intend to do next?' queried Harriet.

'Have a family conference together with Peter Greenhill, who has been our solicitor for years, and then, subject to his advice which I'm sure will be affirmative, confront her with it.'

'Well, I shall be fascinated to hear the outcome. Meanwhile, here is your file. I feel I must say one last thing. Don't underestimate Mrs Weston, will you?'

It was a salutary reminder that the whole affair was by no means over yet.

'I won't.' Sarah picked up her bag. 'Let me have your account as soon as you have made it out, and I'll settle it. Meanwhile, many thanks.' She put the proffered file under one arm, shook the desiccated little hand and left.

After she was gone, Harriet sat staring out of the window for a while. The whole thing appeared now to be cut and dried, and yet, and yet, she had an intuition that there might be more to come. It had all been extremely stimulating, she decided. A welcome change from tracing errant spouses or unearthing

missing relations. Feeling that a small celebration
was in order, she decided to pour herself a very dry
sherry before embarking on her next task.

Sarah drove home in triumph. Rather to her relief
Tom was not in when she arrived back at the Dower
House. Without even taking her coat off she sat down
at her desk, picked up the telephone receiver and
began to dial Marcus's number. After that she spoke
to Mr Greenhill. She told neither of them exactly
what it was all about, but only that she wanted to
arrange a meeting to talk over extremely urgent family business as soon as possible. In the end it was
decided that they would foregather at the solicitor's
office, since he would not be free until 6 p.m. the
following day. When Tom finally reappeared she did
not request his presence but simply informed him
that he was expected to attend whether this was convenient or not.

The evening found her penning a note to Diana.
This was a delicate exercise but one that Sarah felt
must be performed. How to achieve it without upsetting the invalid further was the problem. In the
end she wrote:

> *My dear Diana,*
>   *It is beginning to look as though we may have*
> *found a solution to the Camilla impasse. By the*
> *end of tomorrow I shall know whether this is*

indeed the case. Perhaps, if you are feeling up to it, I could come and see you within the next few days? I shall, naturally, clear this with Sister beforehand. I thought Dr Gresham charming. (She hadn't, of course, but writing without mentioning him at all seemed out of the question.) *He really does seem to have done you a great deal of good.* (Well, that much was true, anyway.) *We are all thinking of you and praying for your return to good health.*

With my love, Sarah.

This alerted without being specific. It would be easier to relate the details face to face when she could stop if the patient became too stressed. Stamping it, she put it out for posting in the morning.

The next day dawned fair. In the garden early varieties of viburnam, jasmine and prunus were beginning to flower and the mildness of the air was more suited to April than January. Mrs Melbury arrived with Camilla's breakfast tray, and having put it on a side table, opened the curtains allowing the pale early sun to filter in.

'Thank you, Mrs Melbury,' said Camilla.

When the housekeeper had gone, she swung her legs out of bed, pulled on the grey silk wrap and walked over to the window. She was, she thought, nearly there. Next week the two Stubbs paintings which were back from New York would be on public view for five days before the auction was due to take place. Although much excitement had been generated by the prospect, especially in the art world, and there had been speculation concerning the owner, as far as she was aware no clue to her identity had leaked out. Her eyes followed the yew-hedged avenue and rested on the graceful goddess of the garden at its end. Camilla liked classical statuary. There were very few things she would miss about Marchants but this was definitely one of them.

Sometimes her thoughts went back to the little terraced house in which she had been born and brought up. Not often though. She infinitely preferred the gilded present. She had always known she was destined for much more than had been apparent to either of her parents, who had been frankly puzzled by this late, longed-for child with whom they appeared to have nothing in common. Bright, and with an innate sophistication beyond her years, it would be true to say that she had virtually outgrown them by the age of twelve. Certainly it was around then that her mother had begun to sense that she had lost the initiative with her difficult and, at that time, rather plain daughter. As when a child prodigy suddenly appears in an otherwise ordinary family, they had little idea how to cope with Christine except to give her her head. The expensive girls' day school which they sent her to at considerable financial sacrifice to themselves became a battle ground of undone prep and confrontations with staff, at the end of which, much to everybody's surprise, their daughter had not only passed her exams at sixteen, the GCEs, as they were then known, but had done rather well. How she had achieved this remained a mystery. After this *tour de force,* however, Christine had announced her intention of going to art school. The very idea gave Mr and Mrs Lombard, particularly Mrs Lombard, palpitations, for were not such places dens of iniquity, and hotbeds of sex, without much art of any kind going on? As usual, having a much stronger character than both of them, their daughter had won the day, the end result, realizing their worst fears, being an entirely unsuitable marriage to the bohemian painter Vane. Having now successfully exterminated all their hopes of a worthy liaison with some boy-next-door archetype, Christine abandoned both Vane and them, leaving her parents, who had done nothing less than their best for her all her life, sorrowfully trying to work out where they had gone wrong. She had never seen them since. They had no place in her world. She had told George they were dead, and, as far as she was concerned, they might as well have been.

It was the most she had thought about them for years and years and still, after all this time, she couldn't, no wouldn't, come to terms with the fact

that somewhere they yet existed, still deeply perplexed, still sad, and still wondering where she was.

Resolutely putting all these unwelcome memories
out of her head, she dressed and went downstairs.
Ensconced at the walnut desk she chewed the end of
George's gold fountain pen. The most imminent decision concerned the timing of her announcement to
the family that she intended (nobly!) to renounce all
claim on Marchants and the income therefrom, and
to return to Rome. She pictured the universal stupefaction this announcement would cause, followed,
she dared say, when she was no longer present, by
euphoria. After some indecision she finally decided
to stage this little scene the day after the sale, preferably in the solicitor's office so that old Mr Greenhill could have a field day as well. Remembering
Jake, it occurred to her that she would have to stipulate that her decision must remain absolutely confidential until he was safely out of the way with his
money. Having thought it through thus far, she
picked up the telephone receiver and rang the solicitor's office with the intention of making an appointment.

Mrs Chance, who had been Peter Greenhill's secretary ever since he joined the firm, and who was a
pillar of rectitude and dependability and therefore
known (naturally) to all the Marchants as Chancy,
took the call.

'Oh, Mrs Marchant, what a coincidence. I was just

about to ring you to see if you could come to a business meeting here this evening at six o'clock. Mrs Marchant senior has one or two family matters she wants to discuss and it appears that your signature may be required on the relevant documents.'

Apart from the exceptionally short notice, this all sounded above board, and Camilla was temporarily at a loss as to how to account for her immediate reaction, which was one of suspicion.

'Do you have any idea what it's all about?' she enquired of Mrs Chance.

'I'm afraid not, Mrs Marchant. However as I'm sure you're well aware things can crop up unexpectedly running an estate the size of yours. I'm sorry about the short notice. If it's inconvenient perhaps we could reschedule it for you.'

On balance Camilla decided not to ask her to do that, though the temptation to be as uncooperative as possible was hard to resist.

'No, no, that's all right,' she replied, more than a little ungraciously. 'I'll reorganize myself around it. May I ask who else is going to be present?'

'Mr Greenhill, of course, Mrs Marchant senior, Mr Tom Marchant and Mr Marcus Marchant, I believe.'

Again that frisson of foreboding. The presence of Marcus did not alert her since he and she would probably have to jointly sign whatever it was, but Tom's attendance was surprising.

After a short pause for reflection she finally said, 'Well then that's settled. I shall turn up at six.'

Sounding relieved, Mrs Chance said, 'Thank you for being so flexible. I'll confirm it immediately with the other participants. And now did you say you wanted to make another appointment of your own?'

With the exception of Tom, they all arrived at the solicitor's office together. Mr Greenhill, who had just concluded a highly satisfactory will reading that day during the course of which the main (unexpected) beneficiary had been assaulted by another member of the family, was in an exhilarated mood.

He consulted his watch. 'Can I offer anybody a drink?'

Sarah, who knew how much the old solicitor looked forward to his six o'clock sip, tactfully accepted. The others all refused. Mr Greenhill's medium sweet Cyprus sherry was famously awful.

'No? Sure? Well, maybe just a little one each for you and me, Mrs Marchant.'

He selected two glasses from the mahogany wall cupboard. Eyes on the old liver-spotted hands as he filled them, Camilla asked herself afresh what they were all doing there. It was typical of Tom to be late, she thought crossly.

'Would anybody like to fill me in on just why we are here, while we wait for Tom?' she said edgily.

'No, I think we should wait until he arrives,' Sarah riposted coolly.

Drinking his sherry, Mr Greenhill said mollifyingly, 'I have to confess that I have no idea what is on the agenda of the meeting either.'

How extraordinary! Camilla looked questioningly at Marcus. He looked away. A silence unnerving in its completeness descended, and it was with relief that they all heard Tom's arrival in the outer office. Characteristically, when he did get round to joining them, there was no apology. He simply greeted the room at large and sat down. It was, thought Sarah, infuriated, as though he considered that the privilege of his company at whatever hour he deigned to turn up transcended everything. Well, as far as she was concerned, it did not. She gave him a chilly look.

'Now you are finally here, I'll commence.'

Peter Greenhill anticipated fireworks. He had, over the years, heard reports of many such confrontations between this particular mother and this particular son. He gave his sherry glass a light tap with his signet ring, and eyed the blue file on the table in front of Sarah with interest. Instinct told him that something momentous was about to be revealed.

Sarah decided not to beat about the bush.

She addressed Camilla. 'Is it true that your name is not legally Camilla Marchant at all, but Christine Weston?'

In the highly charged atmosphere, Mr Greenhill

put down his empty glass noiselessly. He wished he had another. It was days such as this which almost persuaded him that he should write his autobiography. *Memoirs of a Country Solicitor* he would call it. They all looked at Camilla.

Sitting on the same slippery, overstuffed armchair which had been her lot the day of the reading of the will, she gave Sarah a look of such venom that Sarah, in spite of herself, turned her face away. By the time she again looked at her daughter-in-law Camilla had regained her masklike composure. She thought quickly. She had assumed that somehow they might have found out about the Stubbs paintings. It had never occurred to her that they might have investigated her past. But what did that matter, unless they decided to hand her over to the police as a bigamist and she was pretty sure they would not want to do that. She had been planning to bow out anyway and, since, hopefully, no one knew the paintings were connected with her, she might still be ahead of the game. It crossed her mind to deny everything, but one look at the blue file and her erstwhile mother-in-law's implacable demeanour made her decide not to bother. She could still, if she kept her head, be very, very rich indeed at the end of the day. And, of course, if they threw her out and cut her off without even a shilling, Jake could kiss goodbye to his share of the spoils since there wouldn't, as far as he was aware, be any.

'Well?' said Sarah.

'How did you find out?'

'I employed a detective agency.'

Looking at the elegant Mrs Marchant senior, Mr Greenhill could hardly believe his ears.

Camilla laughed. 'How very sordid you must have found the whole exercise.'

'Mrs Weston,' said Mr Greenhill severely 'this is no joking matter. Bigamy is a criminal offence in this country, you know.'

'Ah, but think of the publicity and the scandal if it all came out,' replied Camilla smartly, fixing him with a glittering eye. He subsided. She was right, of course.

Ignoring them both, Sarah said quietly, 'Unless you agree to meet certain conditions which I shall outline in a minute, I shall have no choice but to inform the police about your activities. And I shan't hesitate to do so either. Having come this far, I'm quite prepared to finish it.'

'Okay,' said Camilla, very practical, 'what are they?'

'Firstly, I want you to leave Anthony and his education in my hands. Secondly, you will leave Marchants tonight having first signed a legal document waiving all claim on the estate. Thirdly, you will go abroad, as soon as you have settled your affairs in this country.'

Camilla swept the thick, dark hair back from her

face. She was brazen, exhibiting neither shame nor remorse. Tom, who, along with Marcus had said nothing throughout all this, watched her warily with admiration and desire. What, after all, did it matter that she was Christine Weston, daughter of a plumber? Here he deluded himself. Given his own amorality, he could quite easily have come to terms with her criminal tendencies, but he could never, being the snob that he was, ever have overlooked her roots.

'I agree.'

That was all she said. They all noticed that she made no specific reference to her son. Sarah was uneasy. She had not expected it to be quite this simple. Harriet Golightly's words came back to her. *Don't underestimate Mrs Weston, will you?* Still, she had achieved what she had set out to do, what could possibly be wrong with that?

'I suggest,' she said in a neutral tone to Camilla, 'that you return to Marchants to pack. Anything that is too large for you to take with you we will undertake to send on. By the time you have finished Mr Greenhill will have the relevant documents ready for your signature. We shall conduct the signing session at the big house where Mrs Melbury and Mrs Chance can witness it, and after that there should be no need for us to meet again. Shall we say ten o'clock?'

'As you wish. It seems I have no alternative.'

Camilla stood up. Tall, slim and entirely self-possessed, she gathered up her gloves and bag, and stalked out. As she went, they heard her say to Mrs Chance, 'You can cancel the appointment I made this morning.' The light tap-tap of her high-heeled shoes receded as she walked along the corridor and descended the stairs.

23

When they were quite sure that she had gone, Sarah turned to a shell-shocked Mr Greenhill.

'I assume that you can prepare such a document in time?'

Mixing his metaphors in his agitation, he replied, 'It's all most unorthodox, but I'm confident that something legally watertight can be drummed up.'

He felt mildly peeved as well as elated, for had he not been upstaged by Mrs Marchant in his own office? Still it had been a most fascinating meeting, and certainly a star for his diary. He eyed the fat blue file with interest, wondering what else was in it. Whatever it was, Mrs Marchant had clearly got to the heart of the matter with one Parthian shaft.

Sarah rose and so did Tom and Marcus. Deferentially they stood to one side as she shook hands with the solicitor and then proceeded Boadicea-like to the door. They would not have been surprised to see knives on her chariot wheels.

On the pavement outside, Tom exclaimed, 'Mother, you were quite magnificent!'

'I've always known that, after your father, I was the best man this family's got.'

Although the delivery was ironical, nobody liked this speech very much, but it couldn't be denied that she had brought off a triumph which neither of them could have envisaged. Marcus put his arm around her shoulders. Sarah suddenly felt very tired. Felt her age, in fact. No good flagging now though. She clearly saw that if they were to scotch Camilla's snake it must be tonight, before she had time to think and, possibly, regroup.

'We aren't due at Marchants until ten. Let's go and eat,' suggested Marcus. They struck out in the direction of Compton's only Chinese restaurant.

Driving back, Camilla did have time to marshal her thoughts. She was breathless from the speed and accuracy of Sarah's coup. The fact that she had known about the marriage to Jake, something that Camilla had been at pains to conceal almost since it had taken place, had persuaded her not to try to tough it out. Besides which, the file on Sarah's lap had been a thick one and was probably quite comprehensive. However, she was certain beyond doubt that if Sarah had had any idea that the paintings whose sale was causing such a sensation in the art world belonged to Marchants, she would have raised the matter. Ergo there was still everything to be gained, and apart from the humiliation of the confrontation itself for

which she could not forgive her mother-in-law in a
hurry, if she kept her wits about her she was almost
certain to depart with a fortune which no one knew
about, and without paying greedy Jake. This last was
almost the most satisfying of all.

On arrival she went straight up to her bedroom to
begin her packing. When she had finished she would
allow herself the luxury of telling her husband that
he must depart empty-handed. This happened sooner
than she anticipated because he came to find her and,
on entering her bedroom, discovered her surrounded
by open suitcases and half-packed clothes.

'Has nobody ever told you that it's good manners
to knock before you enter somebody's bedroom?' enquired Camilla pleasantly.

Quite impervious to this sort of sarcasm, Jake said
'We both know I've got no manners at all. What the
hell do you think you are doing and *what* is that?'
She was in the act of slipping a small heavy object
wrapped in what looked like a man's silk handkerchief into a case. Jake, who knew the unmistakable
shape and weight of a gun when he saw one said,
'Give that to me.'

There was no point in refusing for they were alone
together and who would help her if he insisted? She
handed it over. It was a gun, a .25 Browning auto-
matic, very small, very lethal and (he checked)
loaded. Amazed he enquired, 'Do you know how to
use this?'

'Just,' she replied shortly. 'The prince' (a former lover) 'gave it to me. Rome can be a dangerous city.'

'Yes, especially the way you used to operate there.' Handing it back to her, he looked around the room. It was quite obvious from the scale of the disorder that this was not one of her mysterious two-day jaunts to London.

She smiled at him. 'I am leaving. Getting the hell out. The game, my dear, is up. They employed a private detective to look into my past and, naturally yours came under the magnifying glass too. I am told I am lucky not to be pursued with the utmost rigour of the law, but will be if I neglect to sign away any claim I may conceivably have on the estate. Oh, and they want to take over Anthony too. Suits me. Children have never been my forte. My son and I can catch up with each other when he is older.'

He looked at her suspiciously for some time without speaking. She continued to pack methodically, as though he was not there. Finally he said, 'Are you telling me that there will be no money for me?'

With relish came the answer. 'Correct. Not one cent. You are, after all, simply a common blackmailer and, since the family apparently knows everything, there is no longer anything to blackmail me about. Besides which, I myself am being hove out without even a shilling. If you don't believe me, as you probably don't, you are welcome to stay around for the denouement.'

'You're taking this very calmly, aren't you?'

Camilla shrugged. 'What else is there to do? I always knew it was a gamble. And if you'll take my advice you'll make yourself scarce too. They are all turning up tonight with old Greenhill in tow to wrap things up, and you don't exactly smell of roses either, darling, do you?'

This was undeniably true, not that the fact had ever bothered Jake overmuch.

'Where will you go?'

'No longer your business. I hope never to set eyes on you again, by the way. And now, if you'll excuse me, I really do have a great deal of packing to do before the vigilantes arrive.'

He left. There really didn't seem much to stay for. He felt disinclined to wait for the confrontation. She could handle that on her own. He wondered how deeply they had investigated his own background and affairs in the course of looking into Camilla's. Thwarted and enraged he kicked the door of his room open, splitting a panel in the process, and then began to toss his few belongings into a holdall. What a fucking waste of time it had all been. Three-quarters of an hour later Camilla heard the front door slam as he let himself out and then the sound of tyres on gravel as he drove away.

It occurred to her that she must immediately ring Mr Waterhouse to alert him to the fact that she would be staying in London for the next two weeks, or at least until after the auction. It would be catastrophic if he rang her here at Marchants and spoke to Sarah instead. This accomplished, she turned her mind to the journey to London and how to get there. Presumably a departure in George's Jaguar would not be countenanced, so she must organize herself a taxi and find out the times of the trains, and then book herself into the anonymous but pleasant little hotel in Chelsea, where it had been her habit to stay when in London for a day or two. So much to do and so little time in which to do it. Glancing at her watch she was surprised to see that it was already half-past eight.

The family arrived, as Sarah had said they would, at exactly ten o'clock. Mr Greenhill and a scandalized Mrs Chance, who by now had been thoroughly briefed on what was going on had arrived five minutes earlier, and were sitting in the drawing room. Mrs Melbury opened the door to Sarah, Tom and Marcus wondering what on earth could be happening. Mr Greenhill had had an unmistakably conspiratorial air when he entered the house while Mrs Chance looked even more prune-faced than usual— rather, thought Mrs Melbury, as if she had lost ten pounds and found ten pence. Camilla was nowhere to be seen.

'I'll tell Mrs Marchant that you are here.'

'Could you let us have five minutes with Mr Greenhill before you do that, please, Mrs Melbury?'

requested Sarah. 'And then, when Mrs Marchant does come down we'll need you to witness one or two documents, if you wouldn't mind.'

'Very well, Madam.' She went.

Mr Greenhill opened his antediluvian leather briefcase and handed a clutch of papers to Sarah who proceeded to read them carefully before handing them on to Marcus who in his turn passed them on to Tom.

'That all seems to be in order, Mr Greenhill. Congratulations, and many, many thanks for your', here she hesitated, 'discretion over this matter.'

He knew exactly what she meant by that. It was, after all, a criminal matter and should by rights have been reported to the police. As it was, he merely inclined his head slightly, murmuring, as was his courtly, old-fashioned habit, 'My pleasure, Mrs Marchant, my pleasure.'

Sarah rang for Mrs Melbury. 'Could you please let Mrs Marchant know that we are here now, Mrs Melbury?'

When Camilla finally made her entrance they noticed that she had changed. Formerly pearl pale in grey, she was now aggressive in military scarlet, with, Mrs Chance noted disapprovingly, mouth and fingernails to match. She carried only a small Vuitton case and The Coat. Looking at her, Tom could not disguise from himself his own regret that, after tonight, it was unlikely that they would ever meet again. Devoid of all the more civilized impulses, and, indeed, of *any* civilized impulses, she nevertheless possessed three of the qualities he, in his shallow way, admired the most, namely beauty, style and arrogance.

Still, for the next thirty minutes anyway, mistress of Marchants, Camilla proposed drinks. They all, with the exception of Tom who poured himself a large whisky, refused. Mr Greenhill handed the sheaf of documents to her.

'Perhaps you would care to read these.'

'I don't need to read anything,' said Camilla with scorn.

'Very well. In that case, please sign where I have put the pencilled crosses. Mrs Melbury, perhaps you would be good enough to witness the signature followed by Mrs Chance.'

Dimly aware that something of great import was going on but uncertain what it was exactly, Mrs Melbury did as she was asked.

When they had finished, Camilla said, 'I have packed up my personal belongings, but you will appreciate that since I am about to travel by train I'm unable to take more than two suitcases with me. I'm therefore obliged to ask you to send the remainder on to my hotel. Here is the address. I should be grateful if you would not pass it on to Jake Weston. I have made a list of my other possessions such as furniture and small paintings which I shall arrange to have sent to Rome as soon as I arrive there.'

They heard the sound of a taxi drawing up outside.

'I think that's all, apart from the fact that I hope you all rot in hell,' was her vituperative parting shot as she withdrew.

They could hardly believe that they had seen the last of her.

Mr Greenhill said, 'I think I shall drive Mrs Chance home now. Unless, that is, I can do anything else for you. Perhaps it would be a good idea if I took the relevant documents with me and lodged them in the firm's safe.'

'A very good idea,' replied Sarah. She saw them both to the door. 'We shall have to convene another meeting in the not too distant future to sort out all the loose ends now that Mrs Weston has, we hope, finally departed.'

On her return to the drawing room, she said to the mesmerized Mrs Melbury, 'Mrs Marchant will not be returning. She has', added Sarah by way of explanation, 'decided to go back to Rome.'

'What about Master Anthony?'

'Oh, he will continue to regard Marchants as his home.'

It reminded her that she would have to drive to his prep school to apprise Anthony of the latest turn of events. Poor little fellow, she thought, for a mother was a mother, even one as uninvolved as his. She wondered if Camilla would take the time to write to her son, or make any effort to explain her departure. Probably not.

Marcus, who was driving back to London with Jane, transported Tom and Sarah back to the Dower House en route. Nobody said very much. They were all profoundly exhausted.

24

The stir generated in the art and auction world by the advent of two previously unknown paintings by George Stubbs was intensely gratifying for Mr Waterhouse. All his working life he had dreamed of a discovery such as this, and as he worked at his desk in his spacious office every so often would turn appreciatively in the direction of the easels on which they rested. They were truly a feast for the eye, he thought. He would miss their presence after the sale and idly wondered who would buy them. Hopefully a UK resident, either private person or gallery, since otherwise he anticipated difficulties over export licences. They were going on display the following Monday, the auction itself being scheduled for the following Friday. He made a note on his jotter to contact Mrs Marchant who, he had just been informed, was to be rather conveniently based in London for the foreseeable future.

Sarah drove down to see Anthony a couple of days after the confrontation with Camilla. He came into the headmaster's drawing room where they had been tactfully left alone, looking apprehensive. In Anthony's experience this sort of unexpected visit usually augured no good.

He hugged Sarah, who hugged him back, wishing she had better news for him.

After a minute he stood back and said anxiously, 'It isn't Blue, is it? I mean he hasn't died or anything, has he?'

'Oh heavens, no, nothing like that,' replied Sarah. 'No, it's your mama.'

'Oh?' He was instantly apprehensive.

'Yes. I'm afraid she has had to leave Marchants and go back to Italy.'

'Oh.' He said again, clearly nonplussed. 'Why didn't she tell me herself?'

'It was very unexpected, and she had no time to do that. I'm sure that as soon as she has sorted her affairs out she will be in touch with you,' said Sarah, who was by no means certain of any such thing.

Anthony stated with odd clairvoyance, 'She isn't coming back, is she? That's why you've come to see me.' He looked suddenly bereft. 'What will I do in the holidays?'

Distressed, she put an arm around his shoulders. 'Anthony, darling, you'll come to Marchants. We are your family and Marchants is your home. Nothing will ever alter that.'

'Why doesn't she like me? What have I done? Why doesn't she care about me the way other boys'

mothers do?' He felt confused and upset. Mummy
was not after all comfortable to have around. He
wanted her and he didn't want her all at the same
time. Her sarcasm and, worse, her cold rages had
been intimidating, and he had often thought she
seemed permanently disappointed in him, and yet
still he was wounded by more evidence of what he
could only see as her disdain. Her approval mattered
to him, and the fact that she relentlessly withheld it
did his fragile self-esteem no good.

Watching his haunted, introspective look, harrow-
ing in one so young, Sarah thought, *damn that
woman*. The decisions she had taken in advance of
today's trip, namely not to let him know that Camilla
was still in this country for at least another week,
and also to keep from him the true story of her departure, had been easy. Less easy was to explain her
behaviour in any sort of flattering terms. She was,
after all, Anthony's mother and it was important that
he should think well of her, in so far as this was
possible. On the other hand, Sarah clearly saw that
in thinking well of her he would think less well of
himself, since if there was nothing wrong with her
attitude towards him in the eyes of the world, then
the only inference he could draw was that he must
somehow be to blame.

She decided to sacrifice Camilla.

Choosing her words with care, she said, 'Some
women, very few, simply don't like children, their

own or anybody else's. It's something', here she took a deep breath, and then went banco, 'missing in their emotional make-up. I think Mummy is like that. It's very bad luck for you. And for her.'

In spite of himself, Anthony was interested. 'So you don't think it's my fault that she doesn't love me?'

'I think something is lacking in her, not in you.'

Nobody had ever talked to Anthony in this adult way about his unfeeling parent. He had felt himself to be adrift in a sea of other people's tact, whereby, because she was his mother, nobody ever criticized her in front of him, no matter how baffling and unkind her actions were. He knew Sarah to be very forthright and he trusted her, so this was an important point of reference for him and considerably lightened the burden of his guilt. He gave her the benefit of his incandescent, transfiguring smile. 'Do you think,' he said, with concern, 'she's unhappy, being like that?'

Sarah, who had never ascribed such a mundane emotion as unhappiness to Camilla or, indeed, very much emotion at all, replied, 'I think she has no idea what she is missing, and therefore she isn't.'

The compliment implied in this last answer pleased Anthony.

'I think I'll be all right now,' he said.

Sarah caught him to her with tears in her eyes.

'Of course you will, of course you will.'

As she was leaving, having replenished a depleted tuck box, she said, 'I think this conversation should be a secret between us, don't you?'

He nodded gravely. He would, she thought keep his word. He was the sort of sensible little boy who would see the importance of it. After she had gone, Anthony went off to his favourite hiding place with some of his tuck for consolation and thought over what she had said. He felt considerably happier and certain things, though not all by any means, were clearer. Nevertheless, in the small hours of the morning, when the rest of the dormitory was unconscious, he sobbed himself to sleep.

Sarah decided that she would travel up to London to spend a day or two with Marcus and Jane. One of the objects of her trip was to see the Stubbs paintings and the other to shop. Jane had already been to see them and declared them to be magnificent. Before Sarah could leave however she had one or two things to attend to, including a visit to Mrs Seed whom she had finally tracked down through the house agent.

It transpired that the healer had relocated herself in a small semi-detached house on the other side of the town.

'Easier to clean, dear,' was the explanation she offered Sarah. 'Just lie down on the bed and I'll be with you in a minute.'

While Mrs Seed washed her hands Sarah thought

about the last time they had met. Music of a soothing variety was playing in the background, and she began to feel drowsy. She closed her eyes and felt the healer's cool hands brushing her brow.

'Turn over dear, and I'll go down the back,' said Mrs Seed. 'Been troubling you again, has it?'

Sarah nodded. Within her closed eyelids a kaleidoscope of bright colours formed itself, forming, dissolving and reforming. It would have been easy to drift into sleep, she thought, especially as the heat emanating from the hands seemed particularly strong today.

'She's gone, hasn't she? The dark one.' Mrs Seed's question took Sarah by surprise. Before Sarah could reply, she said, 'It isn't over yet, you know.' Her voice, Sarah noticed, had deepened and sounded like that of a man. The persistent, penetrating heat from the hands continued. Because of the position in which she was lying, she could not see the healer, but she was aware that, disconcertingly, Mrs Seed must have slid into trance again.

'Jiggery-pokery with money,' said the voice. 'Something she has that belongs to you. Could be loss of money. Bloody woman's a common criminal!'

Sarah was startled. Oh no, not again! The last sentence was uttered in Osbert's voice. Unmistakable, the intonation and delivery. She felt her flesh creep yet at the same time the very sound of it transported her back to a time of security when the impregnability of her house and belongings had been beyond question, a time when Osbert himself and their love for one another had seemed indestructible. Mind to disembodied mind, Sarah spoke to Osbert. *If there is anything further to be done, I'll do it. That much I owe you, my darling, for all those years of happiness.*

Perhaps he did receive the message for there was a short pause. Apparently nothing more was forthcoming, and then Mrs Seed said in her normal voice, 'That's all for today, dear. You can sit up now. Come back in a month's time and I'll give you a booster.' As had happened the last time, she appeared to have no recollection of what she had just said, or, if she had, made no reference to it. So odd had the whole experience been that Sarah was inclined to think she must have imagined it. And, even if she hadn't, she thought, Mrs Seed must be wrong. One of the first things she had done the day after Camilla's departure was to check the house, and, as far as she could see, nothing was missing. All the same, she felt unsettled and was still mulling the episode over by the time she arrived back at Marchants.

When she entered the drawing room, Tom was there. Tom triumphant. Tom in possession of his inheritance.

As she sat down he said, 'Old Greenhill rang while you were out. He wants to set up a meeting early next week to tidy everything up.'

'Fine by me,' replied his mother. 'You'd better clear a date with Marcus.' She extracted her diary from her handbag. 'The only day I can't do is Wednesday.'

'I don't think,' said her son tentatively, 'that there is any need for you to be there probably.'

Slowly closing her diary while at the same time giving him a level look, she said, 'Are you saying that you would prefer it if I didn't ever come to such a meeting? Or is it that there is simply no need for me to be present at this one in particular? I should have thought that loose ends, which are what I assume Mr Greenhill is talking about, might conceivably have affected me, given what has just gone before.'

'Of course you must attend if you really want to. It just seemed to me that now might be an ideal time for you to…' He paused, intending to choose his words carefully. She was giving him a very uncompromising stare.

'Bow out, perhaps?'

Wanting to say yes, and avoiding her eye, he said instead, though without conviction, 'No. No, of course not. I just thought you'd rather do a bit less in future.'

'You mean *you'd* rather I did a bit less!'

So that was the way things were going to be.

'Tom, you should know, and if you don't know I'm telling you now, that I have no intention whatever in interfering with the running of the estate. But

where decisions are being taken which do concern
me, then I should like you to do me the courtesy of
consulting me.'

He was unconvinced. Mother was a powerful
woman and had run the house and estate for years,
apart from the brief reign of Camilla and even briefer
reign of George. He was in charge now and intended
his rule to be one of autocracy, not consensus. It was,
however, proving an even stickier interview than he
had anticipated. All he had meant to do was to put
down a marker.

'*D'accord,*' he replied easily, and then, changing
the subject, 'What about a drink?'

'No, thank you. I have to get back.' At the door
she paused. 'I shall be away for two or three days
from tomorrow. I'm going to stay with Marcus and
Jane.'

She went. He made no move to stop her. She was
plainly F and O—fat and offended. Too bad. He had
started the way he meant to go on.

Sarah seethed all the way to the Dower House. Not
because she had any wish to go on being the chatelaine of Marchants, or even to take any part in the
running of it, of this she was quite sure, but because
of Tom's sheer ingratitude.

Putting her key in the lock, she heard her phone
ringing and getting to it just as he was about to give
up, found Peter Greenhill on the other end, wanting,
he said, to talk to her on a matter of extreme impor-

tance. Taking her coat off as she listened to what he had to say, she could see that she was never going to achieve a cup of tea.

'If it's as crucial as that we'll have to meet today, as I'm going to London first thing tomorrow.' The thought of returning to Compton whence she had just come was not an appealing one either.

Rather to her relief, he said, 'I was going to suggest that I might call on you this evening at around seven o'clock, if that is not inconvenient.'

It must be something crucial, she thought, as she replaced the receiver. Perhaps Camilla had made some sort of retaliatory move. She rather doubted that though. Greenhill himself had said that the documents she had signed were watertight. She would soon find out. In the meantime she put the kettle on and went upstairs to change.

He arrived punctually looking harassed and she poured him a sherry. When they were both sitting down, he handed her a large buff envelope. Looking at the outside she saw written in what she recognized as George's hand the words: *Only to be opened after the death of my wife and in the event that there is no child of mine to inherit.* It was addressed to Mr Greenhill.

Sarah looked at him. 'You've already read what is inside I take it?'

He nodded.

She drew out what was evidently a legal document, unfolded it and ran her eye over its contents. Ye Gods! She couldn't believe it. When she had finished she read the document all over again to make sure that she had not misunderstood.

She looked at the solicitor.

'You had no idea what was in this?'

'None whatsoever until I broke the seal yesterday. It seemed to me that legally, as far as the estate was concerned, Mrs Weston was, to all intents and purposes, dead. And there is, of course, no child. As you can see, the whole thing has been drawn up by a London solicitor before being lodged with me. Given the bad feeling it was bound to cause, he obviously hoped that there would be no need for such a drastic step.'

'Well, it has to be said that in family terms what he has done is dynamite.'

'Quite so.'

They looked at each other.

Sarah said, 'I should prefer that neither Marcus nor Tom knows that I have already seen this document. I believe they are hoping to have a meeting with you early next week to discuss all the legal implications of what has happened.'

'You can rely on my discretion absolutely, Mrs Marchant.'

'Presumably you'll now want to see them both sooner than that. As soon as possible, in fact.'

'I think it would be advisable.'

After he had gone, she sat for a long time looking into the molten heart of her drawing room fire. Whatever the repercussions, there was no doubt in her mind that George had done the right thing. They had all underestimated George.

25

Jane and Marcus were currently living in Jane's garden flat in Clapham. Sarah, who could tell a great deal about people by the objects with which they surrounded themselves, liked what she saw. Here were ethnic things, personal things and valuable things successfully juxtaposed amid large sofas, kelims and green plants. The whole effect was one of comfort and variety. Magazines and books were everywhere.

Marcus was not yet back and the two women were sitting in the bedroom which was to be Sarah's for the duration of her stay, talking while she unpacked.

'Have you and Marcus decided when you are getting married?' asked Sarah, repairing her lipstick.

There was a perceptible pause. Alerted, she looked at Jane through the mirror. 'You aren't having second thoughts, are you?'

'Not exactly. I know he talked about it in front of you and Tom but he hasn't, in fact, asked me. I think quite a lot about his wife too, and Tom's hostility doesn't help either.'

'Tom,' said his mother, 'made a complete ass of

himself. Some of his values, if not all, are deplorable. And anyway, it's what Marcus believes that matters, surely?'

'Do you think he's still in love with Diana?'

Ah, so that was it.

'I know he isn't.'

'It's just that she and I are so different.'

'Which is a good reason why you and Marcus should marry. Look, let me be frank. I love Diana dearly. We all do. She really is the daughter I never had and, because of the death of her parents, she and the boys grew up together. I expect Marcus has told you all this.'

'Some of it.'

Sarah continued. 'By the time they were all old enough to think about these things, Marcus was in love with Diana, Diana was in love with Tom and Tom was in love with Tom. So, you see, *plus ça change* where my elder son is concerned. Anyway, it's quite true to say that Marcus adored her at the beginning and, in my view, it's equally true to say that she only married him in order to remain in his brother's orbit. Diana really was terribly spoilt, you know. Osbert absolutely doted on her. And I can see now that she never lived in the real world at all. Suffice it to say that the advent of Camilla who you haven't met but who could fairly, I think, be described among other things as a social anarchist, upset all sorts of balancing acts. But by then I think his loyalty to her was under terrific strain anyway. Or, maybe, as I've lately begun to suspect, he switched off long ago.' She appraised Jane, wondering when their affair had actually begun.

Catching her look and correctly interpreting it, Jane said, 'Our affair has been going on for nearly two and a half years. I have no idea if there was anyone else before me.'

'Well, none of us knew anything about it. Diana certainly didn't. Of course, Marcus has always been one for playing his cards close to his chest. When he finally said he wanted a divorce she tried to persuade him to resurrect the marriage, but he was implacable. Now she has at last accepted it,' Sarah decided not to say anything about Dr Gresham at this stage, 'and I gather proceedings have started and they have even hammered out a settlement acceptable to both. So bar the divorce itself, which will happen in the fullness of time, it's all over.'

'Why do you think he waited this long before doing it?'

Sarah shrugged. 'I have no idea. Misguided loyalty? She could be very erratic. Perhaps he thought she couldn't handle it. Or perhaps he had to be sure of you first. I don't know. I've never understood the way Marcus's mind works.

'And her accident...?'

'He must have talked about it.'

'He *never* talks about it.'

Sarah reflected, *aren't men extraordinary?* Aloud she said, 'She's lucky to be alive, but she's getting better. I think he hardly thinks about her these days, apart from sorting out the debris of the end of the marriage, and certainly doesn't feel the need to talk about her. It has never, of course, occurred to him that you might want to.'

They heard the front door open.

'I don't think I do any more.'

That evening, over dinner, Marcus said, 'I'm afraid that I shan't be able to come to the viewing with you. I've had a phone call from Greenhill saying that he's most anxious to get everything concerning the estate settled quickly, and could I spare him some time tomorrow. I did indicate that next week would be more convenient but he seems to think that one matter in particular won't wait, so in the end I said I'd go. But it's obviously going to be a day's trip.'

'That's all right,' said Jane equably. 'The paintings are on show for one more day after tomorrow. We can go then.'

So the following morning found Marcus driving to Marchants, and as he drove he thought of Jane. His thoughts were complex. Jane was not, he recognized, a beauty as such, but she was attractive and outgoing with a certain vivacity of spirit which he admired. She counterpointed his own introspection. In bed where she was sexually uninhibited, aided by a streamlined body, he found her exciting. Marcus knew that he enjoyed making love to Jane, and that physically they were very compatible, but his experience with Diana had made him cynical to the point where sometimes he felt as if he had lost contact with his own emotional base. Was he actually *in* love with her, he asked himself, and did that matter anyway? Being in love the first time around had not done him much good. Importantly she liked the country. Anybody who did not would have been out of the question. Acting on a very atypical impulse, he had stated to Tom in front of their mother that he intended to marry Jane but was well aware that he had not actually asked her. On balance he now thought he should. Some lines of Marlowe were running through his head, relics of his school days when he had actually rather enjoyed poetry,

Come live with me, and be my love,
And we will all the pleasures prove,

He wished he could remember how it went on (something about steepy mountains, he vaguely recollected) but felt it perfectly summed up his feelings. Suddenly certain that he should be reciting it to her, not to himself, he dialled her number on the car phone, and when her quiet voice answered, did just that.

She laughed. 'Marcus, you are a sweet fool.'

'When will you marry me, Jane?'

'As soon as you want, my darling.' Satisfied, he went on his journey rejoicing, confident that he had at last done the right thing.

Peter Greenhill was not looking forward to the forthcoming interview. Even for someone who enjoyed a dramatic interlude as much as he did, there really had been a surfeit of shocks lately. He opened his diary and leafed rather inconclusively through it, wondering if he could possibly fit in a week's holiday, somewhere very remote where the Marchant family had never been heard of. A hubbub in the outer office indicated that both the Marchant twins had arrived together. Mrs Chance showed them in.

'Coffee, Mr Greenhill?' she enquired.

'I think not just for the moment, thank you, Mrs Chance,' he said unwilling to be interrupted while handling such a sensitive matter. Although, on the other hand, when clients got heated it was often an injection of the mundane such as the arrival of tea which calmed things down again.

'Gentlemen.' They all sat down. He pulled the relevant files and document towards him and, with a small twirl, positioned his half-moon glasses on the end of his nose. He might as well get as much as he could out of this.

'I have in my possession a document drawn up by another solicitor. A London solicitor.' Here he looked disapprovingly over the spectacles. 'It is sequential to the original will and was not, in fact, to be opened unless both Mrs Camilla Marchant and any direct heirs there might be (by which I mean sons or daughters of the deceased, Mr George Marchant) died. Since, with the invalidation of any claim Mrs Marchant stroke Weston might have had, combined with her permanent departure from the scene, this is to all intents and purposes what has happened, I therefore felt justified in reading the relevant document.'

They waited. Eyes on the oil painting of his dundrearied predecessor, he did his customary count to ten before delivering momentous news.

'It states that Mr Thomas Marchant is to be passed over as heir to the estate, in favour of Mr Marcus Marchant.' There, now he had said it.

Contrary to what he had expected there was a profound silence.

Into it Tom, in a hoarse whisper, said, 'I don't believe it!' The colour had completely drained from his face. Then, beginning to shout as it sank in, 'I just don't believe it! Do you realize I've been disinherited by my own brother! The bastard!' Sitting in the outer office, sipping her tea, the reverberations of the explosion nearly caused Mrs Chance to drop her cup. Tom was flushed with rage and incoherent with disappointment.

'Marcus won't do this to me!'

He jumped to his feet knocking over his chair as he did so, snatched up the document with a shaking hand and proceeded to read it.

Before Marcus could utter, Mr Greenhill said mildly, 'He has no alternative, I'm afraid. The instruction is quite clear and drawn up in a properly legal fashion with all the necessary witnesses. Even if he doesn't want it, you don't get it, it goes to a cousin.'

Stepping over Tom's chair as he went, he made for the door, opened it and made frantic signals in the direction of Mrs Chance and her ancient Olivetti for coffee. He need not have bothered. Tom erupted through the door behind him, banging it with such force that a *Cry of London* fell off the wall.

'I'll fight this. And I'll win!' They heard him still shouting as he exited in similar fashion through the outer office door.

'Well!' said Mrs Chance, aghast. 'Well, really.' Then, getting a grip, 'Do you still want coffee?'

Mopping his brow with a spotted handkerchief, Mr Greenhill said, 'Make it sherry instead. Coffee for Mr Marchant. Thank you, Mrs Chance.'

He went back into his office where Marcus was standing reading the document by the window.

'So what do we do next, Mr Greenhill?'

'Nothing to be done, Mr Marchant. It's all yours. Unless, of course, you don't want it.'

'Oh, I want it all right.'

Two hours later, having bought them both lunch, Marcus arrived back at Marchants. He parked the car at the front of the house and went in the direction of the kitchen, in search of Mrs Melbury. He found her and Frescobaldi listening to the afternoon play and making pastry. On being asked whether she had seen his twin, she told him that Mr Tom had already left for London adding that he had departed in a great hurry and she had the impression that he might have received some bad news, though, if so, he hadn't told her what it was. Further elaborating, she said that he had had a face like a thundercloud, reminding her very much of what he was like as a small boy when he didn't get his own way. In one sense, this piece of information came as a relief, but the reprieve was still only a temporary one for he and Tom were still going to have to have a talk sooner or later about the situation in which they found themselves.

He said to Mrs Melbury, 'I'm going back to London too, but Miss Prior and I intend to spend the weekend here, so perhaps you would arrange the master bedroom to be prepared.'

The master bedroom? Perplexed, she stared at him. And then thought that perhaps Mr Tom was coming down too, and what he meant was that he wanted that bed made up plus the one in the guest bedroom. It would be a relief, she thought, to get back to normal again now that That Woman had gone.

Marcus went back to London with two bottles of vintage champagne from what was now his cellar. It was hard to believe that when he had set out that morning a nineteen-and-a-half-minute time discrepancy between his birth and that of Tom had stood inexorably between him and any hope he might have had of inheriting his old home. Now nothing did.

Both women were in the sitting room when he finally arrived.

'Champagne! What are we celebrating?' asked Jane. Sarah, who thought she knew, said nothing.

'We, my sweet, are celebrating our engagement.' Here he kissed her. 'And something else besides.' They looked askance. 'My inheritance.'

When he ran out of the solicitor's office, Tom made his way straight to his car and drove out of the town and into the countryside where, to relieve his aggression he began to drive very fast indeed, skidding around the corners and hitting a hundred on the short straights. Eventually he stopped, and with trembling hands lit himself a Gauloise, deeply inhaling the fragrant smoke and willing himself to calm down. He was, he thought, buggered, done for. He would have to get a job now. Tears of self pity started to his eyes. It had never occurred to him that he would not inherit in the event of George dying without, as they say, issue. In fact, as he now saw, this was merely a convention and not in any sense an unbreakable rule, especially if the inheritor looked like being profligate, a possible squanderer of the spoils. And remembering his behaviour over the years, the cheating, the extravagance, the debts and finally, the insider trading débâcle, even he could see that as far as his upright brother George had been concerned all this did not constitute an ideal curriculum vitae. He recalled another family, friends of Osbert and Sarah, who had disinherited their eldest son because of his drug addiction. Now it seemed his fate was to be a similar one. Greenhill had seemed confident that the legal aspect of it was unassailable and, on balance, Tom thought he was probably right. He stubbed out his cigarette, which he really could not claim to have enjoyed very much, dispiritedly started up the car engine and headed towards Marchants. He supposed that Marcus would marry that dreadful, vapid Jane. Just right for the jam and Jerusalem brigade he thought, viciously, but hardly likely to compete with any of her predecessors in terms of élan. Fuming afresh at the very thought of it, he speeded up, slammed the MG into third gear, put his foot down and changed up to fourth and a furious ninety miles an hour on the Compton straight. Blackly brooding on the unfairness of it all, he did not notice the police car slip into the fast lane behind him. By the time it had succeeded in attracting his attention he had hit the hundred. It would be his third endorsement. He had lost his inheritance and now he was about to lose his licence as well.

'Oh, *fuck*,' said Tom. 'Fuck, fuck, FUCK!'

Marcus gave his mother a shrewd look. He had told them everything, but noticed that she had said very little. Sarah was not very good at dissembling and so had decided against artificial cries of astonishment.

'You didn't know about this, did you, Mother?'

'Well, as a matter of fact I did, but for heaven's sake don't ever tell your brother. Peter Greenhill told me the day before I left for London. I have to say I had no idea that anything like this was in the offing. I suppose George wanted a safe pair of hands for the estate and didn't feel that he could rely on Tom. Strictly *entre nous*, I can't say I entirely disagree with that.'

'What do you suppose he'll do?'

'Get on with his life,' replied the Roman mother shortly. 'What else is there?'

'You don't think he'll challenge it?'

'Not if he has any sense. According to Greenhill, legally the whole thing is perfectly sound. It's true to say that what George has done is unusual, but there is no law against it.'

'I feel very sorry for Tom,' said Jane, meaning it.

'I feel *quite* sorry for Tom,' rejoined Sarah, 'but do you honestly think there would have been much left of Marchants by the time he had finished with it? Of course not. He is the archetypal prodigal. And as such he really shouldn't be too surprised at what has happened to him.'

Bracing, but probably correct, thought Jane.

'Mother's absolutely right,' said Marcus. 'It's about time Tom was brought face to face with himself. It may be the best thing that could have happened to him.'

Sarah, who had no faith in the ability of anyone to change their habits much after the age of thirty, rather doubted this, but since it was the well-being of the estate which was at issue rather than that of her eldest son, felt that she could not afford to get too concerned about it. Whatever Tom did next would be the best thing for Tom, no doubt about that. He would look after himself.

Changing the subject, she said, 'Do we still all want to go to Jessops tomorrow?'

26

In her hotel room Camilla was preparing to go out. Ahead of her lay an organizational morning, culminating in a meeting with Mr Waterhouse as this was to be the last viewing day of the paintings. She was looking forward to it since everything completed today took her one step nearer to departure. Very soon she would be able to list counting her money as one of her favourite pastimes. To her relief, as far as she knew there had been no attempt on Jake's part to find her and nor had there been any communication from the Marchant family. She would sort out her affairs there later, she decided, preferably from Switzerland which was where, for several reasons, mainly monetary, she intended to go first. The highest priority was, however, a clean getaway. Jake remained a loose cannon, the threat of whose reappearance there might preclude a return to Rome. This would be a pity but not insurmountable. It was, after all, perfectly possible to have a good time somewhere else, especially with the amount of cash she would have at her disposal.

Still only wearing the sheerest of black stockings and a silk slip, she selected a pair of shoes, put them on, admired her own legs and then rejected her favourite crocodile handbag in favour of the Vuitton case since she would be carrying documents and needed somewhere to put them all. It felt unusually heavy and when she opened it she found inside the little gun, still wrapped in the silk handkerchief. What to do with this was the next question. In the end, rather than risk the hotel chamber maid finding it, she decided to leave it where it was. Sitting down in front of the dressing-table mirror she began to make up her face. She noticed that this took rather longer these days than it once had, though the effect produced was still undeniably attractive. Lastly she outlined her lips in red, sprayed herself with Armani scent, and, having put on the suit she had previously selected, brushed her hair. She consulted her watch. Time to go. Picking up the case, she went.

'They really are quite magnificent,' Jane was saying to Sarah and Marcus as they climbed the stairs to the first floor of Jessops where the Stubbses were displayed. 'I can't wait to hear what you think.'

A small crowd was clustered round each, divided from the paintings by a thick corded rope. Sarah put on her glasses and examined the first she came to. It was the one depicting the racehorse and groom, and Jane had been quite right when she said that it was marvellous. Looking at it, it seemed to Sarah that horses had subtly changed shape since the days of Stubbs. This one, a chestnut, had an arching, strong neck looking almost too powerful for its lean body, and a small, graceful head whose protuberant dark eyes rolled nervously in the direction of the artist. The tail did not stream but had been cut into the equine equivalent of a short clubbed bob. Everything about it was sensitively painted, as was the groom himself, who was dressed in a bottle-green buttoned knee-length coat similar in style to those worn by the grooms at Marchants in the days when there were grooms at Marchants.

'Such a pity that we can't turn up something like this in our attic.'

'We still might. After all we've never bothered to look.'

Jane said, 'Well, perhaps you should. It's worth remembering that these were found in the county.'

The crowd had thinned out a little. People were beginning to drift off to lunch. Jane and Sarah passed on to the next and larger painting, and here it was that Sarah, leaning forward to admire the unusually fine and detailed Stubbs landscape, found herself examining her own family house.

'Good God!' She stepped three or four paces back to assess the whole thing. 'Marcus, come here!'

He joined her from where he was still admiring the racehorse. To Sarah's eyes there could be no mistaking it. Thomas was even wearing the same rather battered coat as in the Gainsborough, School of. It must have been a favourite of his.

'Do you see who they are? It's Thomas and Juliana Marchant, I'm absolutely sure of it.'

She looked at the leaflet provided by Jessops and under Provenance read: *Unknown before its discovery this year in the attic of a country house.* The Provenance of Dash was more specific and said: *Presumably commissioned by Lord Compton, then sold with the horse itself to a country gentleman; thence by descent.*

'Are you telling me that this is a Marchant family painting?' asked Jane, astonished.

They all looked at it again. The eighteenth-century Marchants, if such they were, stared complacently down two centuries at their stupefied descendants.

At last Marcus said cautiously, 'You may be right. It does look like Marchants and it does look like them. But on the other hand there were probably a great many similar country houses and minor country gentry being painted round about then.'

'That,' Sarah pointed at the hound, 'is Ranter.'

'And their similar dogs. All the same the resemblance *is* extraordinary.' As a barrister, the habit of scepticism was ingrained.

A vision of Osbert formed itself in Sarah's mind. *Something she has that belongs to you.*

'Besides which,' Marcus pursued, 'the tree formation round the house is quite different.'

'It is now. You wouldn't know this because you were a very small boy indeed at the time, but Osbert had two trees cut down because they were leaning dangerously after a storm and were too close to the house. Here,' she indicated, 'and here.'

Jane spoke. 'Even supposing it is Marchants, for all you know the painting might have been legitimately sold to someone else a hundred years ago. Which means you would have no claim whatsoever on it.'

'There is a way to find out.' Sarah walked over to the attendant who was sitting on a stool in one corner of the room reading a tabloid newspaper. He looked up reluctantly. 'Could you tell me who is in charge here, please?'

'Mr Waterhouse is,' he glanced at his watch, 'but he may be out at lunch, Madam.'

'Would you mind going to find out for me. It's really very important.'

He was beginning to say that he was not allowed to leave the paintings unsupervised, when his one o'clock replacement arrived.

Sarah persisted. 'Would you mind? I'd be so grateful.'

Rather unwillingly, but feeling in the circumstances that he could not refuse, he agreed. 'Who shall I say wants to speak to him?'

'Mrs Marchant. Thank you so much.'

In the event Mr Waterhouse had not gone out to lunch because he was expecting the advent of another Mrs Marchant who had refused, in her usual tiresome fashion, to let him take her out to a decent lunch where they could discuss matters in a civilized fashion. No wonder she was wafer thin, he thought. By the time this whole exercise was over, he would be wafer thin as well. So when the attendant knocked on his door and said that a Mrs Marchant wanted to see him and should he show her in, he was not surprised, though she was, unusually for her, twenty minutes early.

'Certainly,' said Mr Waterhouse.

As Sarah entered, followed by Jane and Marcus, he said, 'You aren't Mrs Marchant. What's going on here?'

Taken aback, Sarah said, 'I assure you that I am Mrs Marchant.' And it appeared she was for in the face of his scepticism she even produced a driving licence to prove it. Sarah decided to get straight to the point before there was any more confusion. She said, 'I'm here because one of the Stubbs paintings in the gallery is a portrait of two of our ancestors. In the background is the house in which I spent all my married life. We had no idea of the existence of such a painting and I should like to know where it came from.'

This put Mr Waterhouse in a very awkward position, since he had been sworn to professional secrecy. On the other hand, certain things which he had formerly seen only through a glass darkly, so to speak, were shortly going to become known to him as they were known to others, or, rather, to one another. That he could see.

He took his watch out of his waistcoat pocket, looking suddenly absurdly like the White Rabbit. She wasn't due for another ten minutes, and if she was true to form would probably be late.

'Excuse me one moment, would you please.'

Darting through the door he seized the first minion to cross his path and said, 'I want both Stubbs paintings in my office immediately. No more members of the public to be allowed in for viewing. Just put a notice up saying no more viewing today.'

It was done.

Sarah said, 'Am I to understand that you know another Mrs Marchant? Because there is another one, or rather there was. Slim, dark and imperious. Hard as nails. My erstwhile daughter-in-law.'

There seemed little point in denying it. He was just opening his mouth to confirm that he did indeed know another one when the telephone on his desk rang. It was reception announcing that Mrs Marchant was here to see him.

'Show her up, please.' To the room at large, he said, 'She's here.'

Sarah turned to Mr Waterhouse, 'Before she arrives, quickly tell me one thing. Is she the anonymous owner of these two paintings?'

He nodded.

She said, 'I see.'

Mr Waterhouse thought he did too.

At this moment wearing the same scarlet suit in which she had left Marchants, Camilla walked into the room. Marcus, who happened to be standing nearest the door, slipped behind her, closed it quietly and positioned himself with his back against it, precluding any attempt she might make to leave. Camilla took in the scene immediately. She glanced obliquely over her shoulder. No escape there. At bay, she looked from one to the other of them, her uncompromising and malevolent gaze finally coming to rest on Mr Waterhouse.

'Well?'

He jumped.

'Well, what?' he stammered. She had always made him nervous.

'I thought we had a professional agreement that no one should be told my identity.'

'We did and I honoured it,' he nerved himself up to reply. 'Mrs Marchant came to the viewing and recognized her own house. That's what happened.' Why, he wondered, was he on the defensive when it was she who had been caught red-handed in the act of selling two extremely valuable paintings neither of which belonged to her, and had been preparing to pocket the proceeds?

Sarah said, 'Really all this is neither here nor there. I take it I am right in assuming that both the Stubbses were found in the attics at Marchants. In that case they belong to the estate, and must be withdrawn from auction.'

Mr Waterhouse sighed. Part of him had always known it was too good to be true. He was suffused with artistic regret.

Camilla, on the other hand, felt no such pure emotion. She had played for high stakes and lost and felt cold, corrosive hatred for those who had deprived her at this eleventh hour of her winnings. If she couldn't benefit from the two masterpieces which she alone had discovered, then she was going to make sure that they didn't either. She opened the case she was carrying and lifted out the ladies' gun. There was a collective gasp. She pointed it almost thoughtfully at Mr Waterhouse, who to his eternal shame, dropped to his pinstriped knees behind his large old desk, and then swinging the barrel lazily around, she covered the other three, who stood to petrified attention, rather as the Romanovs must have faced the Bolshevik firing squad in Ekaterinburg. Camilla felt very powerful. Penniless but powerful. To the others she looked capable of anything.

'Move away from the door and stand over there,' she ordered Marcus. He complied. Holding the weapon in both hands she levelled it at her targets and fired six shots in quick succession. Shooting was easy she decided. Then she dropped the little gun into the Vuitton case, opened the door and passed through. All that was left on the floor of Mr Waterhouse's office to show that she had ever been there was the purple silk handkerchief in which the gun had been wrapped.

Outside in the corridor, doors were opening and a small crowd had gathered.

'Did you hear a series of explosions?' she asked generally. 'It seemed to me that they came from over there.'

She pointed along the passage. As one they all moved off in the direction indicated. *Like a lot of sheep,* she thought, contemptuously, walking purposefully in the opposite direction. During the ensuing pandemonium no one saw her go. Outside in the street she hailed a taxi and went straight back to her hotel. There she requested her bill, swiftly packed, having first changed out of the distinctive red suit, and took another cab to the airport, where she got a standby seat to Rome.

The shootings at Jessops caused a sensation. That the victims were paintings rather than people in no way muted this. Furthermore speculation was aroused by the fact that the owner had decided not to press charges. Mr Waterhouse, whose office now had six bullet holes in its wall, a fact which upset him considerably, was persuaded to maintain his discretion with the promise that, should the paintings, after repair of course, be for sale again, he would handle them. The reason given for the continued anonymity of the owner or owners (nobody knew) was that both Stubbses were going to be hung on the walls of a private house for the time being, and from the security point of view, therefore, it was obviously desirable that the identity of the owner remained a secret.

Anthony was the principal reason for not prosecuting Camilla. It seemed to all of them that the publicity which would inevitably ensue would further impair a child already damaged by his mother's heartless conduct, and so they decided to do nothing.

It was assumed that she had gone back to her old stamping ground, but nobody knew. Eventually, Sarah and Jane went through the belongings she had left behind at Marchants, throwing most of them away. The exception to this was the carved angel before whose sightless eyes more had taken place than they would ever know about. It was, reflected Sarah, looking at it, a very worldly angel with its heavy-lidded eyes and sensual mouth, which reminded her of Camilla's own. A Luciferian angel perhaps? Well, whatever its heavenly politics, it was undeniably handsome and finally they stood it in the hall, the mischievous aura which emanated from it being too much, Sarah instinctively felt, for a more intimate and therefore vulnerable room such as a bedroom or drawing room.

THREE OF AMERICA'S FAVORITE WRITERS
OF ROMANCE FICTION,

JILL BARNETT,
DEBBIE MACOMBER
and SUSAN WIGGS

WELCOME YOU TO
RAINSHADOW LODGE—WHERE LOVE IS
JUST ONE OF THE AMENITIES....

Rainshadow Lodge may be on a secluded island with
blue skies and crystal waters, but surely that's not
enough to make three utterly mismatched couples jump
over their differences and into each other's arms. After
all, what could a socialite and a handyman have in
common? How could a workaholic and a free spirit ever
compromise? And why would a perfectly nice woman
overcome a bad first impression made by a grumpy
stranger? Must be something in the air...

On sale mid-August 1998
where paperbacks are sold!

Look us up on-line at: http://www.romance.net

MANTHTSP